Deschutes Public
Library

D0339357

DENTON LITTLE'S
STILL NOT DEAD

ALSO BY LANCE RUBIN

Denton Little's Deathdate

DENTON LITTLE'S STILL NOT DEAD

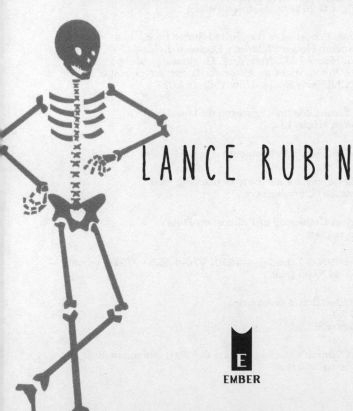

LANCE RUBIN

EMBER

This is a work of fiction. Names, characters, places,
and incidents either are the product of the author's imagination
or are used fictitiously. Any resemblance to actual persons,
living or dead, events, or locales is entirely coincidental.

Text copyright © 2017 by Lance Rubin
Cover art copyright © 2017 by Mathieu Persan

All rights reserved. Published in the United States by Ember,
an imprint of Random House Children's Books, a division of
Penguin Random House LLC, New York. Originally published in
hardcover in the United States by Alfred A. Knopf, an imprint of
Random House Children's Books, New York, in 2017.

Ember and the E colophon are registered trademarks
of Penguin Random House LLC.

Visit us on the Web! GetUnderlined.com

Educators and librarians, for a variety of teaching tools,
visit us at RHTeachersLibrarians.com

Library of Congress Cataloging-in-Publication Data
is available upon request.

ISBN 978-0-553-49700-7 (trade) — ISBN 978-0-553-49702-1 (ebook) —
ISBN 978-0-553-49703-8 (pbk.)

Printed in the United States of America
10 9 8 7 6 5 4 3 2 1
First Ember Edition 2018

Random House Children's Books supports the First Amendment
and celebrates the right to read.

For my aunt Rachel (1946-1996),
an inspiration in so many ways,
and
for Katie and Sly,
my heroes

It's funny that we have no memory of the day we're born.

It's a hugely important moment—*the beginning of your life*—and yet you have to rely on photographs and anecdotes to know what even happened. I mean, in a way, entering the world is kind of like a night of spectacular drunkenness.

Okay, well, being blackout drunk is more likely to result in later discovering that—to use a completely random example—you hooked up with your best friend's older sister, as opposed to learning that you came out of the womb with a conehead or something.

But still.

In both situations, you're only hearing the story from others, so how can you really know what the truth is?

To use another completely random example, if you'd been told your entire life that your mother died soon after giving birth to you, how would you begin to refute that? Why would you even think to try?

The answer is: you wouldn't. You'd take it at face value, occasionally feel bad for yourself, and get on with your life.

But later on, if that life took an extreme detour—a detour that seemed highly connected to things that went down at your birth—you might just begin to question everything.

I wish someone had taken more pictures.

ONE

"Am I dead?" I ask.

I'm supposed to be dead.

My mother smiles. "No."

This would be reassuring, except for the fact that she's supposed to be dead, too.

"I'm alive," she says. "We're both alive. We've been waiting for you, Denton."

Everything spins, and I'm fairly certain the contents of my stomach are about to splatter onto my undead mom's face. But then the spinning stops.

My mom stares at me, more curious than concerned. I don't know if I should believe what she's said or if this is even real, but I'm too damn tired to go anywhere else.

I nod and walk inside.

"Up this way," she says, stepping over an empty can of Mr. Pibb and pointing to a set of stairs. I immediately feel relieved. If this turns out to be some kind of afterlife, stairs that ascend seem like a good sign. Heaven, baby!

But the stairwell smells like fish sticks. And farts.

"It's just this one flight," my mom says, her dark curls bouncing as she leads the way up the concrete steps and stops at a door marked 2D.

Of course. *2D*. As in: a second dimension. As in: the afterlife.

Wow. Here we go.

My mom grits her teeth, fiddling with the key. "Haven't figured this stupid lock out yet," she says. Guess it makes sense there would be tight security. You wouldn't want any ol' schmuck to be able to get into heaven.

"Whew," she says as she finally pushes the door open and gestures for me to head inside. "They don't make it easy, do they?"

"Exactly," I say, pushing past her to see what's in store for me in this other dimension. "Oh." My hopes quickly evaporate. There are no babies playing harps. There are no Skittles raining down from the ceiling. I'm staring at a room with nothing on the walls and only a few pieces of furniture.

This must be a way station between life and heaven.

"Denton," my mother says, locking the door and then coming to stand right in front of me. "You're here. At last." Her eyes sparkle.

"Yeah," I say. I can't believe I'm chilling with my mom's ghost.

"You've grown up into such a handsome young man." She touches my cheek with her cold ghost fingers, and I flinch. "Sorry," she says, retracting her hand.

"No, it's . . ." I can't finish the sentence. My brain is a swirling stew of words, images, and question marks, but none are staying put long enough for me to get a handle on them.

Here's what I do know:

Today—well, technically yesterday at this point, since it must be, like, three in the morning—was my deathdate.

By which I mean, you know, the date I was going to die? Which was determined by a highly advanced test that is given to every baby born in the US? Which is known to be one hundred percent accurate?

Right. So, my deathdate was yesterday.

And I lived through it.

Just . . . did not die.

Or so I thought.

Because now, to add another slice of insanity to this WTF pie, I've arrived at the New York City address given to me by doctor-guy Brian Blum, and my dead biological mother opened the door.

So I'm pretty sure I *did* die.

I finally formulate a question: "We're ghosts, right?"

"What?" my mom says, a grin blossoming on her face like I've just mispronounced a very simple word.

"I mean . . . ," I say. "You're a ghost. And I'm a ghost. Right?"

"Oh, you poor, confused boy," my mom says, cracking up. "I already told you: we're *alive*, Denton."

"This isn't, like . . . heaven?"

My mom laughs harder. "Oh, Jesus. Let's hope that if there's a heaven, it's more appealing than this shit hole."

So this is not heaven.

And I am not dead.

And I am standing here with my mother.

Holy fuckballs.

"I'm sorry to laugh," my mom says, wiping tears from her eyes. "I know you've been through a lot. But you looked so sincere when you said it. *We're ghosts, right?*" She imitates how I looked when I said it, and I notice the parts of her that do, in fact, look like me. Same mouth. Same slightly oversize nose. Different hair, though. And different eyes.

But there's no doubt this is my mother. I know this should be an emotional moment, but I feel nothing.

"I'm sure you have a lot of questions," she says.

Understatement of the century.

"I thought you . . . ," I say. I blink three times, my eyes feeling like they've been coated with a thick layer of glue. "You're supposed to be dead. You died giving birth to me."

"I know, Denton." She looks at me with a sympathetic smile, like she feels bad that I'm the only one not in on the joke. "That's what was supposed to happen. But it didn't."

"You've been alive this whole time?" I ask. "Just living here?"

"Oh," my mother says, running a hand through her brown curls. "I don't live here. This is a temporary situation. A place where we could . . . welcome you."

I stare at the walls, thinking there might be a WELCOME, DENTON! banner I didn't notice when I first walked in.

"I know it seems impossible," my mom continues, "but we both survived. I was part of a team that created a powerful virus, and eighteen years ago, when you were in my womb, we injected this virus into you, and then I contracted it, too. The virus kept both of us alive."

I blink some more. I can barely understand what she's saying. She's definitely using the word *virus* a lot, though.

"The rash you had," she says. "Purple with red dots . . . That was the virus in its activated state."

The splotch. She's talking about the purple splotch that started at my thigh and then spread to cover my whole body. Even in my addled, exhausted state, I remember being purple. "Okay, cool, yeah," I say, the shock of this new reality starting to ebb away. "It was in its activated state. Fantastic. That makes perfect sense." I giggle a little. Maybe it's because I'm ridiculously tired, but suddenly everything seems hilarious.

"Here," my mother says, putting her hands on my shoulders, steering me toward a flimsy-looking gray table and guiding me down into a folding chair. "I'm sure you're hungry. I got you sesame noodles and broccoli. Does that work?"

"Hell yeah it works," I say, not entirely in control of my own words. "Gimme!" I pull the clear top off the black plastic container in front of me and fling it to the side.

"Wow, okay," my mother says, nodding like she's impressed with my initiative. "There's a fork there, but I can find you chopsticks, too. Options!"

"Go for it," I say. "The more utensils, the merrier." I pick up the fork and start shoveling noodles into my mouth as my mom digs around the tiny, uninviting kitchen, aggressively crumpling various paper bags in her search for chopsticks.

This feels like a strange dream, but I don't care. I'm very hungry.

"Bingo!" my mom says, triumphantly holding a pair of chopsticks in the air before sitting down and slamming them onto the table. I continue inhaling noodles. "Geez," she says, "it's like you've never seen food before in your life. Was Lyle feeding you at home?"

It's jarring to hear her say my father's name. I look up at her, a couple of noodles hanging out of my mouth.

There's a quick double knock at the door, which startles the crap out of me and sends the mouth-noodles flying. They land on the table in this formation that looks like a miniature man doing jumping jacks, which cracks my shit up. My mom puts a finger to her lips, so I cover my mouth. She takes silent steps toward the door and puts her ear to it.

A low, muffled voice says something I can't quite make out (sounds like *hippie giant sewer*), and my mother opens the door to let in a tall man in a gray jacket. He has thin blond hair and a craggy face, and he stands politely with his hands in his pockets as my mother shuts the door behind him. I'm still smiling because of the noodle man.

"This," she says to the stranger, "is my son Denton." She gestures to me, and I'm touched to hear pride in her voice.

" 'Sup, homeboy," I say to the random blond dude. I don't think I've ever used the word *homeboy* before, but now seems like a good time to start.

The man gives me a confused nod. "It is pleasure to meet you." He has some sort of thick accent, maybe Russian.

"This is Dane," my mother says. "He's part of our movement. He—"

"Part of our *what*-now?" I interrupt. You can't just casually throw out a word like that without explaining it. "Movement? What do you mean by that?"

My mother looks to Dane. "Denton's very tired," she explains, like she's trying to excuse my strange behavior. She turns back to me. "You don't need to worry about the movement right now. But Dane is on our side, and he needs to do some quick tests on you."

"Tests?" I say, my inner red flags flapping wildly. "No thanks! Pass!"

"How you feel?" Dane asks my mother, really hitting the *f*. She doesn't respond. "Is he deaf as well as tired?"

"Denton," my mom says. "He's asking how you feel."

"Oh, he's talking to me?" He must be one of those people who look past you even when you're the one they're talking to. "I couldn't tell, because of the . . ." I start to point to Dane's lazy eye, but then I stop. It's rude to point.

"Yes, I talk to you," Dane says, suddenly unhinged. "Who else? *How you feel?*"

"Look," my mom says. "Denton thought he'd be relaxing in a coffin by now, not getting pestered with questions by a couple of people he just met. Let's cut him some slack."

I'm not sure if *relaxing* is the right word for what I thought I'd be doing once I was dead, but I appreciate my mother coming to my defense.

"Sorry," Dane says, one apologetic hand floating in the

air. "I get antsy because car is parked illegal out front. Just don't want ticket."

"Well," my mom says, shaking her head, "that's your problem, isn't it? No one forced you to park illegally."

Dane snuffs out air through his nostrils and looks toward the blank wall behind me. "I am sorry I put on pressure," he says. "Worry for my car overcomes me."

"That's okay, man," I say. "I loved my car, too." A tear comes to my eye as I think about my small silver car, Danza.

Dane perches on the chair formerly occupied by my mother and stares at me intently. (Well, as intently as he can with that lazy eye.) "I do not know if your mother has told you yet, but you are very important person."

"Excuse *moi*?" I say.

"So that is why I need ask these questions and do tests. Please tell me how you feel."

"Uh, well," I say, looking to my mother, who nods vigorously. "I guess I feel like I want you to tell me more about this whole me-being-an-important-person thing, because it sounds both interesting and intimidat—"

"No!" Dane interrupts. "How you feel in ways of *health*?"

"Oh," I say, trying to understand why exactly I'm being shouted at by this Eastern European. "Well, I mean, I'm alive, right? Which is much healthier than being dead."

Dane clenches his jaw and looks down at the table. "You making joke?"

"I guess so," I say. "Sorta."

"This now is important. Save jokes for your mother later."

"Dane," my mother says. "Denton can make a joke if he wants to."

"Fine," Dane says, arms in the air. "I think important situation as this one calls for serious, but you are always joke joke joke. I see how son is like mother."

He thinks we're alike. That's oddly comforting.

"So," Dane tries again. "You feel healthy? Yes or no?"

"Yeah, pretty mu—"

"YES or NO?"

"Yes," I say, annoyed that Dane had to come here and ruin all the fun.

"You had the purple all over?" he says, gesturing with one hand to his arms, legs, and chest. "With the red dots?"

"I did, yes."

"And it turn all red?"

"It did." I can still see those moving electric red dots, the way they combined and solidified at the end of my deathdate, making me look like a red freak instead of a purple one.

"What happen when it turn red?"

"It was pretty nuts," I say. "As parts of my body changed color, I stopped being able to move them. Once all of me was red, I was, like, paralyzed, which turned out to be a good thing when I was in that car accident. I didn't get hurt at all."

For the first time since I walked into this insanity, I think about my dad and my stepmom, how I left them in the hospital after we all got in that car accident. I hope they're okay.

"You see?" Dane whispers, looking to my mom. "I tell you this was possibility. . . ."

My mom is shaking her head, one hand on her mouth

covering a huge smile about to bust forth. "Wow . . . ," she says. "That's . . . I can't believe this."

"What?" I ask. If I have to sit here, I want to at least understand the exciting thing that's happening.

"It means the virus worked even better than we anticipated," my mom says, looking just past me, like she's trying to imitate Dane's lazy stare. "It means the others should also survive. And if it turns out you—" Her eyes lock back onto mine. "Oh, it means so much, Denton. We did it!" Then she looks to Dane, her arms spread wide. He rises from his chair, and they share an awkward celebratory hug.

"This just the beginning," Dane says, mid-hug. "We are finally ready."

"I know," my mom says, a bit teary-eyed. "I know."

"Um, *okay*," I say, rolling my eyes for the benefit of approximately no one. I feel like I'm watching the season finale of a TV show I've never seen a single other episode of. Not only that, but it occurs to me that my mom hasn't offered to hug *me* since I arrived.

As if she's received a transmission of my thoughts, my mom breaks from Dane and walks over to me at the table. "Denton, come here," she says, suddenly pulling me into a hug. She smells like coconut.

"All right," Dane says, sitting back down across from me. "Must do tests so I can leave."

"I'd still prefer to pass," I say.

"Great," my mom says, patting me on the back and not listening at all to what I've said.

"While I do this, you check on car?" Dane asks my mother. "Make sure no ticket?"

"Just do the damn tests and get out of here," my mom says, laughing. "It's late. *My son* is tired."

I'm touched and unsettled by the way she emphasizes the words.

"All right, all right." He brushes back some of his thin hair. "But if there is ticket, maybe you split with—"

"Dane," my mom says in this calm, forceful way, all traces of congeniality vanished.

They exchange a tense look before Dane says, "I apologize," bowing his head like a dog at obedience school. It's pretty bizarre.

"Now," Dane says, turning his head back to me. "I take hair and saliva. And blood." He pulls tweezers, a paper packet, a plastic bag, a petri dish, and a vial out of the pocket of his coat, haphazardly placing them on the table.

"Seriously, I'm really not feeling this." I look to my mom, panic rising in my chest.

"It's vital that we do it now," my mom says.

I turn to Dane. "Are you a doctor?"

"Sort of," Dane says, reaching into his pocket once more and pulling out what looks to be an alcohol swab, which gets chucked onto the table amongst the jumble of medical accessories and chopsticks.

"What does *sort of* mean?" I ask. "Are you a nurse?"

"I take anatomy class at university." He grabs the paper packet, rips it open, and pulls out a syringe.

"Ha, so you do know how to make jokes after all."

"This no joke," Dane says, sternly looking past me at the wall. "I get all top marks in anatomy."

"All right, hold up," I say, standing and turning to my mother. I want to address her by name to more strongly make my point, but I have no idea what to call her; feels too soon to bust out Mom and too strange to call her Cheryl. "Mrs., um, Birth . . . Mom," I say instead. "I think I might prefer to not get syringed by this man right now."

"We don't want to mess with timing because of mice," Dane says.

"Wait, mice?" I ask. "What does that mean?"

My mom sighs. "Look, this has to get done. We need to know if the virus is still in you and how it's changed. Dane'll make it quick and painless."

"I do hair first," Dane says. "Is easy." He's holding the tweezers. I don't fully understand why this is happening, but the sooner I let him do this, the sooner I sleep. I sit back down. "Good choice," he says, leaning over me. I can smell his coffee breath. "Wait, I need precise record of time."

"Right, it's"—my mom looks at her phone—"three-twenty-seven and thirty-six seconds."

"Excellent. We need that for cross-reference with astrological charts," he says to me, as if that made any sense. "I take five hairs."

He plucks them in quick succession, placing each one into his plastic bag.

"See? I perform with speed."

"Impressive," I say.

"Now, for next, you spit."

"Beg your pardon?"

He holds the petri dish annoyingly close to my chin. "You spit into this."

"Fun," I say, and spit into Dane's dish.

"Much thanks," he says, putting a lid on the petri dish and shoving it into his back pocket, the strangest handling of scientific material I've ever seen. "Now, which arm you prefer me to shoot?"

"Neither."

"I will do left."

I am very opposed to having this brusque Russian jab something into my arm, but I'm too wrecked to put up a fight. I roll up my sleeve, and Dane grabs the alcohol swab from the table.

"You got this," my mother says, appearing behind me and squeezing my left shoulder kind of hard.

Dane holds my arm with one hand, swabbing and tapping my vein with the other. "I count to three. Don't be nervous."

I close my eyes, thinking maybe I can sleep through this.

"One . . . two . . ." Dane sticks the syringe into my arm. I gasp. The ol' skipping-the-number-three trick. I should have known.

And not one second after he's stuck it in, a loud, abrasive buzzing echoes throughout the apartment.

Dane freezes, looking to my mother.

"Was that the doorbell?" I ask.

"Shhh!" Dane says.

My mom nods. It's clear they have no idea who could be buzzing. And that Dane is very afraid.

It's also clear that Dane has forgotten there's a syringe jutting out of my arm.

"Anyone follow you?" he shout-whispers at me, both hands on the table, neither one holding the freestanding syringe, which is slowly starting to Pisa sideways.

"What? Here?" I ask.

"Yes, here! You go other places, too?"

"No, no, I came right here! Are you just gonna leave that thing sticking in me?" I gesture wildly with my head to the syringe.

He looks down, surprised, and grabs on to it. "I had not forgotten," he says, focusing again on drawing my blood, moving faster than before.

The buzzer screams out again, two quick staccato bursts.

"You were followed!" Dane says, his eyes darting around.

"Quiet!" my mom says. "It's probably just a wasted teenager pushing the buttons to be obnoxious. That happens all the time."

"Not probable! It is the DIA!"

A chill runs through me. The DIA is the Death Investigation Agency, whose existence I learned of yesterday, when my best friend's mom revealed she was a DIA agent and tried to kidnap me.

"I wasn't followed," I say, hoping that if I speak with enough confidence, it will be true. But, really, I have no idea.

Dane pulls out the syringe—the vial it's attached to now filled with my blood—and crams it into his front pocket. I pull my sleeve down over the puncture. "What will happen to me if it is the DIA?" I ask, absorbing some of Dane's panic and getting to my feet.

"What will happen?" Dane cries. "Put it this way: you will not be here any longer to contemplate the theoretics of what could happen!"

This has gotten so nuts so quickly.

My mom moves toward the window.

"Don't let them see you!" Dane says. My mom holds out a hand to him, like, *Shut up,* and continues across the apartment. "Think about this, Nadia," Dane says.

Nadia?

My mom peers out the window. Dane stands there like the Tin Man in the midst of getting oiled—frozen to one spot as a zillion tiny muscles all over his arms, hands, and face come to life.

"Yup, it's the DIA," my mom says, unnervingly calm. "That's a shame."

"No!" Dane says, the fiercest shout-whisper I've ever heard. "The kid *was* followed! What a huge fuckjob!"

I resent—and am amused by—many things Dane has just said, but I'm too terrified at the prospect of being kidnapped again to dwell on them.

"Dane," my mom says.

"Now it all is ruined!" he continues. "All of it for nothing! Matilda! Yuri! NOTHING!"

"DANE," my mom says again.

"We must escape," he says, wild terror Ping-Ponging in his eyes.

"I was kidding," my mom says.

"Huh?" Dane says.

"I was kidding," my mom repeats.

"No," Dane says.

"Yes. There's no one down there. I'm sure it was a drunk buzz-and-run."

Dane's face drops. I understand how he feels. I exhale and grab the back of my neck, my hands shaking.

"I couldn't resist," my mother says, an impish smile on her face.

"That was not okay," Dane says.

"You thought it was funny, didn't you, Denton?" she says, walking back over to us.

"Well . . . ," I say. I laugh nervously. I did not find it funny. I found it scary. My heart's still beating double time.

"See? Like mother, like son," my mom says as she puts an arm around my shoulders. "By the way, Dane, there's a policeman writing out a ticket and putting it on your windshield."

"I not fall for joke again," Dane says.

"Sadly, this one's for real," my mother says, shaking her head.

"What?" Dane shouts, grabbing the plastic bag with my hair in it, jamming it into the same pocket that has my blood, and making a beeline for the window. "Shit my ass!" he says, staring down at the street. He races out the door, his footsteps echoing down the stairwell.

"So that's Dane," my mother says. "He can be a lot sometimes."

I've moved past shock, past exhausted hilarity, and now I just feel like a mush-brained zombie. A scared, confused, mush-brained zombie. "This is all kind of a lot."

"We're not going to let the DIA get you. Just so you know."

"Thanks?" I'm not sure who the *we* she's referring to is, but it makes me feel a little bit safer. I guess.

"Sure." She scratches her ear and looks around the apartment, like she's not sure what to say next. I yawn and rub at my right eye with the heel of my hand.

"Good God," my mom says. "Why are you still awake?"

She ushers me into a small bedroom, about half the size

of my room at home. I don't take in anything else about the room other than the bed.

"So this is where you'll be sleeping," my mother says.

"Okay," I say, plopping down on the edge of the twin. There's a light brown blanket on it that's covered with lint balls. "Thanks."

A silence floats up between us. "Speaking as someone who also lived through a deathdate," my mom says eventually, "I can say that it might feel weird at first, but with time, it'll all get easier."

I know that's supposed to be comforting, but instead it just makes me feel worse. How long do I have to live like this before I can go back to my actual home and my actual life?

"Sleep well, Denton. It's great to meet you."

My head sinks into the pillow. I'm too tired to get under the covers. Too tired to take off my clothes.

She might be your mother, a voice in my brain calls, *but you can't stay here. You know that, right?*

Maybe, I think in response.

My inner dialogue doesn't go any further, because I'm out within seconds.

TWO

I open my eyes and stare up at a crack in the ceiling.

I don't think this is my bed.

Waking up confused is my thing now.

I peer around at blank walls, and the lunacy of last night comes rushing back to me. Oh right, I'm hiding from the US government in my dead mom's apartment.

As one does sometimes.

I hear the muffled sounds of my mom talking in the other room, a man's voice responding. Probably Crazy Dane. I don't want to go out there.

As my grogginess melts away, I remember everything I left behind when I didn't die.

Oh God. Paolo, my best friend. His deathdate is in twenty-six days. Wait, no, twenty-five days now.

Is it possible he could live, too? I passed him the virus on my deathdate. His purple splotch didn't have the red dots like mine, but he still got something.

I rip off the hoodie I've been wearing since the train station, followed by the button-down I've been wearing since the prom. I can practically see the stink lines emanating off my body, but even if I showered, I don't have any other clothes to change into. So, for the time being, I throw the hoodie back on. Now I'm in that and powder-blue suit pants. Ridiculous.

I move to the window on the other side of the room, pushing aside the green, scratchy curtain. It's morning. I wouldn't have minded sleeping till the afternoon, but oh well.

I met my mom last night. And she was kind of intense. (And I was kind of punchy and nonsensical, but I'm choosing to block that out.) I'm not sure I'm ready to face her frenetic energy again. I know I should be ecstatic to have met her—not to mention grateful, seeing as she saved my life—but every cell in my body is screaming that I need to find a way out of here. Nevertheless, I take a deep breath and swing the door open.

And I'm staring at my older brother, Felix.

"That's not what I do!" he's saying to our mother. They're sitting at the small table, laughing together as they eat waffles and bacon.

"It absolutely is," my mom says, turning her body toward me while her head stays with Felix so she can get in the last word. "I know you, so don't even bother trying to deny it." Her head joins her body. "Well, good morning! At last, he rises."

"Hey, Dent," Felix says, smiling as he stands up and gives me a hug. "Nice outfit."

"Hi," I say. Part of me is relieved to see my brother, but

the other part feels like I've stepped into some alternate universe.

"You sure you don't want to sleep some more?" my mom says. "Thirty hours may not have been enough."

"Thirty . . . what?" I ask. "Didn't I go to sleep at, like, three a.m. last night?"

"Try three a.m. the night *before* last night. It's Sunday morning."

I look to Felix, confirming that this isn't one of our mom's hilarious jokes. He nods.

"From what we've seen," my mom says, "living through your deathdate completely saps the body. We thought you might sleep longer, actually. After mine, I was so wiped I slept at a Super 8 motel in Poughkeepsie for almost two full days straight."

"Oh," I say.

"To be fair, I'd also just given birth. To you!" She shouts that last part, like, *What're the chances?*

I must look terrified or, at the very least, befuddled, because Felix says, "I know this is a lot to process. But you were absolutely awesome on your deathdate."

"Thanks," I say.

"I was awesome, too, of course," he says.

My mom cackles at this.

"While you've been sleeping, I've been in jail for hitting that cop with a bedpan to save you."

"Whoa, what? I'm so sorry," I say.

"All good," he continues. "I got bailed out, and you got here, so it was totally worth it. Though . . . you don't seem too excited about the whole being-alive-instead-of-dead thing. I would think that might be a boon to your spirits."

"A boon?" I ask.

"Yeah, a boon."

"That's a word?"

"Yes," Felix says. "It's, like, a helpful addition. A lift."

"Sounds made up." For pretty much my whole life, Felix was predominantly an absent brother, always busy, but then on my deathdate, he became this ever-present guardian angel, saving my life on at least two occasions. I was incredibly touched, but it's suddenly hitting me that he was probably just doing it because our mom asked him to.

It also occurs to me that Felix can probably provide information I desperately want. "Are Mom and Dad okay?" I ask.

Felix's eyes flick over to our mother, then back to me. "Um, you mean Raquel and Dad? Mom's sitting right here."

"You know what I mean," I say. He can be just as much of a fart-face in the afterlife as he was in the real world.

"You can call me whatever you want, Denton," my mother says, adoringly rolling her eyes at Felix, who sneers back at her.

"So, are they all right?"

"Yeah," Felix says. "I talked to Dad on the phone, but you know how that goes; we didn't actually say much. Sounds like they're fine, though. They were discharged from the hospital yesterday afternoon."

Thank God.

"Sweet of you to be concerned," Felix says, putting one hand on my shoulder, "but I'd say the bigger news here is that you're alive. And so is Mom." His face is barely able to contain the smile that's broken out. "Can you believe that?"

"Not really," I say. "I also can't believe you knew about this and never told me."

Felix scratches the back of his head as he nods. "Yeah, I apologize for that, I really do, but there was no way we could tell you. If you'd let someone know Mom was alive, you would have jeopardized everything we'd been working for."

"It's the truth, hon," my mom says. "Plus, we didn't know if the virus was going to work. We didn't want to get your hopes up for no reason."

I'm sure they're right, but that doesn't make me resent them any less.

"Look," my mom says, getting up from her chair and walking toward us, "like Feel said, you're here now, which is all that matters." She's in a lime-green running ensemble: skintight shorts, T-shirt, and sneakers. "Oh," she says, glancing down at herself. "Yeah, I ran this morning. Didn't know you got that from me, did you?"

Felix must have told her I'm a runner. And, no, how the hell would I know that when NO ONE TELLS ME ANYTHING?

"Mom is pretty hard-core," Felix chimes in. "She runs almost every day." He has this idiot glow about him, the same look he used to get when he'd tell me stories that painted our mom as a near-mythological figure.

"Yeah, I'm kind of an addict," she agrees. "Gotta stay healthy, you know?"

I obviously never knew my mother, but being here has the strange effect of making me feel like I don't really know my brother either. My chest tightens, and the room spins. I don't want to be here. "I might actually go for a run myself this morning," I say, looking at the floor and trying to get my bearings. "Get some fresh air, move around a little."

My mom and Felix share a look.

"Running isn't an option," my mom says.

"Sorry, Dent," Felix adds.

I don't understand. Does living through your deathdate make your body lose its ability to run?

"You can't go outside," my mom says.

"I can't— Wait, what? I can't go outside today?"

"Not only today," my mother says. "For the indefinite future. Until things settle down a bit."

The floor lurches beneath me, and I lean back onto the doorframe to keep myself from falling.

"Dent, you okay?" Felix says, reaching out.

"I'm fine," I say, forcing myself to make eye contact to prove my fineness. "Is this a joke?"

"Look," my mom says. "It's for your own safety. The DIA came way too close to getting you, and you can be damn sure they have teams of people looking for you now. If anybody saw you get on that train, they'll definitely be searching New York City. So we have to be careful."

Oh my God. She's serious. "I can't leave here?" The place looks even sadder in the daytime, if that's possible. Other than the folding table where breakfast is happening, there's a ratty gray couch, an old TV that's box-shaped instead of a flat screen, a closet-size bathroom, and a kitchen with a yellowing fridge and a stove, three of its four burners rusted over.

"It's not as bad as it sounds," my mom says. "You can get on my laptop whenever you need to. I've blocked all the email and Internet phone sites—don't want you to be tempted—but otherwise you can look up whatever you want to."

Because using search engines all day is exactly how I want to spend my post-deathdate existence.

"I brought over my Wii for you," Felix says, pointing to a little black box standing up near the TV. "It's got Netflix." He gives me this grin, like fucking Netflix is going to make up for the fact that I'm essentially going to be a prisoner here.

"And," my mom says, racing to the kitchen cupboards, really pushing the hard sell now, "I have no idea what teenage boys are eating these days, but I tried to stock this place to the gills with tons of snacks you'd like. Ho Hos, Ding Dongs, Starbursts." Those are all foods my stepmom would never let us keep in the house. "And the fridge is packed, too. Peanut butter, jelly, eggs. Tons of frozen dinners. And there's ham. If you want to make a sandwich or something."

I'm not fully clear on what's happening here. Are my mother and I going to stay in this nondescript apartment eating ham and Ding Dongs for the rest of our lives?

"Here," my mom says. "Sit down. Have some food. You'll feel better. I made waffles and bacon, Felix's favorite, so maybe that's something you like, too."

I take a seat at the table with my mother and brother. As the two of them continue to engage in their cutesy mom-and-son-comedy-team bullshit, I chomp down on a piece of bacon. It pisses me off that my mom knows Felix's favorite foods and not mine. I know they had nine years together before she fake-died, but it still makes me feel outside of the world's best inside joke.

Ohmigod. I wonder if my dad knows, too. I mean, in the hospital, he saw that I had survived, and he hardly blinked an eye. It was like he'd always known I was going to live through my deathdate. So why wouldn't he know this, too? How messed up would *that* be? He knows his wife isn't actually dead, but he remarries anyway?

I wait for a lull in the banter and turn to my mom. "Dad knows you're alive, doesn't he?"

She looks at Felix, then slowly nods. "He does."

If Felix and my dad both know about my mom, is it something they talked about on a regular basis? Am I the only one not in on this secret? There's no way my stepmom knows, right?

"I don't . . . ," I say. "I mean, Felix, how long have you known?"

A small smile curls on his face as he looks to his mom. "Pretty much the whole time," he says.

I'd thought my brain had already exploded, but I was wrong. *Now* it's exploded.

"Yup," my mom says. "He was nine, but I thought he was mature enough to understand. And to keep the secret."

In other words, nine-year-old Felix could be trusted, but I had to wait until I was seventeen and fake-dead.

"I know it seems crazy, Dent," Felix says. No wonder he was never around. Probably too worried he'd accidentally spill the beans to me, the oblivious idiot. "But it wasn't like Dad and I ever talked about it. He refused. Just like he waited almost eighteen years to give you the letter Mom wrote."

"I'm so pissed at Lyle about that," my mom says. I have to agree. She wrote me a letter before I was born, and my dad didn't give it to me until my deathdate. "He knew the whole point of that letter was to establish a code, a way to communicate with you when the time came. *Happy dinosaur.*" (And here I thought the point was to let me know she loved me, even though she was about to die.) "That's also why I gave you that dinosaur toy, so it would further cement the code in your head." (She's talking about my favorite stuffed animal of all time, Blue Bronto. Who, apparently, was just a pawn in my mom's scheme.) "But thanks to Lyle, I'm sure you thought my top-secret Happy Dinosaur messages were actually real ads for erection pills."

"I did," I say.

"Geez!" my mom shouts. "I spent so much time on those, too."

"Anyway," Felix says. "My point is, Dad wanted nothing to do with it. And for a lot of years, Mom and I were just communicating through old-school mail, letters sent back and forth. I didn't start seeing her in person until . . . I think . . . late in high school?"

"Right, yeah, because I helped you with that college essay, remember?" my mom says.

"But," I say, completely unable to wrap my head around the idea of my dead mother guiding Felix through the college application process, "if you guys were able to see each other, I can do the same, right?" My voice is all shaky. "I mean, like, I can see Dad and Raquel, right? And my friends?"

My mom looks at me, then Felix, then me again, her eyes apologetic.

"No," she says, "you can't."

THREE

I stare at my mom, unable to speak, as the abyss below me grows vaster. I don't think she's joking. This is my life now. I survived my deathdate for . . . whatever this is.

"It's just not possible, Denton," she says. "At least not for a long time."

"But . . . ," I say. "Then what's the point?"

"What do you mean?"

"I mean, what's the point of living if I can never see my family again? Or my friends?"

"The point is, you're *alive*," my mom says, looking personally offended. "Most people think that's better than being dead."

Right. Without meaning to, I've crapped on the choice she made when she ditched my family for all this. I should probably feel bad about that. But I don't.

"Look," she says, softening her tone. "I understand. It wasn't easy for me when I survived. At all. But you *do* have family in your life: your mother and your brother. That's more than a lot of people have, Denton. You should be grateful."

"I am," I say. "I just don't get why it's not possible."

"It's too risky," my mother says, banging on the table and accidentally sending a fork clattering to the ground. "You're supposed to be dead. Someone happens to see you, they tell someone else, that someone tells someone else, and it eventually gets back to the DIA, who will find you and then, you know . . ." She lets the sentence hang in the air.

"Wait, no," I say. "I *don't* know. Find me and then what?"

"Well, any number of things, really," my mom says, leaning over the table and looking straight into my eyes. "None of them good."

"I was told the DIA would take me to DC and run tests."

"Sure, they'll definitely do that."

"But you're suggesting they'll also do other stuff to me?"

"Look," my mom says again, raising her hands in the air exactly the way Felix does. "I don't know for sure what they would do, but I'm pretty sure none of us would ever hear from you again."

My stomach drops.

"Yeah, Dent," Felix says. "This is no joke."

"How many people have lived through their deathdate like this?" I ask. "Has anyone been taken before?"

My mom grimaces. She looks away for a few moments

before turning back to me, incredibly serious. "Five of us have lived. One's been taken. Dane's wife."

I can't believe what I'm hearing. "What the hell? Why did they take her? Is she all right?"

"We don't know! This is what I'm trying to tell you, Denton," she says. "The DIA is not to be taken lightly. Don't you think, after I lived through my deathdate, I would have wanted to keep my life? To stay with your dad and Felix? And you, my new baby? Of course!" She gestures wildly. "But I didn't, because I'm not an idiot. At the time, there was a scientist doing the same work we were doing, trying to find a way for people to live past their deathdates. But, unlike us, he made no effort to keep what he was doing quiet. The *New York Times* ran an article about him, and the next day there was a huge fire in his lab. All his work was destroyed. A few days later, he went missing."

"But," I say, trying to process all this as quickly as I can, "what if that was completely unrelated to the DIA? What if he was sabotaged by some rival scientist or something?"

My mom looks me in the eyes. "Don't be naïve."

"Are you saying the US government would *kill me*?" I can't believe that Paolo's mom would purposely lead me to my death. But I also wouldn't have believed that my best friend's mother was actually a spy who'd been watching me my whole life.

"Denton," my mother says, her eyes boring into mine. "What I'm saying is that your existence is a threat to a multibillion-dollar industry that directly benefits many of the people *in* the US government. Would they go so far as to kill you? I can't be sure. But, honestly, no one would know the difference anyway. You're already listed as dead."

"Holy shit," I say quietly. I thought the whole point of living through my deathdate was that I'd escaped death for the foreseeable future. Incorrect.

The table buzzes. My mom grabs her phone from where it was hiding between her plate and glass.

"Hey," she says into it. "Yeah, he's awake." She looks at me. I take a bite of cold waffle. "He's doing all right. A little confused, but he's hanging in there. Sure." My mom holds the phone in my direction. "It's Brian."

"Oh," I say, grabbing the phone. It's my mom's old college friend, the doctor who helped save my life. "Hello?"

"Hey, Denton. How goes it?" I'm surprised how comforted I am to hear the voice of this man, who, as recently as a week ago, was a complete stranger.

"You know, glad to be alive. But totally disoriented."

"I hear you, my man, I hear you," Brian says. "I hope you understand why I couldn't tell you about your mom."

"Yeah," I say. "But there's a lot I don't understand."

"Your mom is going to tell you everything you need to know, so don't worry. But if you ever want to talk, get on your mom's phone and give me a call." Brian must know that I already threw my phone away in order to stay off the grid.

"Thanks," I say. "Are you gonna come by here to hang out or anything?"

There's silence on the other end of the line. Just as I'm starting to wonder if Brian lost reception, he speaks. "Not likely, no. I'm, um, pretty busy. But never too busy if you need my help. You understand?"

Not really. "Sure," I say.

"All right, just wanted you to know that. Be good, buddy. Enjoy this new life."

"Oh," I say, surprised that the conversation is suddenly ending. "Should I put my mom back on?" But he's already hung up. I hand the phone back to my mom.

"Wow, a phone call from Brian," Felix says. "Like Halley's comet. Happens once every seventy-six years."

"Ha," my mom says.

I'm so confused. "But aren't you and Brian, like, good friends? Since college?"

"Well, we used to be," my mom says.

"So, what happened?"

My mother sighs. "He fell in love."

"Oh," I say. "And you were . . . jealous or something?"

"Jealous? No. I was happy for Brian. But then his husband, Langston, started putting ideas in his head that what we were doing here was a waste of time. He just didn't get it. A lot of people don't."

Felix is shaking his head, like, *It's a damn shame.*

"That's kind of sad," I say.

"Tell me about it," my mom says. "Brian was my best friend. When deathdates were made mandatory, he was the one by my side protesting against it. When we were forced to find out anyway, and I learned I was going to die at thirty-two, he was the one comforting me." This reminds me that Brian said they used to date and have sex a lot. Narsty. "But things change."

"So why did he help me on my deathdate?"

"Brian feels like you're partly his responsibility," my mom says, running a hand through her curls, "because he was so involved with the creation of the virus. And he's the one who injected you with it."

"You guys mind if I take the last piece of bacon?" Felix asks.

"Okay, hold on a second," I say. I'm finding it hard to organize my thoughts on all this, because the gaps in my knowledge are boundless.

"I'm happy to flip a coin for it if you want to," Felix says.

"No, that wasn't about the bacon. I don't care about that—"

"Sweet." He grabs the final slice.

"I'm just wondering if we can talk about this virus situation," I say. "Like, um, isn't a virus a bad thing?"

"That's a common misconception," my mom says, "because all of the famous viruses happen to be bad ones. But, really, a virus is just a vehicle for carrying other things into the body, and it's an effective one, because it can reproduce quickly inside cells."

"So, how did it make us be still alive?" I'm immediately embarrassed that I've phrased that in such a stupid-sounding way.

My mom looks at me, then Felix, who doesn't notice because he's savoring his bacon with his eyes closed.

"The short version is: the virus canceled out our death-dates by rewriting our DNA." My mom takes a drink of water, then puts it down and looks at me, like she's not going to say anything else.

"Okay," I say. "Um, what's the long version?"

"Dent," Felix says, licking bacon crumbs off his fingers, "you know how undated people don't know their deathdates because of a defective gene that the ATG kits can't read?"

"Yeah," I say, remembering when my dad first explained all that to me when I was five.

"Well, that's the gene the virus goes after. It incorporates itself into that gene, effectively scrambling the genetic information. So then the deathdate you were given when you were born becomes incorrect."

"Right," my mom says. "But since the virus has melded with that gene, it still knows the deathdate you were supposed to have. The day before, the virus activates and spreads throughout the body, into every tissue, almost like a protective force field or something."

Science was never really my thing, so I'm focusing hard. "But how . . . ? Like, on my deathdate, I almost got hit by a car, but then I tripped over the curb and didn't. Are you saying the virus made me trip?"

My mom and Felix share a look before she turns back to me. "Dent, it's complicated. Think of it this way—the ATG kits draw upon not just biology but also astrology and statistics to predict what would seem impossible. The virus does everything it can to mess up that prediction."

I just stare at my mom. I didn't think it was possible to get more confused, but apparently it is. I mean, it all sounds kinda ridiculous. Then again, I *am* alive right now.

"There's so much more going on in the world than science alone can explain," she says, standing up and starting to clear the table. "But we're working on it. And with you here now, we've got so much more to study. Starting tomorrow, I'm going to be at the lab with Dane, working with your samples."

"What lab?" I ask, so I can ignore the rest of what she just said.

"I'm a tech in a diagnostic lab. It's my part-time job." She turns on the sink and begins washing dishes. "And they let me use the facilities for my own work as well."

"Oh. That's how you make a living?"

"Well . . . not really. There's a . . . benefactor who believes in our cause, who helps support our movement, and that allows me to devote most of my time to it."

"Which is great," Felix says. "Not all of us can."

"But, anyway, you'll have this place to yourself for a good chunk of time." She smiles and winks. I really don't like when adults wink at me. "If you're anything like me, you probably go a little crazy when you don't have any alone time."

I'm honestly not sure I *am* anything like her.

"Make sure you let him know where you keep your stash of adult films," Felix says.

"Ha!" my mom says.

I don't laugh, because it makes me uncomfortable.

All of this does, really.

"You're hilarious, Feel," my mom says. "Either of you want a Ho Ho?"

Welcome to your new life, Denton Little.

FOUR

The first thing I do on my first day alone in the apartment is get on my mom's laptop.

That's not entirely true. The first thing I do is lie awake in bed, waiting for my mom to go out for her run, come back from her run, shower, get dressed, eat breakfast, and leave for the lab. Where she will mess around with mice and my saliva all day.

Maybe it's sad that I'm deliberately avoiding any interaction with my newfound mother, but then again, isn't this what typical teenage boys are supposed to do?

Once she's gone, I take a shower and put on an outfit from the bag of clothes my mom has provided for me (predominantly T-shirts that feature funny sayings that aren't actually funny, like *My swag is so bright I gotta wear shades* and *I may be wrong . . . BUT I DOUBT IT*).

Then I walk into the kitchen and grab a chocolate croissant.

And *then* I get on my mom's laptop.

I plop down on the couch and look at the screen, which is almost completely covered with a jumbled mess of folder and document icons. She needs some serious guidance in desktop organization.

I click on a folder labeled *Travel,* and four more folder icons appear: *Portland, Chicago, Austin,* and *LA.* Maybe cities where my mom has lived? I click on *Portland* first, and I'm greeted by a document filled with symbols instead of letters, like that font Wingdings or something. I try to change it to a font I can actually read, but it doesn't work. I click on the folder of every other city, and it's the same frustrating nonsense. I click on a document called *Overview,* one called *Implementation,* one called *DDA,* and six or seven others, and it's all the same. I don't know if it's a code or an encryption or just a formatting problem, but it's totally snoop-proof, so I move on.

As I'm about to click on Firefox, I notice the name Nadia Forrester at the top right corner of the screen. I hope my mom didn't steal this laptop. I put it out of my mind and get to work. My mom, Felix, and Dane have been filling my head with facts and stories, and I need to see if I can get confirmation on any of them. I'm trying to keep my Google searches vague because of possible government surveillance and whatnot—because I am now *that* paranoid—so it's difficult.

I Google: *deathdate virus.* I come up with a bunch of horrible articles from all over the world about different people and the viruses that have killed them. Downer.

I Google: *deathdate movement.* I come up mainly with Wikipedia entries featuring birthdates and deathdates for famous historical figures behind important movements: Martin Luther King Jr., Elizabeth Cady Stanton, Marcus Garvey. But then I see the link for a Wikipedia entry titled "Deathdate Protests."

I click on it, and I can't believe what I'm staring at.

At the top of the page is an old photo of a throng of protestors, and smack-dab in the middle, there's my mom and Brian Blum. There isn't any caption, but it's unmistakably them. When they were my age. Wow.

So my mom was definitely telling the truth about at least one thing.

In the photo, she's mid-shout, wearing a bandana Rosie the Riveter–style and holding a sign that says WE SHOULDN'T HAVE TO KNOW WHEN IT WILL END. I quickly skim the page. Apparently, protests started immediately after it was announced that deathdates were becoming mandatory. The government said it would be an incredible benefit to the nation, "especially in regards to federal budgeting and military strategizing," but the protestors thought it was about personal profit, pure and simple, with the company that makes the deathdate kits funneling money into the campaigns of the politicians who would put this into effect.

I stare at the fury frozen on the faces of my mom, Brian, and the rest of the throng, and I don't fully get it. I mean, it never occurred to me to think about what it would be like to *not* know. I'm embarrassed to admit it, but I always thought knowing was pretty helpful.

Fired up and confused and wanting to learn more, I Google: *living through deathdate*. I have to scroll through four pages of search results, but finally I stumble upon a couple of message boards where people are going back and forth, discussing rumors that there is a way to live through your deathdate. Apparently, one commenter says, there's a woman from New Jersey who did just that and is now in hiding somewhere.

And there it is.

I know it's foolish to put your faith in a message board, and the most recent comment is from more than ten years ago, but this still seems like confirmation from someone outside this apartment.

Suddenly everything's feeling a little too real. In a desperate attempt to remind myself that I used to have a life before this, I go to Facebook, my first time there since my deathdate, when I used it to bestow love and praise upon my peers.

Problem: the site's been blocked by my mom.

I'm even more cut off from my former life than I realized. I've lost access to everyone. All my friends. All their Timelines. All their funny cat videos.

I'm panicking way more than I should over the loss of Facebook.

Okay, let me think. Maybe she doesn't know about Instagram? I type Paolo's account into the URL header (KaPowInYerFace), and I'm staring at a goofy picture of him wearing sunglasses that I took at Six Flags last summer. Instagram's not blocked. Thank God. The last photo on Paolo's page is a candid he took of me talking with my grandpa Sid at my Sitting. The caption says: *dent's grandpa be mad cool but dent is mad cooler #ripdenton*. I refuse to still be stuck in this apartment when Paolo dies. I can't think of anything more horrible.

Of course thinking about Paolo leads my brain to his older sister, Veronica. Who, you know, took my virginity. NBD. I type in her account next (VMDSelfiesSuck), and naturally it's set to private, but I can still see her profile pic and bio, which consists of one line: *Sometimes I drink orange juice.* She's so cool. I stare at her photo, which is shoulders-up of her smiling in this big way you'd never see her do in real life. A superhuge, sarcastic smile that melts my heart. I think about how awesome it was to make out with her in the bathroom, our bodies pressing up against each other. I'm starting to get aroused, and even though I'm highly tempted to give myself a little release (the first one in at least four days, which is a long time), the idea of my mom, Felix, or Dane walking in and seeing me jerking off in front of a laptop sounds worse than getting kidnapped by the DIA. There'll be time for that later. In the privacy of my own room.

Instead, I go back to Paolo's account, thinking maybe he'll have some more pictures from my Sitting. I notice that one of the names that's favorited the picture of my grandfather and me is RLittle916. I'm shocked; my stepmom joined Instagram, and I didn't even know.

She has no photos posted other than a profile pic, where her eyes are blinking shut. "Geez, Mom," I say aloud. "You couldn't find a better picture?" Then my eyes land on her profile: *I love my family and the beach. Right now devoting most of my time to my son Denton, who won't be around much longer : (*

My throat tightens up. It's that damn emoticon that really gets me. I miss my stepmom. The screen is blurred. I'm all snot and salt.

I shut the laptop and wipe my face. This is nuts.

I go into my room and put on the green-and-yellow off-brand Puma sneakers—the brand is called CatScratch, not even kidding—my mom bought me. I wonder if she chose embarrassing clothing as a way to further deter me from leaving the apartment.

I go back out into the front room, looking around for any hidden cameras.

When I don't see any, I walk to the front door and try to open it.

Locked.

With a deadbolt that needs a key to open it on both sides of the door. Who has that? Why would you even want that *unless you were planning to hold someone hostage*.

I try again, yanking at the door, which moves back and forth, but less than an inch. I yank again. And again. And again. Nothing.

I put both hands on the knob, get one CatScratch on the doorframe, and start pulling as if my life depends on it. Which maybe it does. I hear myself grunting like a professional tennis player. Sweat is dripping down my face.

I need to get out of here. Now.

I back up from the door and ram my shoulder into it.

I realize this is a pull door, but I'm thinking maybe I can loosen it or something.

I ram into it again. And again. And again.

Nothing's happening.

I lean back against the door.

I scream.

I scream for the life I used to have.

I scream for the parents I might never see again.

I scream for the best friend getting closer to death every minute that I'm here.

And I scream to remind myself that, even though this hardly feels like a life at all, I am alive.

It probably lasts a total of three seconds, but my throat feels ragged and torn.

I slowly walk back to the couch and sit down.

"Hey," an older man's voice says from outside. "Everything all right in there?"

Shit. Why did I call attention to myself like that?

"Hello?" the man says.

"Oh," I say, my voice hoarse. "Everything's fine. I just . . . Um, I got laid off from my job today." I said *laid off* to make it seem more adult.

"Jesus," the man says. "Sorry to hear, but keep it down next time. Sounded like someone was getting murdered in there."

"Yeah," I say. "Will do, sorry."

I hear the man walk away.

I sit there in silence, utterly spent. Utterly defeated.

This is my life now. No use fighting it.

I stare at the television and the little black box next to it.

Well. If you can't beat 'em, right?

FIVE

My soul is slowly dying, one Netflix episode at a time.

In the three days since Monday, I've watched almost three seasons of *Danger People*. It's a drama about two cops who go undercover in all these crazy ways: the first season, they're stunt people on a movie set; the second season, they're firefighters; and the third season, they're circus performers. It's better than it sounds.

It's one of those shows I'd always heard people talk about but had never gotten around to watching, especially as my deathdate got closer and binge-watching started to feel like a sad use of my time. As with a lot of popular entertainment in the post-deathdate era, the protagonists, Brannigan and Rodrigo, are undated. Writers are fairly unanimous in their feeling that known deathdates suck the drama and high stakes out of most narratives. So, conveniently, most action heroes are born undated, with the genetic flaw that prevents them from learning their deathdates. I always found that to be sort of hilarious.

Danger People is sort of hilarious, too. But it's helped distract me from the nothingness my life has become. My mom has been gone a lot, working at the lab with Dane, doing God knows what with my bodily fluids, which they take new samples of every other day.

I'd like to say I'm getting to know her better, but I don't know if that's true. I know a lot about her hatred of the government and mandatory deathdates, and how much she adores Felix. But she never really asks me anything about myself. It bums me out.

Last night, she came home and started watching an episode of *Danger People* with me. She really related to the whole undercover thing, and I thought we might be having some kind of bonding moment, but then Felix showed up, and they proceeded to loudly talk through the rest of the episode. I hate that.

Now I'm watching the last episode of season three. I'd like to say I'm really invested, but at this point all the episodes are blurring together, and I just want to get through the damn thing.

This is my life now.

Brannigan is in the middle of this difficult trapeze act— and he has no idea the scaffolding's been rigged to break— when I hear the lock jiggling, and my mom opens the door. I think it's the afternoon, which means she's home earlier than usual.

"Hi hi hi!" she says, clearly in one of her up moods. I

watch her close the door and lock it again with one of her keys.

"Howdy," I say, pausing the episode. "You're early today."

"Things have been going well," she says, still wearing a white lab jacket, "so we gave ourselves the afternoon off. Also I have something for you." She pulls a stiff piece of paper out of a manila envelope and places it down next to me on the couch.

I lean over to look. "Who's Frank Biggs?" It's a birth certificate with that name on it.

"You," my mom says with a smile.

"Huh?"

"It's your new name!"

No.

"You can't walk around having people call you Denton Little. Denton Little is supposed to be dead." This did not occur to me, and I find it very upsetting. "You don't hear people calling me Cheryl. I'm Nadia Forrester now. And Dane's real name is definitely not Dane. So, you're not alone in this."

I stare down again at the words on the paper. Frank Biggs.

"Do you get it?" my mom asks.

I'm not sure what she means until I read the name a few more times.

"Instead of Little," I say, "it's Biggs." I want to cry.

"Yes!" She claps her hands once. "Fun, right?" There's nothing fun about that. "I know it might seem strange now, but you'll get used to it."

"I guess," I say. If I'm getting a new name, I should

at least be allowed to pick it myself. Something cool. Like Nick Chambers. I don't know, maybe not that. But definitely not *Frank*.

"Okay, good. Because it's impossible to change it at this point."

There are three knocks at the door. "Oh, they're here," my mom says. She puts her ear to the door, and unlike the first time he showed up, I understand what Dane says: "Happy dinosaur." I feel kind of flattered that the phrase from the letter my mom wrote me is, like, the go-to password.

She lets Dane in, and I'm surprised to see there's a dark-haired little boy holding his hand. "Hey there, Yuri," she says, crouching down to the boy's level.

"Hello," he says.

It's jarring to see a kid in the apartment.

"It smell like body in here," Dane says. He's not wrong.

"Denton," my mom says. "Or, I should say, *Frank*. Since we have some downtime today, Dane wanted to introduce you to his son. Yuri really wanted to meet you."

Dane has a *son*? Who wants to meet me?

"Hi there," I say, getting up from the couch and walking toward them. Yuri smiles and mushes his face into Dane's leg. It's pretty adorable.

"He get shy sometime," Dane says. "Yuri, you finally here in the room with Denton. You say hello."

I crouch down, and Yuri's face reappears. "Guess what?" he asks.

"What?" I say.

"The day they say I'm gonna die isn't actually the day I'm gonna die." He smiles so big I can see all his teeth, including the gaps where he's lost some. I'm so confused, but I can't help but smile back.

"He like you," Dane says.

"Yeah, that's so sweet," I say. "I like him, too."

"No," my mom says. "Dane means that Yuri is *literally* like you. He was injected with the virus in the womb."

"Oh," I say, the blood draining from my face. I suddenly feel so bad for this little guy. He's wrapped up in all this, even though he never asked to be.

"Here," Dane says, pulling a book out of his back pocket and handing it to Yuri. "You go sit and read. Have good time."

Chills run down my spine as I see it's the book I was reading in kindergarten when I first met Paolo, the one about the bear who bakes a birthday cake for the moon.

"Okay," Yuri says. He grabs the book, gets a running start, and vaults onto the couch.

I look back at Dane and my mom. "I don't get it," I say. "He has the virus, and he *knows*?"

"He does," my mom says, taking Dane's jacket from him and putting it in the closet. "Dane and his wife, Matilda, decided to start new lives after she lived through her deathdate. New identities, new home. And they took Yuri with them."

I glance at Yuri, who's laser-focused on his book. If my dad had decided we should go with my mom when she started her new life, that would have been me.

"How did you decide you wanted to inject Yuri?" I ask Dane. "Just because you wanted him to be undated? For the movement?"

Dane looks at me like I'm stupid. "What you mean?"

I asked because I'm curious, but now I wish I hadn't.

"Actually," my mother says. "Dane and Matilda found me, because they'd heard about our movement. They'd heard I could provide a way to live through your death-date."

"We did not make decision to inject Yuri," Dane says, as if my ignorance has physically wounded him. "We make decision to *have* Yuri. To save Matilda's life."

I'm not following.

"I've told you this," my mother says, seeing my confusion. "You were injected with the virus in my womb, and I contracted it through you. That was the only way I could get it."

"But I thought . . . ," I say. "Weren't you trying to save me?"

My mother looks down and sighs, the three of us still hovering awkwardly near the front door, like she wishes she didn't have to go into this right now. "We did extensive testing on mice, but the virus never worked when injected directly. But"—she looks back up at me—"we discovered it *would* work on a fetus.

"And not only that, once a fetus had the virus, it would pass it along to the mother, who would live through her deathdate, too."

"Oh," I say.

I get it now.

My mom decided to get pregnant because it could save her life. That's the only reason she wanted me.

I remember the talk I had with my dad in the kitchen during my Sitting. He said he hadn't wanted to have another child after Felix, and I flipped out, offended that he'd never wanted me to exist. He said my mom had gone off birth control without telling him, and that's how I was conceived. I thought this explained everything about my dad's behavior, why he so often seemed emotionally detached from me.

But I had it all wrong. My dad didn't want me . . . because he didn't want to create a human being solely in the service of my mom's mad-scientist urges, even if it was going to allow her to live longer.

"Now you comprehend," Dane says. "We inject Yuri so Matilda can live. But then the government snatch her away. The work we do, your mother and me, this will bring the system down." He grips my arm right below the shoulder and stares past me, his eyes nearly popping out of their sockets. "The work *you* do, this will bring them down. Expose the government. And give them no choice but to tell us what they have done with Matilda!"

I look at my mom, who's nodding, smiling, getting revved up by Dane's speech.

I look back at Yuri, who mouths silently along as he continues to read the book that first brought Paolo and me together.

I look at the door of the apartment.

I know what I have to do.

SIX

I'm again sitting and watching *Danger People*.

But this time, I'm not actually watching it.

I've been fully dressed—jeans, sneakers, and a gray T-shirt that says, *Dude Gotta Party*—for at least thirty minutes, and my heart is beating so fast.

Even though my mind is mainly focused on what I'm about to do, I'm seeing the images on the screen—Brannigan and Rodrigo dealing with this huge-ass fire in season two—and they're inspiring me to channel my inner Danger Person. If these cops were in my situation, they would do whatever they had to in order to get the hell out of here. It wouldn't matter that they were undated and knew they could die at any moment.

Because the way I look at it, if there's a chance Paolo can be saved, I have to get to him. Of *course* my mom's going to tell me that the DIA will kill me if I leave. She'll say whatever it takes to get me to stay here and do her bidding. Just like she did whatever it took to save her own life. Matilda was taken away, but I don't know the full story—hell, maybe she *ran away* from Dane. I wouldn't blame her.

I hear the front-door lock making noises. My mom is back from her run.

I strike as casual a pose as possible, doing my best impression of me the past few days, in a total TV coma.

"Hey," she says, locking the door with her key, then lightly jogging in place as she messes with some electronic doodad on her arm.

"Hi," I say, not even looking up.

"Having a good morning?" she asks, doing a few squats.

"Yeah, you know," I say. "Really into this show."

"Oh, are you?" she says. "Hadn't noticed that." She heads to her bedroom, then into the bathroom. She closes the door, and I hear the shower turn on.

Go-time.

I pop up from the couch, moving as quickly and quietly as I can. My mom's showers generally only last four to seven minutes. I go into her bedroom and—YES!—there are her keys, lying smack-dab in the middle of the bed.

I grab them.

I'm inordinately proud my logic was correct; I figured my mom would assume I was so into my Netflix that she wouldn't think twice about leaving the keys out. It's almost touching that she trusts me enough to no longer worry that I might try to escape.

Once I reach the front door, though, I realize there's something my logic hadn't accounted for: there are seven keys here.

I grab a silver key first. I try to direct it into the lock, but my hand is shaking so much that I miss, and the whole key ring clatters to the floor.

I freeze, waiting to see if my mom heard.

She didn't.

I pick up the key ring, and this time I get the silver key into the lock. I try to move it back and forth. It won't budge.

I'm looking at the keys and trying to picture which one of them is in my mom's hand every day when she walks in and locks the door behind her. Why didn't I take note of that? Or at least check what color it is? Such an idiot.

I try a bronze key next, then a round silver one. I can't tell if they don't fit, or if, like my mother, I'm just struggling to use them correctly. There's no way this plan is going to work. The shower is still running, but who knows for how much longer.

My hands are shaking more than ever.

I try another bronze key, and this one, too, won't move in the lock at all. "Please," I whisper. I wriggle it around, moving it up and down, and suddenly the key finds the groove and turns to the left.

Yes.

At that exact moment, as if this key has powers beyond just opening doors, the shower turns off.

Ohmigod.

I want to throw up, I'm shaking so much. But I've come this far; I can't give up now. Sorry, Mom. I pull the door open, tiptoe out, and hop down the stairs to the building's front door.

I'm outside.

The sun hits my face, and I want to scream, this time triumphantly, but I don't.

Instead, I'm running.

I can't believe I got out of there. I *did* something.

I've been alive a week longer than I thought I would be, and yet this is the first moment since my deathdate that actually feels like living.

Now I can get back to New Jersey, find Paolo, and let him know he might be able to survive, too. I'll be super-stealth, so his mom never finds out I'm in town. And then the two of us will come back to the safe house, where my mom can collect samples and run tests and stuff on Paolo, and figure out what's what.

Maybe I'll also find my dad, talk to him about all of this craziness.

Also wouldn't mind finding Veronica. Maybe squeeze in a quick, triumphant make-out sesh.

I realize this is not the most well-thought-out plan.

But, again, it's something.

I've been running in the direction I came from the night of my deathdate, thinking that will lead me back to the train station, but now I take a left turn when I'm pretty sure I'm supposed to take a right. I need to think smart; this is, after all, a game of chess I'm playing, with the DIA agents on my tail and with my mom, who I'm sure has already noticed my absence and is using her super-human running ability to come after me. (I've never actually played chess. If I survive all this, I'm going to make that a life priority.) I run from Fifty-Third Street up to Fifty-Fourth, then Fifty-Fifth, even though Penn Station is somewhere in the Thirties. I'm glad I'm taking a route they won't expect, but I'm thinking this might not be the most productive way to actually get somewhere.

I make a left and find myself walking toward a huge four-lane highway. Even though I was dazed and exhausted the night of my deathdate, I'm sure I didn't pass anything like this. I walk back the other way. My impulsive exuberance is already giving way to neurotic paranoia. There are more people on this street, and though none of them seem like obvious candidates to be government agents, who really does? Paolo's mom certainly didn't.

I pass two teenagers in basketball jerseys. I pass a skinny man wearing lots of eyeliner. I pass a mother and her daughter. "I told you, we'll go for ice cream after dinner," the mother says.

"But I want it before!" the little girl squeals.

"No, Dylan," the mom says, making brief eye contact with me and smiling as I walk by.

I walk three more steps before stopping in my tracks as an alarm bell goes off in my head. A little girl named Dylan sounds awfully familiar, and now I remember why: on the train ride here a week ago, at two in the morning, a mother and her little girl were a few seats behind me. I thought it was strange for the girl to be out so late at night, but then I promptly fell asleep and forgot all about it.

But now I've just passed another mom with another daughter named Dylan. Is that woman a DIA spy? Is her daughter? Can three-year-olds be spies? I can't remember if that's what the mom looked like or not. Should I turn around and get a better look? No, that makes no sense. Why would I start following a spy who's following me?

A deafening car horn interrupts my train of thought, and I turn to see a yellow car bearing down on me.

In my panic, I'd stopped dead in the middle of the street.

A shudder runs through me as I brace for the impact, in disbelief that the yellow car has found me after all.

This is how I was meant to die. Destiny.

But the car, trying to turn onto the street I'm crossing, stops about a foot before it hits me.

"What the hell you doing? MOVE!" the driver shouts.

It's not my stoner classmate Willis Ellis, and it's not even the same car that he was always driving.

It's a yellow taxicab.

One of thousands that roam the streets of New York. So, it's less of a destiny thing and more of a moron-who-doesn't-understand-the-rules-of-the-city thing. Well, great.

"Sorry, sorry!" I shout as I scurry to safety.

I press onward, my heart still pumping wildly, trying to blend back into the sidewalk traffic after calling such attention to myself.

I make a right, and a street sign tells me I'm now on Eighth Avenue, where I encounter thickets of men and women in business attire. This is good: these crowds give me something to work with.

I walk briskly, weaving in and out of people, trying to stay aware of any potential followers. The street numbers get lower. I'm already at Forty-Seventh Street. I'll be at Penn Station in no time.

"You like comedy?" a guy in a baseball cap, a little older than me, asks, popping out at me from my right.

I jump a little, though I assume he's talking to someone else.

"Hey, man, don't ignore me," the guy says again. "Don't you like comedy?"

"Um, sure," I say. "But I actually—"

"Awesome!" He adjusts the clipboard he's holding. "Then you're in luck, my brother, because I've got a great deal for two tickets to the Gotham Chuckle Club for the low price of—"

I actually wish I could take in some comedy right now. That sounds nice. "Sorry, I have to catch a train."

"No, you don't! Take a later one! It's Friday, man. It's a beautiful day for comedy."

"Sorry," I say, walking away.

"Dick," the comedy guy says in my wake.

That was mean.

As the street numbers tick down lower and lower, I begin to relax. Is it possible the DIA has already given up on searching for me in New York City? And that my mom was overreacting? And/or trying to manipulate me?

I hit Forty-Second Street, and as I stand at a corner, waiting for the walk sign, I take a minute to breathe. My New York City geography's never been that good, but I think Times Square is somewhere around here. I've been there with my family a few times, and it always astounds me. Big-ass TV screens and crazy-bright lights. We went through it at night once, and I swear, all of that wattage made it seem like daytime.

But I don't have time for sightseeing. I need to get to the train and get home. The light switches from red-orange hand to white walking man, and I step off the curb, in sync with about a dozen other people. I can see the appeal of living in this city. You really feel like you're a part of something bigger, this living, breathing, pulsing thing.

As I'm reveling in the beauty of it all, I feel an arm hook around mine from the left. I'm fully expecting to look over and see that obnoxious comedy guy again, so I'm already preparing to tell him in great detail why there's no way I'll be able to take in a show today. But it turns out none of that is necessary.

"Well, here we are again," a familiar voice says.

"Oh," I say.

"Just keep walking," Paolo's mom says. "Let's not make this any harder than it needs to be, sweetie."

SEVEN

I can't believe I've let this happen again. Paolo's mom has a firm grip on my arm as we continue walking down Eighth Avenue. Unlike the last time she kidnapped me, though, I'm not paralyzed. I can run.

"I know there may be a temptation to try and wriggle away from me," Paolo's mom says, like she's reading my mind, "but I promise it's not worth it. We have agents surrounding us on all sides."

I glance over at her as we walk. The entire right side of her face is bruised a purplish brown. For a brief moment, I think she's gotten infected with the splotch virus, but then I remember the car accident.

"I'm sorry about your face," I say. Even after all that's happened, I still think of her as my best friend's mom.

"It looks worse than it is," she says. "But thank you." She's keeping up a steady pace, occasionally glancing around.

"How's Paolo?" I ask. Probably a strange time for that, but I don't care.

"I'm not really sure, Denton," she says. "He's not speaking to me these days."

"Oh," I say, unable to hold back a smile. My best friend still has my back.

We pass Port Authority, the gray, unappealing bus depot that I was in once with my family when we missed the train and took the bus to the city instead. A large man in tattered pants stands out front and asks us for three dollars so he can get to Albany and see his daughter. Paolo's mom doesn't even look at him. "Where are you taking me?" I ask.

"To a car," she says. "Not very original, I apologize. We're parked closer to the Lincoln Tunnel. Didn't want to risk getting stuck in Times Square traffic."

"What if I don't want to go?" I ask.

"I'd say I'm truly sorry, Dent, but you got away from me once, and I'm not going to let it happen again. But this is for the best, I promise."

I'm once again trapped, forced to listen to someone tell me what's best for me. I look around to assess my options and possibly identify any of these other agents she's talking about. There are too many people around to pick any out.

"I can't imagine what it felt like when you learned your mother's been alive all these years. Pretty disturbing, right?" Two teenage girls walk by, giggling and belting out a show tune. Probably not DIA agents. "I don't know what she's been telling you the past week, Denton, but you don't owe her anything. She's a very misguided person. Who's using you."

I don't want to hear this.

"What did she have you doing today? Running some errand for her?"

"She doesn't know I'm out here," I say. I make my own choices. Paolo's mom should know that. Somebody should, anyway.

"Oh," she says, a note of surprise in her voice. "Then what were you doing?"

We make a right turn at the corner, moving away from Times Square, away from Penn Station.

"I was trying to get home." I immediately regret saying that. I try to change the subject. "How did you even find me?"

She turns her head and looks straight at me for the first time. "We're the government, Denton. We have our ways." At first I think she's joking, but once I realize she isn't, it just seems terrifying.

"Okay," I say, wondering if that woman and her daughter, Dylan, actually were spying on me.

"It wasn't as easy as we thought it would be. Let's leave it at that."

So my mom was completely justified in keeping me on lockdown. But who cares? Whether I'm with her or the DIA, I'm somewhere I don't want to be.

"You know, you're using me, too," I say. "You don't care what happens to me. You just care about your job."

"That's not true, Denton," she says, guiding us through a pack of elementary-school kids on some kind of field trip. "I care about you a lot. Coming with me is the best thing for both of us. You'll be treated very well; I promise you that." She sounds sincere, but I don't believe it.

"My mom says you're going to kill me," I say, deciding now is as good a time as any to drop that bomb.

Paolo's mom stops in the middle of the sidewalk, still gripping my arm tight. "She said *what*?"

"That you'd kill me. That it wouldn't even matter, because the world thinks I'm already dead."

"Oh, Denton." Paolo's mom looks to the left and right, not really seeing things, more for dramatic effect. "Your mom has gone further off the deep end than I thought. You don't believe her, do you?"

"Honestly, Cynthia," I say, "I have no idea. I mean, I've been thinking about Paolo a lot, how maybe this same virus that saved my life could save his. But clearly you don't care about that. You seem to be fine with letting your son die."

Paolo's mom swallows twice, then looks at me with daggers. "That's not fair, Denton."

"Oh no?" I say, feeling bolder by the second. "Then explain it to me."

"The system is so much bigger than one person," she says through gritted teeth. "Paolo has an early deathdate. It's a raw deal, but it is what it is." She looks to the right and blinks four times in a row. "Come on."

We walk in silence, Paolo's mom's grip tighter than before.

"There's our car up ahead," she says. "Here's how this is going to—"

A man coming from the opposite direction jostles Paolo's mom hard. She loosens her grip on my arm as she stumbles to the sidewalk, and I'm thinking this is just something that happens in New York, until I hear my brother's voice.

"Run, Dent! Get the hell out of here!"

Holy shit, it's Felix. Saving my ass yet again.

I run forward, immediately think better of it, and run the other way. I'll have a better chance of losing people if I head for the insanity of Times Square.

"Dammit, Felix! Denton, come back!" Paolo's mom shouts as she gets up from the ground and begins to run after me.

I pick up speed, running across the street as the orange hand blinks, signaling it's almost time not to walk. The icon solidifies as I reach the middle of the street, and I hear cars zoom by, inches behind me. Paolo's mom is still on the other side.

I run through and around throngs of slow-moving people, past Broadway theaters with huge signs I don't have time to read. What am I doing? Where am I going? I should stick with my original plan, I guess: get on a train to New Jersey, find my parents and let them know I'm all right, then get Paolo. If I really want to save him, I need the knowledge my mom has. If she used me, I can use her back. So once I find him, I'll bring him back to the safe house. That plan has approximately one zillion holes in it, but it's the best I can do at the moment.

I emerge into the center of Times Square, and the hugeness of everything makes me aware of the panic growing in my chest. This is all so much bigger than me. I'm mesmerized for a split second by a gargantuan TV screen straight ahead of me—a man is grilling something on a barbecue while wearing no pants—but then I turn left and keep running.

It's harder to dodge and weave through the people here.

My path is suddenly blocked by Elmo and Buzz Lightyear. They look sad and strange and not quite themselves, and they're both wearing backpacks. Elmo silently extends an arm around my shoulders, and Buzz Lightyear holds up both hands, making the international sign for camera. "No, no," I say, pushing Elmo's arm off. "I don't want to take a picture with you. I'm sorry, guys."

"Only five dollars!" Buzz Lightyear says, a far less inspiring catchphrase than his usual one. I dash away, thinking that whole exchange was creepier than anything that's happened with the DIA thus far.

I make it about seven steps before I encounter a thick barricade of tourists extending across the whole sidewalk. "Excuse me!" I say. A family looks back at me, their eyes wide. They make space for me to pass by. "Thanks!" I shout. The father says, "You're welcome," with some kind of accent.

But it doesn't matter, because now there's a new slow-moving herd of tourists. And I realize I'm heading away from Penn Station. Shoot. I look behind me to get a sense of how close Paolo's mom is, but I don't see her. I'm also on the lookout for the other agents she mentioned. Maybe she was bluffing. I can't worry about that now, but I can avoid running into her by continuing to move in this direction. I'll just double back later.

Before I understand what's happening, an arm pops out from an open door and yanks me inside. It's Dane.

"Move off to side," he says, pushing me away from the glass door and then staring frantically out at all the people passing by. "Move further to side!" he shouts. "So you cannot be seen!"

I turn away from the door, and I'm looking at manne-
quins in women's clothing and a huge sign that says FOR-
EVER 21. A nice idea, but first I gotta focus on making it
past seventeen.

I inch back toward Dane, who's continuing his jumpy
surveillance.

"Why you leave apartment?" Dane asks without looking at me. "Now everything compromised!"

"Dane, look, I'm sorry, but I want to go home. I need to."

"This is not possible! You know this!" The door opens,
and a mother and daughter in matching blue fanny packs
walk in, forcing Dane to step to the side. They give him a
dirty look as they pass, and he looks a little embarrassed,
but this doesn't stop him from resuming his post once
they're gone. "Your mother is very upset about this, you
should know."

"Honestly, I don't care what my mother thinks. I'm
upset with her, too. And I'm still going to catch that train,
all right? Sorry." I run deeper into the store, past scores of
lady blouses, and bound down an escalator.

"You don't do that!" Dane shouts, trailing behind me.

Loud, pulsing music plays as I speed past racks of dangly jewelry and head down another escalator. I don't know
what my plan is.

"I am not messing, Denton!" Dane shouts, still hot on
my heels. "You cannot just run away!"

"Watch me," I say. I realize I actually have an excuse
to do something Brannigan did during a chase in the first
season of *Danger People:* I leap from the down escalator
over to the up one. It's very awesome. Dane is surprised,
and I'm back on the first floor before he's even made a

move to follow. I sprint out the door and back into tourist land.

Being alive is cool.

Riding this wave of empowerment, I turn back in the direction of Penn Station. I push my way through the throngs of people, not even bothering to say excuse me. I'm acting like a real New Yorker, and it feels great.

The crowds thin as I pass block after block, fewer tourists and more businesspeople, and no one seems to be following me. I'm starting to get worried that maybe you can't get to Penn Station from Seventh Avenue when the overhang comes into view.

It's the NJ Transit entrance of Penn Station.

I can't believe I've made it. I'm going home.

I take the escalator down and head to the ticket machines, still peering around occasionally for suspicious characters. As I grab my one-way ticket from the machine, a woman with wrinkly skin and glassy eyes asks for a dollar, and I give her one, pulling from the same wad of bills Felix gave me the night I didn't die.

I find a monitor with train times. There's a train leaving in three minutes that goes to my hometown; it's already waiting on track four. Amazing. I hold my ticket tight and head straight for the platform, taking the stairs two at a time.

"There he is!" Paolo's mom shouts, barreling down the platform toward me, followed by at least two other agents.

SHIT.

That's why my journey was so easy. They knew I'd be coming here.

I guess getting on the train is no longer an option. I turn back up the steps, pushing against the tide of late passengers.

My body is getting tired of all this running, but I need to keep moving. I careen across the dirty floors of Penn Station, less focused now on where I'm going and more focused on getting away.

"Stop, Denton!" Paolo's mom shouts. "Please! We don't want to be forced to take extreme measures."

What does that mean? Would they shoot me?

I glance back quickly to see that Paolo's mom is accompanied by two broad-shouldered men—one white and one Asian. They are fast.

I skid past a cart selling pretzels as the glassy-eyed woman from earlier appears in my path, asking for a dollar. "I already gave you one!" I shout.

Up ahead are stairs that lead to the street.

Dane and Felix are waiting at the bottom of those stairs.

"Quickly, Dent!" Felix shouts. "They're right behind you!"

"Yeah, I know that!" I shout back at him.

I make a quick left turn down a corridor. I'm not going with Paolo's mom, but I'm not going with them either. Not yet anyway.

"What you doing?" Dane shouts.

What I'm doing is trying to get away, which is probably dumb, foolhardy, careless, but I have to at least try. I'm not sure if Dane and Felix have joined the chase or not; they might not want to be caught by those agents either.

I have to say, running full speed through one of New

York City's biggest transportation hubs while being chased by at least three very official-looking people is probably not a fantastic way to stay under the radar.

There's a sign ahead showing the way to the A, C, and E subway trains. I contemplate it for a second, but the subway's too claustrophobic and risky, especially since Paolo's mom and her dudes aren't far behind me. I veer left instead, up a bunch of stairs under a sign pointing the way to Amtrak.

And again, I ask: what the hell am I doing?

I find myself back on the upper level of the train station, staring at a huge board of train times, wildly looking around for a way out. I see a nearby exit to Eighth Avenue, and I dash toward it. There are more steps, and I take them three at a time, extending my legs as far as they can possibly go, until I'm aboveground, back on the chaotic street, surrounded by shouts, whistles, and car horns. I try to decide whether to go left or right before remembering it's completely arbitrary and I should just pick one and not waste any more time deciding.

So I've gone left, and the air is in my ears, and my heart is thumping, and I don't know how much longer I can keep this up. As I'm literally pounding the pavement, a car horn beeps loudly behind me. I ignore it, just part of the cacophony of the city. But it doesn't let up, and I'm terrified to realize it might be beeping at me. The DIA must have troops on foot and in cars. I pick up my pace, trying to call on my expertise from four years on the high school cross-country team: *Pump your arms,* Coach Mueller used to say. *Breathe in through the nose, out through the mouth.*

He never gave guidance on what to do if being chased by federal agents.

I refuse to look back at the relentlessly beeping car. It gets stuck at a red light, and I zip across the street, even though it's a *Don't Walk*. Screw you, car.

But I'm not as smart as I think I am. Up ahead of me, the white DIA agent catapults himself around the corner onto my block, effectively cutting off that route. I quickly turn back and see Paolo's mom and the other agent coming at me from that direction, about a block away. I can't run into traffic. I'm screwed.

And to top it all off, the car continues its horrendous beeping. Then the light turns green, and it moves toward me. Now that I've turned around, I can see it for the first time, and my whole body starts to tingle as it pulls up alongside me.

Because it's not just any car.

It's *my* car. Danza.

And in the driver's seat is my best friend, Paolo.

EIGHT

"Dude!" Paolo says, leaning out the window. "You're not making it very easy for us to save you!"

"Pow!" I shout. "Ohmigod, you're the beeper!"

"Hey, Dent," Millie says, leaning forward in the passenger seat, her dark hair swinging to the side.

"Millie! It's so good to see you guys!"

"Yeah, great, get in, man!" Paolo says. "Get in the car!"

"Right right right," I say, whipping open the back door. I'm almost in, but before I can get the door closed, there's an arm around my shoulder, trying to yank me out.

"I don't think so, kiddo," the white agent says. "You're not going anywhere."

"We'll . . . see . . . ," I say, focusing all my strength on trying to get the door shut. Paolo reaches out and grabs my shoulder to help keep me in the car.

"Paolo Luis Diaz!" Paolo's mom says, maybe ten feet away. "You shouldn't be here!"

"Start driving," Millie says.

"Can I do that?" Paolo asks through gritted teeth. "With the door open? What if this agent guy gets hurt?"

"I think he'll be okay. He looks tough."

"Okily-dokily . . ." Paolo lets go of me, and the agent and I are flung toward the open door as the car revs forward. I'm sure I'm about to fall out onto the street, but Millie grabs my hand and whisks me back into the car.

"Holy crap," I say, breathing heavily. "Nice catch, Millie."

"I have catlike reflexes," she says, gripping my hand a moment longer before letting go.

I slam the door shut, and we leave Paolo's mom and the two agents in our dust. "You guys have impeccable timing."

"I know!" Paolo says. "That couldn't have been more badass if we tried. Though I really was trying. Hey, watch it!" He slams hard on his horn at another car. "Man, these city people drive like maniacs. I love it!"

Paolo's never been a very good driver, and under any other circumstances, I would be completely mortified to see him behind the wheel of Danza. But now I'm just so happy to see him at all. Millie, too. And, of course, Danza. Sitting inside my old car, inhaling its familiar strawberry musk, feels like coming home.

"How are you guys?" I ask.

"Dude," Paolo says. "This has been a crazy week."

"No shit," I say.

"Hope you don't mind that I took Danza. Still had that extra set of keys in case you locked yours in the car again."

"Uh-oh," Millie says, looking behind us.

"What?" I turn, too, and see that Paolo's mom and her

two cohorts are getting into a black car that's pulled up to the curb. "Oh shoot."

"What? What is it?" Paolo asks, swerving around a biker.

"You're gonna have to do some serious driving in a second," Millie says.

"This isn't serious already? What do you mean?"

Millie turns back around to face front. "They are also in an automobile now."

"Aw, geez, I'm about to be in another car chase with my mom?" Paolo looks up into the rearview mirror. "Hey, Dent, I hope you appreciate all the shit we're going through for you."

"I'm sorry, man," I say. "I really do."

"Aw, that was such a genuine response. I was just kidding, bro. Kinda. Anyways, everybody buckle up. We don't want a repeat of that last car chase."

"Right," I say.

"Although, technically, that crash helped you get away," Paolo says. "So maybe we do want a repeat."

The black car is just four cars behind, weaving and passing and beeping, trying to catch up to us.

"You need to make the speedometer needle go farther to the right," Millie says. "And make more crazy turns."

"Oh, you wanna see crazy turns? Check this out!"

Paolo cuts the wheel hard and turns onto a cross street, barely making it.

"Nice!" I say. "Terrifying but nice." It was actually an impressive maneuver. Maybe I've never given Paolo's driving enough credit. But then something immediately feels wrong because all the cars parked along the side of the road are facing in a different direction than our car is. "No no no no, this is bad."

"You just said it was nice," Paolo says.

"Not nice," Millie says, her voice slightly tightening, which is her subtle way of exhibiting panic.

"We're going the wrong way," I say. "This is a one-way street, and we're going the wrong way."

"Oh shoot, you're right!" Paolo says. "We might get a ticket or something, huh?"

"Uh, or have a head-on collision with another car," I say. "You know, one of those."

"There are no cars coming, so I'm not gonna stop driving, right? Or should I? Kick it into reverse? What do I do, what do I do?"

"Your deathdate is in, like, three weeks," I say. "And Millie doesn't know hers, and who the hell knows about me! Clearly we're about to die." I grip the armrest on the car door. "We're going to die. And poor Danza's gonna be smashed to pieces."

"Dude, could we have a little positivity and stop with the dunesday routine? It's not helping."

"Did you just say *dunes*day?" I ask as the car continues moving forward, the way still miraculously clear.

"Yes! Okay? Dunesday! You're being all end-of-the-world. Bleak! Post-apocalyptic!"

"That's *doomsday*," Millie says.

"*Dooms*day? Like Dr. Doom? That's weird."

"And *dunesday* isn't?" I say.

"No, *dunesday* makes perfect sense. When the world ends, it will be covered with sand, thereby—"

"Holy shit," I say. The traffic light ahead of us has

turned green, and since we're going the wrong way, it means cars have just been given permission to drive directly into us. "Ohmigod, all those cars . . . Shit shit shit shit. Do something, Pow!"

"Well, it's too late to hit reverse now!" Paolo says.

"Just keep going," Millie says. "They'll stop."

"What the hell, Millie?" I shout.

"They will," she says.

The car heading straight toward us isn't a car at all but a huge truck, its front grille smirking at us like a lunatic. Its low and powerful horn blares, and the world starts to spin as I brace myself for the impact.

But it never comes, because, as Millie predicted, the truck has no choice but to come to a screeching halt, blocking all the cars behind it and leaving a perfect-size gap for Paolo to maneuver off the street and onto the avenue, once again facing Danza in the correct direction.

"Wow," Paolo says.

"Yeah," I agree.

"People always say you have to be more aggressive when you drive in the city," Paolo says. "It's really true."

"I thought we were going to die together in this car, no joke," I say.

"There are worse ways to go," Paolo says.

"Millie," I say, "how'd you know the truck would stop?"

"I didn't," Millie says. "I just hoped it would. I was also pretty sure we were about to die."

"What?" Paolo says. "You were casually instructing me to drive into a truck you weren't sure would stop? Damn, General Mills, you're even more baller than I thought. That's some real *Thelma and Louise* shit."

"Still finding ways to relate everything back to *Thelma and Louise*," I say. "That's comforting."

"You know it, bro," Paolo says, steering around two delivery guys taking hundreds of soda bottles out of the back of a truck.

I unbuckle my seat belt and stare out the rear window, scanning the traffic for any sign of the DIA-mobile. "I think your little one-way turn actually bought us some time, Pow. Whew."

As I sit back and rebuckle, I'm able to take a moment to appreciate the fact that I'm in my car with Paolo and Millie. After the lonely, confusing week I've had, it feels amazing.

"So," I say. "How the hell did you guys find me? How did you know I'd be coming out that exit of Penn Station? I mean, I would be so screwed right now if you hadn't been there. I'd probably be on my way to DC with your mom, Pow."

"Yes, you are correct," Paolo says. "You would have been screwed. We are your personal gods."

"I always wanted to have my own personal god," Millie says.

"Like I said," Paolo continues, "we had a busy week." He glances over at Millie, and she glances back at him. It's sweet. I guess as I was languishing away in a tiny apartment, they were getting closer. "Once my mom came home from the hospital, I straight-up interrogated her about everything."

"Seriously? Good work," I say.

"Well, she wouldn't tell me that much, so I said I wouldn't tell her anything either. And I stopped talking to her! My own mom! It's so nuts."

"Wow."

"Yeah. And then Millie and I were trying to figure out how we could find you, and we realized: if my mom's gonna do some spying, then we could do some spying, too."

"It's mainly been a disaster," Millie says.

"This is true! I tried to hack my mom's computer, and I ended up downloading about eight hundred porn viruses onto her hard drive. But never mind that! We figured my mom would eventually get some kind of call about you. And we were totally right! Once she hit the road, so did we."

I'm so touched. I hoped I was in Paolo's thoughts, but this way exceeds my expectations. "Were you guys, like, spying around the clock? What about school?"

"Eff school!" Paolo says. "I'm a dead man anyway."

"This is the first day I'm missing," Millie says. "I was in gym class when Paolo texted that he was going to pick me up in two minutes. I told Mrs. Pinkus I was having Lady Problems and then walked out of school. It was surprisingly easy."

"Has Veronica been around for any of this?" I ask.

"Dude," Paolo says. "Don't even get me started on V. She's taken this whole our-mom-is-a-government-agent thing really hard." Part of me is thinking/hoping that what she's really taken hard is my absence. "I have no clue what she's been doing all week. She's out all day, comes home to sleep, then leaves early the next morning. I tried to do an intervention on her, but she just got pissy."

"I told you, Paolo," Millie says. "She's grieving."

"Dent didn't even die, though!"

"Not Denton. She's grieving for the loss of the mom she

thought she knew and trying to align that with the reality of who your mom really is."

"Damn," Paolo says, opening his eyes wide and shaking his face back and forth, like he's been splashed with water. "Some deep shit right there." He leans his head back toward me. "She blows my mind all the time with crap like that."

"I'm right here," Millie says. "So you don't need to talk about me in the third person."

"I know, babe. It was just, like, a stylistic choice, you know? For humor."

"Hmm," Millie says.

"Where are we going right now, by the way?"

"I have no idea," Paolo says. "I figured I'd keep driving straight until you told me to turn."

"Oh." I look out the window. A street sign says Seventeenth Street. "No, this is good. The numbers are going down, so that means we're going south." My dad taught me that on our first family trip to the city. "I don't think they'll expect us to do that."

"They might," Millie says, looking in her side mirror.

"What do you mean?" I whip my head around and see that a black car is about five cars behind us. "You sure that's them?"

"Not entirely."

"Damn, I'm blowing up," Paolo says. "Mills, wanna grab my phone out of my back pocket? It's near my butt." He contorts his body awkwardly and lifts his pelvis in the air to make it easier for Millie, who gingerly tugs the phone out.

"It's your mom," Millie says.

"For reals?" Paolo asks. "Answer. Put her on speaker-phone."

"You sure?" I say, but Millie's already done it.

"Hey, Mama," Paolo says. "How's things?"

"I don't know what you think you're doing, Paolo, but this is highly inappropriate," Paolo's mom says, her voice all speakerphoney. "And what the hell were you doing turning the wrong way on a one-way street? Trying to get yourself killed early? Almost gave me a heart attack."

"Sorry 'bout that. But if I remember correctly, I'm not on speaking terms with you at the moment. So I guess I'll hang up now."

"Wait, please!" Paolo's mom says. "We don't want this chase to continue. We're drawing too much attention to ourselves. People could get hurt. It's stupid."

"I agree," Paolo says. "We're totally in favor of you not chasing us."

"Is Denton there?"

"Hey, Cynthia," I say.

"Hi, Denton. I think you've gotten the wrong idea about us. We're really on your side. Would you please tell your friend to pull over so you can come with us and end this craziness?"

"Um . . . I don't think so, Cynthia," I say.

She sighs. "Well, okay, then. But you know we're going to catch up to you. We've got more cars on the way."

"I may have more cool tricks up my sleeve, though," Paolo says. "Get you guys off our tail."

"Seriously, please don't do anything like that again, Pow," his mom says. "I don't think you understand. Nothing you do will shake us. We will *always* know where you guys are, okay?"

And something about the way she says it flips a switch in my brain. We can't stay in Danza anymore. We need to get out of this car as soon as we can.

"Yeah, yeah, blah, blah, you work for the government, you know all, we got it," Paolo says. "You can hang up, Milltown." She does, just as Paolo's mom is starting to say something else. "You know, I love my mom," he says, "but she's really pissing me off right now. And it's so weird to feel pissed at her! Because she's always been the best mom! But now she's being the worst mom. It is confusing to me."

Millie pats his shoulder.

"Thanks, babe." The car suddenly revs forward, gaining speed as Paolo blasts through a light just as it's turning red. "I'm not gonna let her get us, Dent. Don't worry."

"I appreciate that, Pow, but I actually think we need to get out of Danza."

"No offense, Denter, but now is no time to be worrying about me driving your precious car."

"It's not that. I think as long as we're in the car, they know exactly where we are. Your mom must have put some kind of tracking device in it, probably way before my deathdate. Probably the first day I got the car." I shiver as I consider all of the different ways and times Paolo's mom may have been spying on me while I was completely oblivious.

"Whoa, don't you think you're being a little paranoid, bro-bro?" Paolo asks.

"Pow! Your mom was spying on me the whole time I knew you!"

"A good point," Paolo says, looking into his rearview

mirror. "Man, they're gaining on us. I'm not good at fast driving."

"I am," Millie says.

"Seriously?" Paolo says, looking over to her. "Why have you never mentioned that?"

"It never came up."

"You should be driving right now! Not me!"

"Okay, look," I say. "Whoever's driving, I think we have to find a way to lose the black car, get out of sight, and then—as much as I hate to say it—ditch Danza." Damn, I don't want to have to say bye to this car again.

"Dude, why would we do that? A car is faster than walking."

"Oh, is it?" I say. "Guess I hadn't thought of that. Never mind, then."

"Wow, this past week must have really shaken you up, man. Because that is a very basic fac—"

"I know a car is faster than walking!" I shout. "We need to get out of the car so your mom won't be able to find us. Remember the tracking device we discussed thirty seconds ago?"

"Ah, yeah, now I do, now that you reminded me," Paolo says, completely earnest. Our car stops at a light, and he turns to Millie. "So let's switch," he says.

"Okay," Millie says.

"You're doing this right now?" I ask as they enter into a minute-long negotiation of limbs and torsos—Millie's skirt at one point getting stuck underneath Paolo's leg—which ends with them having traded seats. The whole time, I'm wildly looking back, half expecting Paolo's mom to get out of her car while we're stopped and try to get into Danza with us. But just as Millie settles herself and clicks her seat belt in, the light turns green.

"Do you mind if I turn this on?" she asks, gesturing to the radio.

"Uh, yeah, go for it, babe," Paolo says.

"Thanks." The radio comes on, and Millie turns the knob all the way up. Beyoncé reverberates throughout the car. "I drive better with music," she shouts.

We rocket forward, and, holy shit, Millie wasn't kidding around: she is good at driving. We're weaving, passing car after car, making last-second turns onto streets, and somehow avoiding having to stop at a single traffic light. Paolo looks back to me, like, *What the hell is happening?* I just shrug as I grip on to the armrest for dear life.

"Where'd you learn to drive like this?" Paolo asks.

"I'm not sure," Millie says. "*Mario Kart,* maybe." She looks up to the rearview mirror. "Dent, where do we want to end up?"

"Um, well, don't worry about that, because you're not driving us there. We have to ditch the car, remember?"

"No, I'm asking so I know which subway line to drive us to."

"Oh, gotcha," I say. Millie knows the subway system? "Um, well, I was thinking maybe we could go back to Jersey first, so if we could get to Penn—"

"Back to Jersey?" Paolo interrupts. "You crazy, boy?"

"I think it might be nice to see my parents, let them know I'm okay."

"Not happening, dude," Paolo says as his body gets propelled toward the car window by one of Millie's turns. "My mom has so many agents staked out around your house, it's not even funny. There's no way you'd be able to get inside. I'm sorry, dude."

"All right," I say, feeling my heart pulse with disappointment.

"Let's catch whatever train will take us far, far away," Paolo says. "Why the eff not, right? We can get polka-dot sacks to hang on sticks! Hobo it up on freight trains across this glorious country!"

"I could be down to hobo it up," Millie says.

"Okay, that does sound beautiful," I say, "but—"

"Yo, bro," Paolo says. "Not to be obnoxious, but perhaps my input should get priority, what with me dying in two and a half weeks and everything."

"I totally agree, Pow, but about that . . . I learned some things, and I'm thinking maybe since I spread the virus to you, it might make you live through your deathdate, too."

"Wha?" Paolo says, turning around in his seat to face me, his mouth agape. "Are you for serious?"

"It's just a theory at this point," I say. "But maybe."

"Holy poop machine," Paolo says. "I mean, the thought did occur to me, but I assumed it was just wistful thinking." I decide not to ruin this poignant moment by correcting him. "Who told you this stuff? Have you been staying with that cool Brian dude?"

"No, actually. I've, um, been staying at this safe house with, uh, my mom."

"What. The. Hell." Paolo looks over at Millie in disbelief. "You were in Jersey this whole time? Just hiding in your own house? That's bonkers! How'd you get to the city?"

"No," I say. "I haven't been in Jersey. I was talking

about my actual, biological mother. You know, the one who died giving birth to me? Yeah, turns out she didn't actually die. She's totally alive."

"*Cómo*saywhatnow?"

"That is the most ridiculous thing you've ever said," Millie says, zipping us past two slower cars.

"You're not messing with us?" Paolo asks. "Your mom is alive?"

I nod.

"Holy crapoly mustard sundae with Polly-O string cheese on top, this shit keeps climbing notches on the Paolo Diaz scale of mindblowery! What's she like?"

"Um," I say. "She's . . . interesting."

"MILF . . . ?" he asks.

"I'm not going to answer that," I say. "But that's why we can't hobo it up. She might know how to save your life, Pow."

"Well, when you put it like that . . . ," Paolo says. "No hobo!"

"Where is the safe house?" Millie asks, all business.

"I don't remember exactly. I think Fifty-Third Street near, like, Eighth or Ninth Avenue?"

"So, Hell's Kitchen?"

I have no idea what that means. "Yeah, maybe?"

"All right, I've come up with a plan," Millie says. "We're gonna leave Danza at the corner of Canal and Varick, and hop onto the A-C-E line to get back to this safe house you speak of."

"There's another notch," Paolo says.

"Sounds amazing, Millie, thanks," I say. "But, uh, how do you even, uh—"

"My dad's office is in the city. I'm here a lot. Oh, there they are."

I turn back, and the black car has made its triumphant return. No matter how fast we're going, they always know where we are and always catch up.

"Not to worry," Millie says.

A police siren cuts through the air.

"Oh shit, is that for us?" I say.

"Probably," Millie says. "I'm going really fast."

Sure enough, there's a cop car with its lights on several blocks back. "Dammit, there's always cops!"

"You sound like a criminal when you say that," Paolo says.

"We can't not stop for the cops, can we?"

"We'll be fine," Millie says. "As long as we jump out of the car immediately after we get to the subway."

"But they can trace this car back to us," I say.

"Not to us, just to you," Millie says, wiping at the steering wheel with her sleeve. "A dead teenager. They'll assume the car was stolen. It shouldn't be a problem."

Wow, Millie is beyond impressive today. I'm sort of in awe and also astounded that I never knew about this side of her. And to think, if I'd died, I never would have found out.

"We're almost there," Millie says. Suddenly the car is slowing down, and the subway entrance is right outside my window. "Okay, let's go!"

"Now? Ah, that was too quick!" I shout, frantically trying to open my door. "Goodbye again, Danza! You're amazing!"

"I agree!" Paolo shouts, flinging himself out of my car.

Millie is somehow already waiting at the top of the subway stairs for us.

"Stop right there," a voice says through a megaphone.

But the three of us are already hurtling, nearly tumbling, down the steps into the station. "This seems like a terrible idea," I say.

"I think I have a stitch in my side," Paolo says. "Can we take a breather?"

"We just started running!" I say.

"I know—it's the kind of stitch that you get when you start exercising without stretching. Ahhhh."

"We can't stop for a breather, dude. We're being chased by, like, fifteen different people." We reach the entryway to the uptown train platform. It's not your normal turnstile; it's a giant turning cage. "Where do we pay to get on the train?"

"Don't worry," Millie says. "I'll swipe you guys in."

"Where did you get that?" Paolo says.

She shrugs and slides the yellow card in her hand through the entryway-swipe thing, and one at a time, we go through the slow-moving spindle. There's a gradually building roar as we go down more steps, and just as we set foot on the platform, a train comes barreling into the station.

"Paolo! Denton!" Paolo's mom shouts from the upper level of the station. "Do not get on that train!"

"She's persistent," Paolo says. "Gotta love her for that."

"How long is this train?" I ask, watching car after car pass us.

After what feels like hours but is probably closer to ten

seconds, the train finally stops. Its doors open, and we cram onto a fairly crowded car. We try to move deeper in, but there's a large, bearded man with two dogs blocking our path. Instead, we stand by the open doors, feeling insanely vulnerable. I just want the train to take us away from here.

Paolo's mom has made it through the turnstile and is racing down the steps toward the train. My heart rate accelerates. This is where it ends, I guess. "Come on, let's move!" I shout to no one in particular, trying to will the doors shut.

Maybe my plea worked or maybe it's just a coincidence, but there's a ding and a pre-recorded voice saying, *"Stand clear of the closing doors, please,"* and, thank God, the doors are closing. Just in time. I exhale.

"That was close, huh?" Paolo says.

Before I can say yeah, an arm shoots through the small gap left between the doors just before they smack together and grabs on to me. Paolo's mom stares at us through the glass.

"Ohmigod!" I shout.

"Stand clear of the closing doors, please," the pre-recorded subway voice says again.

"Please!" Paolo's mom says. "Get off this train and come with me!"

Paolo and Millie pull at my shoulders as the bearded man's dogs go into a barking frenzy.

"They might open the doors for her," Millie says. "Get ready to run."

"Stand clear of the closing doors, please."

The bearded man has no idea what's going on, but joins Paolo and Millie anyway in trying to save me from Paolo's mom's grip. He's strong. They free me almost instantly, and Paolo's mom's arm slides back during the tussle, so only her hand remains between the doors. She uses her other hand to try to pry the doors open, but she's unsuccessful and has no choice but to extract herself.

"Sorry, Mama-Lady," Paolo says as the train dings and slowly pulls away.

She stares at us through the glass, more sad and defeated than angry. For a brief second, I wonder if maybe we're not doing the right thing, but that thought's quickly replaced by an overall feeling of relief. We're actually getting away.

"Me and my mom," Paolo says to everyone in our train car. "We got in an argument."

But no one seems to care. Most of them are looking at their phones.

"Get in!" Dane shouts. He's standing next to a blue CR-V and waving frantically at us from farther down Fifty-Third Street. "Quickly! Come on!"

Paolo, Millie, and I pick up our already brisk pace.

"I actually thought we could go in and talk to my mom," I say once we're within speaking distance.

"Your mom is not inside that apartment anymore. And never will be again."

"What do you mean?"

"They went ahead," Dane says, anxiously staring down the street behind us. "I stay here in case you come back. Now please! No time to talk. DIA could be here any minute."

I look to Paolo and Millie, who are even less equipped to decide what to do than I am. "All right, I guess," I say, getting into the front seat.

"No!" Dane says, putting a hand on Paolo as he tries to open the back door. "Only Denton."

"These are my friends, Dane," I say, climbing back out of the car. "You can trust them."

"Felix has told us that this one is son of DIA." Dane points to Paolo. "And I don't know about the other." He flicks a hand at Millie. "But better to be safe."

"You don't understand, Dane," I say. "Paolo has nothing to do with his mom's mission."

"Do you want to come or not?" Dane shouts. "We do not have time to dally!"

"You should just go, D," Paolo says.

"No way," I say. "If they don't come, then I don't come. That's the deal."

"You don't know of what you speak," Dane says. "You see the DIA mean business, and you know they take my wife, and still you think this all casual, fun games?"

"I don't think it's a game," I say, "but I'm also not going to leave Paolo and Millie. Paolo's gonna die soon. If we see my mom again, he needs to be there."

Dane's entire body shakes as he looks down the street once more, jumpy as hell. "Goddamn, fine!" he says. "They can come, but they need give me their phones."

"What? Why?" Paolo says.

"You want to come or not?" Dane says, his arm extended, his hand open.

Paolo and Millie look to me. I shrug and nod. Millie hands hers over.

"Okay," Paolo says. "But can I just check one more thing real quick?"

"Give!" Dane says.

He sighs and reluctantly passes it over. "You'll give them back later, though, right?"

Dane grunts as he hurls the phones down onto the street, where they crack into several pieces.

"All righty," Paolo says.

"Get in car." Dane gets into the driver's seat.

"That was kind of cathartic," Millie says, sliding into the backseat right before Paolo.

"Shit! Close doors! Lower heads!" Dane says, looking into the rearview. The doors slam shut, and the three of us crouch down as our car pulls away. I peek behind, and from a block and a half away, I see the familiar black DIA car drive up and park in front of the safe house. Paolo's mom and the other two agents pour out and stand in the middle of the street, wildly looking around.

"Holy shit, that was close," I say.

"My mom found us?" Paolo says, still crouching. "Damn, she's good."

"Not good," Dane says, steering us onto that big highway I saw earlier, just after I first escaped. "She track your phone. That is why I dispose of it."

"Oh," I say. Considering I'd already ditched my own phone to get off the grid, I feel kinda dumb for assuming they were tracking us through Danza. We just abandoned my car for no reason.

"See? Sometimes it is good to trust instead of behaving like slippery spider." Dane looks away from the road to glare at me.

"Sorry about that," I say, remembering our insane encounter in Forever 21.

"You can get up now," Dane says into the rearview. "We are in clear."

"Thanks, Mr. Dane," Paolo says as he and Millie sit up.

Dane doesn't respond, because he's got his cell phone pressed to his ear. "Hello, yes," he says. "I got him. Yes, he is safe." I'm guessing he's talking to my mom. "But I could not take him without taking the friends, too. He refuse; I have no choice! Yes, sorry. I understand, I will." He chucks the phone, and it lands at my feet.

I want to know what he's just told my mother he'll do, but it doesn't seem like now is the best moment to ask.

As the car rolls onward, I stare out the window, where there's a view of a river. On the other side, there are buildings, the sky around them a brilliant blue. It looks like a painting.

"That's New Jersey over there," Millie says, noticing me staring.

"Oh," I say. "It's pretty." I feel like I've spent the last week on an entirely different planet, but the place where I'm from has been right over there the whole time, just a strip of water away. I think about my dad and stepmom, how I won't get to see them after all. But then I remember that Paolo and Millie are immediately behind me, and I breathe easier.

"Hey," I say, looking over to Dane, who's finally cooled down a bit. "Where are we going anyway?"

"The safe house is no longer safe. We start there because we don't know if we could trust you. Don't know if you will do something to expose us."

"Well, that's a little insulting," I say. Dane shoots me the most deadpan look, and I'm mortified to realize they were completely right to think that. "But, you know, always good to play it safe. Smart thinking."

"No more room for mistakes," Dane says. "We go now to Brooklyn. Where your mother actually live."

"Whoa, cool!" Paolo says from the back. "Maybe we'll meet some hipsters!"

Brooklyn. Huh.

I press my face against the window and look at New Jersey some more.

NINE

"Do you know why we're here?" my mother says, staring at me with intensity.

It's a tough question to answer, as it's open to interpretation. *Here* could mean the coffee establishment we're in. Or it could mean Brooklyn. Or, if she's getting really existential, *here* could mean the earth. Whichever version she's thinking, I don't know the answer.

"Um," I say. "Because I messed up?"

My plan didn't play out the way I intended, but I did exactly what I set out to do: I got out of that claustrophobic nightmare of an apartment; I found Paolo; and now I've brought him to the one person who might be able to save his life.

I assumed Dane would bring us to the place where my mom "actually live," but instead he brought us to the back of a cavernous coffee shop—exposed brick walls and couches galore—where my mom and Felix were waiting for us.

We've all taken seats in various mismatched chairs around a low oval table. I'm between Paolo and Millie, and my mom is sitting right across from me. She doesn't look happy.

"Yes, you did mess up," my mother says with hushed force, making sure no one around us can hear (even though most of them are working on laptops and wearing headphones), "and I'll get to that, but, no, we're here because you insisted on bringing these two along." When she says *these two,* she flicks a hand at Paolo and Millie. It really pisses me off. "They can't know where I live. Even them knowing I'm in Brooklyn is a huge risk. You're a smart kid; I'd think, after all you've been through, you would have understood the importance of extreme confidentiality with all this."

"Sure," I say, impressed by how unintimidated I'm feeling. My mom might be the only person who can save Paolo, but I'm the only person right now who can help her movement. She needs me. "But I trust Paolo and Millie. And I want them here with me."

"Oh, you trust them?" my mom says, chuckling. "Well, why didn't you say so? I didn't realize that you *trust* them. We're all set, then!" I'm learning that my mom and I both have a penchant for sarcasm, but she wields hers more like a weapon.

"Look," she says, the fake smile disappearing, "if we were talking about two random friends of yours, maybe we could figure something out. But this one?" She points to Paolo without looking at him. "This is the son of the *main DIA agent that's trailing you.* He is the absolute *last* person, other than Agent Diaz herself, we should be welcoming into our ranks. And the girl that's with him," she says, waving a hand at Millie, "well, I don't know enough about her yet."

"She is little bit shifty," Dane says.

My mom turns to Felix for his opinion, like he's her advisor or something.

"That's Millie," he says, putting his coffee mug down on the table. "I don't think she's a threat."

"You don't think?" I say, astounded. "Of course she's not a threat! She's lived down the street from us forever."

"Dent," Felix says, "people can be a threat without even meaning to, by inadvertently exposing our secrets to . . . other people that shouldn't know them."

"So why aren't you a threat?" I'm trying to keep it together, but my voice is getting louder. "You've known about this movement for years, been in touch with our mother all that time."

"That's because Mom trusted me," Felix says, taking on his most patronizing tone. "And in all these years, *I've* never revealed her secret."

Ouch. But, okay, fair enough.

My mom puts her face in her hand, and everyone is silent for a moment. Then she lifts her head back up and looks right at me. "Do you think this is some kind of game?"

The way she says it is pretty scary. "No, I—"

"Because it seems like you don't understand how high the stakes are here. That I, along with many others, have been waiting almost *eighteen years* for your arrival, and now you're going to throw that all away because you want to dick around with your friends?"

"I wouldn't put it like that," I say.

"Why did you steal my keys and leave the safe house?"

She stares at me, waiting for me to respond, but as soon as I start to, she cuts me off again. "Do you know how dangerous that was? If Felix hadn't been there to save you—*again*—you'd be halfway to DC by now. Do you think they'd be taking you down there for lemonade and some swings at a piñata?" I'm tickled by her choice of party references, but I restrain my smile. "Because if you couldn't handle being in the safe house for less than a week, you sure as hell won't like what they have in store for you."

"I'm sorry," I say. "I wasn't trying to be reckless. And I'm not trying to ruin your plans. But . . . they're *your* plans. I just . . . I appreciate that you've helped me live, but being locked up in a 'safe house' and getting stuck with needles every day isn't exactly the new life I would have chosen for myself. There are things I want to do. Things *I* care about." Out of the corner of my eye, I can see how tense and uncomfortable Paolo and Millie look, and I'm once again sorry that I've pulled them into this madness.

"Oh yeah, like what?" my mom says. "How many likes you got on Twitter? Who they're going to cast in the next Spider-Man movie? Where to take the girl you like out on a date?"

This is so incredibly insulting I'm shaking with anger. I can't believe how mean my mother can be. (Though I can't help but wonder if the Spider-Man thing was a random reference or if they've just made an announcement that they're rebooting the franchise yet again.)

"Paolo is going to die in nineteen days," I say quietly. "That's what I care about. And you're the only person who might be able to save him. That's the only reason I'm even sitting here. So, really, you should be thanking Paolo."

My mother looks, at least temporarily, like she's been put in her place. I'm about to tell her that Paolo's one of the people I gave the virus to, but I'm interrupted.

"Um, Mrs. Little?" Paolo says. My mom's head snaps toward him. "Or Ms. Little." My mom looks around, super-paranoid that someone's hearing him. "Or, you know, Denton's Real Mom. Whatever name you like to be called. Sorry to jump in here, but, um, first of all, congrats on still being alive. Really great news."

My mom stares at Paolo like he's a stain on the carpet.

"Secondly, you should know that my sense of direction is disturbingly bad. Not only do I have no idea how we got to this coffee shop, but I don't even know how to interpret very basic directional terms, like *east* and *north*. So you definitely don't have to worry about me knowing where you live. Thirdly, and most importantly, your son Denton is my best friend in the whole world. I'd honestly rather be dead than betray him. And I know Mills feels the same."

Millie, looking terrified, gives a tiny nod.

My mom is still staring at Paolo, but now it's like he's a famous painting and she's trying to figure out why everyone loves it so much. "You're saying you choose Denton over your own mother?"

"That's exactly what I'm saying, Denton's Real Mom. I've only talked to my mom once since she kidnapped Dent. And that was just to give her what for."

I can tell my mom is at least a little bit charmed by Paolo—because Paolo is magic—but there's too much at stake. "Well. Be that as it may. It's still too risky."

"In that case," I say, surprising myself by standing up, "I must take my leave." Not sure why I said it like that, but all right. "Because if Paolo and Millie can't stay, I can't either."

The two of them look up at me, like, *Are we seriously leaving?* I don't look back at them because I'm not sure of my answer.

"Don't be stupid," my mom says.

"I'm serious. Whatever it is you need me here for, I'm going to need help."

My mom is already shaking her head. "You have help: me, Dane, your *brother,* Felix. Who's closer to you than your own brother?"

I look over to Felix, the brother who was never around until I was going to die. I look back to my mom. "Paolo is. No one's closer to me than him."

"Oh man, really?" Paolo says. "I thought I was at least third-closest, but first? This is such an honor."

"I mean, he's literally so close to me that he's one of the three people I passed the virus to on my deathdate. Or some part of the virus, I really don't know. He didn't have the red dots."

My mom scratches her neck and looks at the floor for a second. "Uh, Felix?" she says.

"Yeah?" he says.

"You didn't think it was worthwhile to mention that Denton passed the virus to his best friend, who happens to be the son of a DIA agent?"

"Yes, this is what I am thinking as well," Dane says.

"I just forgot, Mom," Felix says. "In all the craziness. I'm sorry."

"Huh," my mom says, the wheels in her brain spinning as we sit and wait and listen to the seventies funk song playing in the coffee shop. I glance at Paolo and Millie, who look back at me like a pair of deer in headlights. "This changes things," my mom finally says. "We can work with this."

My heart leaps, even though I'm not down with her phrasing, like this is all a business arrangement and not human lives we're talking about. "Wait," I say. "So, do you think there's a chance Paolo could live, too?"

My mom raises her eyebrows and shrugs. "I don't know. We'll have to do tests, see what state the virus is in. I certainly wouldn't rule it out."

Holy shit. Paolo might live.

"Holy shit," Paolo says. "I might live?"

"It depends," my mom says. "But maybe."

"Dude!" Paolo says, standing up and hugging me. "Maybe we're both not dying! Wow, this is such an insane moment!"

"I know," I say, sort of in shock.

"Shhh!" my mom says, understandably, as we are in a public place talking about crazy shit.

"Mills!" Paolo says. "Get up! We're all gonna be one big undated family!"

Millie stands up from her chair and hugs us, but I can see in her eyes she's not entirely convinced.

"Sit down," my mom says. "Stop drawing so much attention!"

But, really, nobody's looking; they're all typing away in their respective laptop bubbles. We sit back down anyway.

"So, Paolo and Millie can stay?" I ask.

"They can," my mom says. "For now." I want to hug the entire earth. "But there are going to be restrictions."

"Of course, DRM," Paolo says, smiling and giving a little salute. It takes me a moment to realize he's made an acronym of Denton's Real Mom.

"And for the record," my mom says. "No other friends are allowed besides these two. Okay? Felix told me that Agent Diaz has got a daughter you've been a little, uh, friendly with?" She smiles at me in this jokey, suggestive way that should never be employed by a mother with her son.

"Veronica," Felix says. "Denton passed her the virus, too, Mom."

"Yeah, well, I don't care," she says. "We've got Paolo as a sample for how the virus spreads. We don't need another. And from what you've told me, Feel, I don't trust this Veronica, and I don't want her around."

"That's bullshit," I say. I was hoping to get Veronica in on this deal, too. . . .

"You really want to fight me on this?" my mom says. "Why don't we just get your entire high school class to come visit? Does that sound fun?"

I probably shouldn't press my luck. "Fine," I say. I'm sure I can find a way to see Veronica at some point.

"Good," my mom says, standing up and finally taking a sip of the iced tea that's been sitting in front of her this whole time. "Now let's blow this Popsicle stand."

TEN

"I finally get why it's called happy hour!" Paolo says, half falling off his chair, a beer called Enthusiastic Yell in his hand. "People are happier because all the drinks are cheaper during that limited window of time. It's so obvious now! Oh, and the more you drink, the happier you get! Wow, double meaning, that is so smart."

"I'm not sure you're using the word *smart* correctly," Millie says, taking a sip of her Shirley Temple.

I can't believe we've been granted permission to be out of the apartment at night. We've been at this bar called Chair for about an hour. It's pretty cool. The concept is they only have one type of furniture for sitting: chairs. There are no couches, booths, benches, or even any barstools; the bar is lower so that you can sit next to it on chairs.

"I love Chair!" Paolo says. "Brooklyn, baby!"

It's been a few days since we got here. After we left the coffee shop on Friday, my mom led us to her apartment, which makes that rinky-dink safe house seem even more pitiful than it already did. Put it this way: I didn't know apartments in New York City could have stairs inside them. It feels like a house. Not only does the place have two levels and a shiny, state-of-the-art kitchen, but it's fully furnished with leather couches, puffy orange chairs, and a larger-than-life nude painting of a woman who bears an uncomfortable resemblance to my mother (that last one I could do without). This benefactor who's supporting my mother and her movement must be super-loaded.

Suffice it to say, even though my mom mostly didn't want us to leave the apartment, it was a much more enjoyable lockdown experience. Having Paolo and Millie around didn't hurt either. Other than when Dane took some of Paolo's blood, saliva, and hair for testing ("Hey, Dane, we're blood brothers now!" Paolo said), we mainly just hung around, watching movies and playing board games.

My mom hasn't talked about the movement that much, both because they're waiting on a couple more mouse deathdates before they can interpret the results and because she doesn't want to say much in front of Paolo and Millie. It's been kind of nice. I wouldn't go so far as to say I fully understand what goes on in her brain, but she's been able to relax a bit more, let down her guard.

In fact, she's trying to take a more relaxed approach with me overall, which is pretty miraculous. "That strict-mom routine didn't suit me," she said on Sunday. "And obviously it didn't suit you either. I trust you and your friends, so if you want to go out sometimes, that's all right with me. Rather have you do that than cook up another terrible escape plan." Fair enough!

Her one condition was that I change up my look: she gave me a pair of black nerd glasses, and Millie bleached my hair blond. I know. But it had to happen. On Sunday, Paolo, Millie, and I took a walk around the block. It was beautiful. Then yesterday was Memorial Day, and the three of us spent a couple hours in the park, weaving our way amongst picnicking families as the sun burnt our necks. It made me miss my parents pretty bad, but it was also a reminder of how quietly spectacular life can be.

Both of those outings went well (insomuch as they seemed to have gone completely unnoticed by the DIA), so, in the spirit of her new lenient approach to parenting, my mom granted us permission to have our first nighttime excursion. She even gave me a Frank Biggs debit card and a Frank Biggs license. (Paolo wanted an alias, too, so he's Steve Pickle now.)

"I hooked you up when I had those made," Felix said later, helpfully pointing out that Frank Biggs's age is three and a half years older than mine, making him twenty-one. "Don't say your older bro isn't looking out for you." He winked in a big, exaggerated way. "And also don't tell Mom about this."

I definitely won't. The fake ID has been very helpful.

And anyway I told my mom we were going to a diner tonight. (Untrue.)

"Hey," I say, holding up my bottle of beer. "I want to make a toast. To you guys, for saving me and for being amazing friends."

"Aw, no," Paolo says, raising his beer. "To you, for living. And maybe helping me live, too! Denton lives!"

"Shhh," I say, looking around. "You can't say that too loud."

"Oh right, right," Paolo says. "Everybody, I was just saying that, uh, there's a *dent* in my *liver!*" He's really proud that he came up with that on the fly.

"To Frank Biggs and Steve Pickle," Millie says, clinking her Shirley Temple with both of our bottles.

"There you go," I say. "And to Millie, a very excellent driver."

I take a swig of my beer, a bittersweet brand called Arthur's Great-Aunt's Ale. I don't really like the taste, but I like the idea of it.

"I gotta say, dude," Paolo says. "This intellectual albino thing you got going on is really starting to grow on me."

"Thanks." It might be growing on me, too. I like having glasses I can adjust all the time.

"There's no reason why this look should work on you, but somehow it does," Millie says, her head tilted like a bird's as she gazes at me. "You look like a handsome tool."

"Thanks?" I say.

"Yeah, that's exactly it!" Paolo says. "A handsome tool!"

"Cassandra!" a bartender shouts from the other side of the bar. "Food's up for Cassandra!"

"Oh, that's me," Millie says. Paolo and I stare at her. "What? You guys shouldn't be the only ones who get fun names."

"She's so cool," Paolo says once Millie's a few steps away.

"Quick, man, tell me everything," I say. It's the first

moment Paolo and I have had alone together since arriving in Brooklyn. "What's going on with you two?"

"What do you mean?"

"What do you think I mean?" Paolo usually revels in hookup stories, so this is bizarre. "Are you guys, like, doing stuff?"

"Oh. No," he says, shaking his head like I could never understand. "Not yet, man, it's much deeper than that."

"Is it?"

"We just get each other. We don't need to express it with our bodies."

"Have you, like, kissed or anything?"

"Well, what's your definition of *kissed*?"

"What kind of question is that? You know, like, two mouths and tongues mushing up against each other."

"We—" Paolo begins to say, but then Millie sits back down, setting her plate on the bar and staring at it.

"What are those, babe?" Paolo asks.

"Pomegranate mozzarella sticks," Millie says. "They sounded nice on the menu. But now I'm having doubts."

Paolo grabs one of the purple, gooey sticks and takes a bite. "Oh sweet Ryan Phillippe! These are delicious." He pops his chomped-on mozzarella stick back onto her plate. "Don't ever doubt yourself, Mills."

"Thanks," she says, still looking unconvinced.

"You know what? I gotta do something," Paolo says as he stands up on his chair. "Everybody, I am so happy to be alive! Living is the best!" A couple people cheer, but most just look annoyed. "I gotta say, these past few days have been awesome," he says, sitting back down. "Every time

I remember that I might not die in a couple weeks, I get so happy. And Brooklyn is great. And, you know, I was so pissed at Dane for smashing my phone into pieces, but it's actually been quite liberating. Everyone should try disconnecting for a while." Paolo takes a deep breath, inhaling the world.

"Speaking of disconnecting," Millie says, "I should probably get going. I told my parents I'd be camping all weekend and wouldn't have cell reception, but by now they'll be starting to freak out about me missing school. They're chill, but not *that* chill."

"What? No!" Paolo says, tugging on her arm. "Don't leave, WindMill. At least finish your sticks!"

"Thing is," I say, "I think my mom might have a meltdown if you leave. Plus, I don't think she'll let you come back."

"Well," Millie says. "That may be true. But I give my own parents' meltdowns priority."

"That's fair," I say.

"And if I can't come back to the apartment," Millie continues, "we'll have to meet elsewhere, then. Maybe we can find a bar called Table. That only has tables."

"Whoa, do you think that exists?" Paolo asks.

"Also," Millie says, "I need to go to school so I don't get suspended."

"Ah, yeah, that's also fair," I say. "You don't have the dying excuse."

"She *could* die, though!" Paolo says. "Seriously, she's undated. She can die whenever. So that means you should stay. Cassandra would!"

"I don't disagree," Millie says, and Paolo's eyes light up. "But I just stopped being Cassandra thirty seconds ago. Sorry, Stevie."

"Aw, you called me Stevie," Paolo says, finishing off his second beer and gesturing to the bartender for another.

"I did," Millie says. She goes to hug Paolo, and he goes in for the kiss. She angles her head a little bit, so he gets part of her cheek and the corner of her mouth. He stays there for a solid five seconds. It's awkward to watch.

Once she pulls away, Paolo stays where he is with his eyes closed, swaying slightly.

"Um," Millie says, looking at me before swiftly changing the subject. "Don't forget to watch out for any government weirdos lurking around."

"Will do," I say.

"I don't know if they're with the government, but we definitely got some weirdos up in this piece," Paolo says, a little too loudly, as he gestures to a mustachioed man in a seersucker suit.

"You all right getting back to Penn Station on your own?" I ask Millie.

"Thanks for asking, Blondie." She gives me one of her trademark, barely perceptible grins and ruffles my hair. "But I'm tougher than I look. Later, Stevie. Later, Franklin."

"Peace out, Cassandra," I say. "See you when we see you."

Millie puts two fingers to her mouth, then raises them in the air and leaves. I can't get over the fact that somehow, right before I was supposed to die, she became such an important presence in my life again. I'm glad I hit her with my car.

"Did you see that moment Mills and I had when she was leaving?" Paolo asks. "Wasn't that beautiful?"

"It was," I say, and I instantly feel the guilt of lying to my best friend.

"I seriously feel like I could marry her, you know?"

I start to laugh, but Paolo doesn't seem to be laughing along with me, so I stop. "But . . . ," I say. "Maybe you guys should, I don't know, kiss first before you talk marriage."

"Kissing before marriage is so 1992, dude," Paolo says.

"I don't know what that means."

Paolo puts his arm around me. "It's so good to be hanging out with you," he says.

"I know," I agree. "It really is."

"We've never been to a bar together!" Paolo says. "This is, like, the first taste of what life could be like as grown-up people." He takes a sip of beer.

Paolo's words knock me in the gut. I don't know why I hadn't thought of this yet: it's possible I'm going to live to be an adult.

Paolo might, too.

It should obviously be cause for celebration, but instead I feel a hard knot of anxiety form in my stomach.

"Wasn't that cool," Paolo says, "how after I said 'first taste of what life could be like,' I *tasted* my beer?"

"Ha, yeah," I say, trying my best to get back into the moment and out of the terrifying blankness of my adulthood. "That was really cool."

"You okay, D?" Paolo says, chugging more of his alcoholic beverage. "You usually love my puns."

"I don't think that counts as a pun."

"Yeah, you're right. Probably more of a homophone."

There's a melancholy song playing in the bar, overly affected vocals and soft guitar. It's only feeding my existential crisis.

"I'm just . . ." I shift around on my bar chair. "I mean, I never mentally planned to be a grown-up, you know?"

"Nobody plans to be a grown-up, dude. It just happens."

"I guess," I say.

"And anyway," Paolo says. "Look around this bar! Lots of these people might technically be grown-ups, but they're wearing the same shit that people in our high school wear." He cocks his head sideways. "Well, maybe not that mustache, seersucker-suit guy. Or that chick over there in the Jane Eyre dress. Superhot."

I follow Paolo's gaze to a girl in a huge, fancy blue dress holding a beer. "That is pretty hot," I say. "But if you and I really do live . . . We haven't applied to college. We haven't even taken the SATs!"

Paolo starts cracking up. "Only you would say something like that, Dent. Seriously. You beat death, and you're worried about a standardized test?"

"All right, fine," I say, swigging some of my beer. "But I mean, we probably at least want to graduate from high school."

"Not sure how that one's gonna play out," Paolo says, grabbing two of Millie's abandoned pomegranate mozzarella sticks and shoving them both in his mouth at once. "Graduation's the same day as my deathdate."

"Oh man. I'm a terrible friend. I never even realized that." My deathdate was prom, and Paolo's is graduation. Hard to say which is worse.

"Why would you, dude? You were supposed to be long gone by then." Paolo always cuts me so much slack. "And anyway, even if I do end up surviving, I think I'd rather spend that day getting high or something. To commemorate the Day I Was Supposed to Die—you know?"

"Yeah, I hear that," I say. "But, like, if you survive, have you thought about what your career would be?"

"Hell no!" Paolo says, making a twirly signal in the air so the bartender will bring him another beer. "But I'll figure it out. Maybe do a bunch of things: grocery cashier, newspaper writer, zookeeper. . . . Oh! Actually, I just remembered, I'd love to be one of those people who say stupid shit to celebrities on the red carpet."

"Really?"

"Yeah! It's such a cool skill, to be able to have conversations that are about absolutely nothing. Doesn't everybody want that job?"

"No." I grab a mozzarella stick. "I have no idea what I'd want to be. Maybe I could write movies or something." It sounds silly to even say it aloud. I don't know the first thing about writing movies. I've just watched a lot of them.

"Yes! That's it!" Paolo says, standing up from his chair. "You should write movies! And then you can write a lot of sexy scenes. That I'll act in!"

"So, you're basically saying I should write porn so you can act in it."

"I hadn't thought of it that way, but, oh man, would you be down to do that?"

I take a sip of my beer so I can watch Paolo sweat out my decision. "Sure, Pow. I'll write pornos for you to be in."

"Woo! Planning our futures is awesome!"

It, of course, occurs to me that maybe none of this will be an option for me. Maybe my anxiety should be redirected to the idea that I might have to live off the grid with my mom, Felix, and Dane for decades, allowed to do nothing except help them with their virus mouse missions or whatever the hell it is we're going to do.

And also redirected to the idea that maybe Paolo won't survive. Maybe he will die on his deathdate. And I'll be forced to live in this world without my best friend. Knowing my deathdate was before his meant I never had to think about that.

"Check this," Paolo says, legs straddled over his chair in a compromising position. "There's no way this move has been done before. I've watched pretty much all the pornography that exists, and I've never seen it."

"Do you seriously watch that much porn?" I ask.

"This could be our ticket to a porn Oscar!"

"I hope so," I say, grateful to be pulled out of my own head.

We sit there for a couple of hours, joking and laughing and talking. It's nice. I take my time with each of my beers, so I'm buzzed but not wasted. I figure I should try to keep it together; one dumb move, and my mom might change her mind and put us back on lockdown. Paolo, however, is more than buzzed. I've lost track of what number beer he's on.

"Hey, look at this guy," he says, his eyelids half closed, his smile wavering like a lava lamp. "Maybe you could write movies with him."

Right near us, there's a bearded dude in a white tank top, suspenders, and jeans holding court amongst several other aggressively eccentric-looking people, at least two of them wearing aviator sunglasses, even though we're inside and it's nighttime. "*All* of his work is overrated," Beardy Suspenders says. "He's never *not* been overrated. Anybody can point a camera at people and underscore it with cool music. That doesn't mean it's *good.*"

"Who're you talkin' about?" Paolo calls out, much to my complete mortification. "Steven Spielsberg?"

Beardy Suspenders looks over at us. "No, we're not talking about Steven Spielsberg, my friend. Did you add the extra *s* for *sauced?*" His eccentric cronies laugh.

"Sorry," I say. "He's had a little too much."

"No need to apologize. I'd love to hear more of your little buddy's insightful thoughts on cinema." This horrible beard guy loves the sound of his own voice.

"Well," Paolo says. "For example: everybody loves E.T., but he makes me feel weird inside. And didn't it always trip you out when you see that E.T. comes from a whole species of creatures that look exactly like him? It's like, *You're not as special as you think you are, E.T.*"

"Sure, right, of course, of course," Beardy says, nodding exaggeratedly at Paolo, some alcoholic drink with a lime in it in his hand. "Tell me more."

"Give it a rest, man," I say to Beardy. It just comes out, and I instantly regret it. This guy looks like he's at least twenty-five. But, on the bright side, I'm not guaranteed to die today, so that's something.

"I'm not doing anything," he says, shoulders and arms raised up. "Just talking shop with your friend."

"Okay, sure, you're not doing anything," I say, trying to speak his language of Douchey Sarcasm.

"Hey," Paolo says, sticking one finger in the air. "You gotta respect what my man's saying. He's an effing rock star, this guy."

"Oh?" Beardy Suspenders says. I can tell where Paolo's going with this, and I don't like it.

"Check it: He was supposed to die, like, a week ago. But he lived through his deathdate. Magic, man." Paolo fans his fingers out with a flourish.

I can't believe he just said that.

Beardy runs his hand over his beard and narrows his eyes. If I don't do some damage control, this could be very bad. Like, permanent-lockdown bad.

"He's wasted," I say. "Obviously that's not true."

"But he seemed kinda sincere when he said it, right?" Beardy asks his friends.

"I dunno," a girl with pink-and-blond hair says.

"And guess what, Paul Bunyan," Paolo says. I'm hoping he'll pass out before he can say anything else, but no such luck. "My deathdate is in, like, two weeks, and because of my man Dent, I'm gonna live through mine, too! Oh, I mean Frank." Paolo nods at me, like, *I got this*. He is quite drunk.

"Well, that's special." Beardy turns to one of his friends, a guy whose head is shaved except for one black tuft in the front. "Our man Jefferson over here is gonna die in a couple years. Can you save him, too?"

"Yeah, man," Jefferson says in a low voice dripping with irony. "Can you save me?"

"No, because the things my friend is saying aren't real," I say.

Beardy Suspenders scoffs in my face and throws back

the rest of his drink as he turns back to his friends. "Enjoy your night, Goldilocks. Ha."

There's been something oddly familiar about this entire exchange, and I pinpoint it now: this dude fits in the same Extraordinary Douche category as Phil Lechman, my ex-girlfriend Taryn's dickhead ex-boyfriend, who tried to shoot me on my front lawn.

Making that connection taps into some repressed anger or something, and suddenly all my concerns about playing it safe go out the window. I very much want to capitalize on the boldness I feel knowing that today is not my deathdate.

"What'd you just call me?" I ask.

"Huh?" Beardy says, turning back. "I thought we were done here. I don't know. Goldilocks?"

"Yeah, that's what I thought," I say. I put my half-full bottle of beer down on the bar and give Beardy a hard shove. He falls back into his friends, completely surprised, which feels good, until I trip into a table and bump a couple of beer bottles to the floor, where they shatter.

"Whoa!" Paolo says.

"What the hell was that, dude?" Beardy says, taking two steps back and rubbing at his chest. "I was just messing around. I don't wanna fucking *fight* you. My God."

"You all right?" single-tufted Jefferson asks.

"I'm fine," Beardy says, adjusting his suspenders and leading his posse to the other side of Chair. "Can't believe this kid pushed me."

All the anger I was feeling has quickly dissipated, and now I just feel dumb. I was thinking that since this was New York City, everyone would be up for a fight. Or something. I don't really know what I was thinking.

Paolo's eyes and mouth are wide open, emanating pure joy. "Why did you do that? That was the best thing I've ever seen! We were having a nice talk about cinema, and you're like, *I think I'll fight this guy now.*"

"He was making fun of you to your face, Pow. And, man, you absolutely cannot go around telling people about the deathdate stuff. What if those guys were spies?"

"Those guys?" Paolo says. "Ha! Spies don't wear suspenders, bro."

"Hey," a short man in glasses and a blue button-down shirt says. "I'm going to have to ask you to leave."

"Yeah, okay," I say, turning my head away so he can't get a good look at my face. I'm mortified that just happened and terrified it's going to somehow help the DIA find me. I'm such an idiot.

"We gotta go now?" Paolo asks.

"Yeah, bud," I say. I get an arm around him, and I'm walking us out the front door when a girl in a black hoodie comes charging in past us.

"Hey, V made it," Paolo says, almost like an afterthought.

"What?" I turn and see the girl stop deeper inside the bar, frantically looking all around. Sure enough, it's Paolo's sister, Veronica. My heart starts pumping double time.

"Yo, Veronica," I say. "You looking for somebody?"

She turns around, sees us, and rolls her eyes.

ELEVEN

"Wow," Veronica says. "You look like an even bigger nerd than usual in those glasses. And what the hell happened to your head?"

"Great to see you, too," I say.

"Were you guys about to leave? How would I have found you if you left?"

"I had no idea you even knew we were here."

"Millie and I called her from a pay phone!" Paolo says, his head resting on my shoulder. "Pay phones still exist here."

"Oh." I forcefully twitch my shoulder to nudge his head. "That might have been a nice thing to let me know about."

"We wanted it to be a special surprise."

"Is he drunk?" Veronica asks.

"Spectacularly," I say.

"Please, gentlemen," the man in the blue shirt says, appearing next to Veronica's shoulder. "I don't want to have to ask you again."

"Sure, sorry. We're just going."

"Whoa," Veronica says. "You guys got kicked out of here?"

"Yes," Blue Shirt and Glasses says. "Your friend tried to assault one of the patrons in our bar. They need to leave. Now."

"You tried to assault someone, P?" Veronica looks shocked.

"Not me, V," Paolo says. "Frank."

"Who the hell is Frank?"

"I'm Frank," I say.

"Uh, okay. And you attempted to assault someone?"

"I mean, kinda. Not really."

"You pushed that man with the beard," Blue Shirt says. "I saw it happen."

"We should leave," I say.

"Wow." Veronica laughs.

Back outside, I walk in between Veronica and Paolo, who's still leaning on me.

"I gotta say, Dent," Veronica says. "I'm impressed and a little disturbed by this new life-after-death you. Already getting into bar fights, that's hilarious."

"Wait," I say. "Can we back up? How are you? I'm so happy to see you."

"Yeah," she says, looking away. "Same."

Paolo starts taking very deliberate breaths. "I feel like I may blow some hunks."

"I think you mean *chunks*," I say.

"Whichever."

"Guess it's only fair that we all take a spin in the vomit

van," Veronica says, possibly smiling at me for a second, but I'm not sure.

"Yeah, true." Paolo's vomiting would complete the trifecta, so to speak: my funeral-morning throw-up in Veronica's bed, her prom-night hwarf on my shoes, and now this.

"I do not want to spin on any such van," Paolo says.

Veronica's walking next to me so casually, like it's no big deal to see me, like we're not going to even acknowledge the intense moments we had during my deathdate, which included: (1) an incredibly hot make-out session in my bathroom and (2) Veronica telling me, right before I escaped to New York City, she felt all the things for me that I felt for her.

"Heard you saw our mom," Veronica says to me. "That must have been fun."

"Pow told you?"

"Nah, my mom's been back home since then. I eavesdrop." She chews on one of her hoodie strings. It's pretty sexy.

"Oh. Well, yeah, it was intense," I say. I'm reminded that we're currently breaking one of my mom's main rules. I am not supposed to be hanging out with Veronica. "Actually, shit, she's not going to be able to track you here, is she? Is your phone's GPS on?"

"Turn off the GPS!" Paolo shouts, suddenly roused from his nauseated half sleep. "Very important!"

"Of course my GPS is off," Veronica says. "What do you think I am, stupid?"

"It woulda been . . . an honest mistake," Paolo says

before leaning over to his right and vomiting onto the street. "Hunks blown."

"Bonus points for aiming in that direction," I say.

Paolo rises back up, wiping his mouth. "I'm classy, man."

"Ew," Veronica says. There's some throw-up on his cheek that he missed. "Try again."

Paolo lifts up the bottom of his T-shirt to clean off the rest.

"You sure your mom can't track your phone even without GPS, though? I mean, since she's, like, got all these government resources and stuff?"

"Dude," Veronica says. "I turned my phone off as soon as I got onto the train to come to the city. You need to give me at least a modicum of credit here."

"Modicum," I say. "Nice."

"What? I know words," Veronica says.

"Heh heh," Paolo says, re-energized postpuke. *"Modicum.* Sounds like a type of ejaculate."

Veronica shoves Paolo hard into a white Audi parked by the curb, and its alarm goes off, shrill beeps piercing the night. Paolo freezes by the car, like a prisoner who's been caught by a spotlight mid-escape. "What did you do?" he says, eyes huge.

"Come on, keep walking," Veronica says, grabbing Paolo by the arm. "It's not a big deal. It'll turn off in a second."

"I hope that car wasn't a spy," he says.

"Where are we going anyway?" Veronica asks as we turn the corner, the beeps fading away behind us.

"Um . . ." I trust Veronica, but I hear my mother's strict

warning ringing in my ears nevertheless. "I don't know if you can come with us. It's kinda top secret."

"Yeah," Paolo says, "Dent's Real Mom gets *intense* sometimes. And it's like, *Whoa, Mama, let's all be cool, aight?*"

"What do you mean, *Dent's Real Mom?*" Veronica asks, looking at me with narrowed eyes.

"We're staying in an apartment that belongs to my . . . Well, it belongs to my biological mom."

Veronica stops in the middle of the sidewalk. "Hold up. She's alive, too?"

"She lives, baby!" Paolo says. "All the dead Littles live! And I'm next! WOOO!"

"What the hell? Your mother's been alive your whole life?"

"Yeah," I say. "The same virus thing that saved me saved her, too."

"Wow. Guess that explains why my mom and her people want to get their hands on that virus so bad."

"Wait. What've you heard?"

"Not much, really," Veronica says, kicking at an empty Vitaminwater bottle in our path. "I've pieced stuff together from the limited eavesdropping I've been able to do when I'm home. But Mom knows we're both on your side, so she's been as confidential as ever with all this shit. I've had to be real stealth about it."

"Very pink ninja," I say.

One side of Veronica's mouth curls up first, the other pulled along moments later. I forgot how magical her smile is, especially when it happens because of something I said.

"I picked this up," Paolo says, holding up the Vitamin-water bottle. "So we can recycle it. Not cool to kick trash, V."

"Um, all right," Veronica says. "The important stuff we're talking about sorta takes precedence over recycling someone else's beverage."

"It's that kind of attitude that's killing this earth," Paolo says, shaking his head.

Veronica and I look at him for a moment.

"Anyway," Veronica says. "I've never seen our mom like this. She's so worked up about it. She got demoted after you got away from her this last time."

"Seriously?" I almost feel bad.

"I think she's worried she could lose her job if they don't end up finding you, Dent."

"Oh," I say. "But if the alternative is having to kidnap her son's best friend, who is also her daughter's, well"—I want Veronica to finish the sentence for me, but she doesn't—"maybe she should just give up her job, then."

"For realsies," Paolo says. "Mom's gotta get a new job."

"I told her that," Veronica says. "We talked in the hospital the day after you left. More of a fight than a talk, really. But she started crying when I said that. I mean, if she lost her job with the DIA, she'd have to find something else to do. And the economy sucks right now."

"I guess," I say.

"Oh!" Paolo says. "Maybe the government can transfer her to a job as a congresswoman or something. So then her responsibility would be something else, not kidnapping Denton."

Veronica looks so offended. "Pow. You can't just—
Don't you know how democracy works?"

"Oh, pardon me," Paolo says in a snooty-person voice.
"I didn't realize you were so touchy about democracy. Hey,
you guys, look at how pretty the moon is tonight."

We both look up. The moon is barely visible.

"Zing! Made ya look!" Paolo giggles. "Got you back,
sucka. That was classic." His drunkenness is severely affecting his judgment.

"All right, then," Veronica says. "My point is, she can't
just quit, Dent. She's a single mom trying to put me through
college."

"Oh shoot," Paolo says. "If I survive my deathdate, too,
she'll really be screwed, because she'll have two kids to put
through college. Ah man." He puts his face in his hands
and shakes his head. "Wait! I'll take some time to travel
after high school. Yeah, that's perfect! Maybe hit up Asia,
Paris, the Grand Canyon. Problemo solved-o!"

Doing my best to ignore Paolo, I process what Veronica
is saying, and something occurs to me. "Assuming all that's
true," I say. "Wouldn't it be in your best interest to make
sure your mom finds me? Since you don't want her to lose
her job?"

"Ooh," Paolo says. "*Such* a good point, V."

Veronica looks away and takes a deep breath. Suddenly
I'm very worried about what she's going to say. What if this
is all a trap and she's been stalling to give her mom time to
come get me? "She wanted me to help her," she says, still
looking away. Then she turns back and looks right at me.
"But I wouldn't do it."

I rub the back of my neck and look up at the non-impressive moon.

"You have to trust me, Dent," Veronica says.

We're the only people on this block right now, and for a moment, there's just our silence and the distant sound of cars moving along on neighboring streets.

"His name is Frank now," Paolo says, pulling at his bottom lip like it's Play-Doh.

"I do trust you," I say, realizing as soon as it's out of my mouth that I mean it. I hope.

"Good," Veronica says, her relief visible. "But I'm not gonna call you Frank, all right?"

"Thank you," I say.

"Thank you?" Paolo asks. "Why are you saying 'Thank you'? I thought you wanted to be Frank!"

"I hate the name Frank. I was just doing it because my mom said I had to."

"Oh, screw that," Paolo says. "I'm not calling you Frank either, then. It was really hard for my brain to remember."

I look up and realize we're in front of my mom's brownstone.

I look at Veronica and make a snap decision. Screw my mom's rules. "This is us. You can stay here, too, if you want."

"Um, maybe, yeah," she says, unusually flustered. I wonder if she thinks I'm asking if she'll stay in the same bed with me. I hope that's what she's thinking. "If that's all right."

"Lemme just check something first." I go through the gate, quietly unlock the front door, and step inside. I tiptoe down the hall, and, just as I hoped, my mom's bedroom door is already closed for the night. Score.

"Okay, come on in," I say, popping my head back out.

"Did you just go and take a dump?" Paolo asks.

Veronica and I both choose to ignore him. The three of us head inside.

TWELVE

I lead them quietly down the hall, stopping in front of the room Paolo's been sleeping in. He's nearly asleep on his feet, his eyelids heavy as he sways left and right.

"Veronica," I whisper. "Head upstairs and chill while I help Pow. I don't want us to accidentally wake my mom."

She nods and goes upstairs. I open the door to Paolo's room and try to lead him inside, but he's rooted to the ground. "Hey, Pow," I say, giving him a shake.

His eyes snap open. "Did somebody pack a bowl?"

"What? No, man. It's time to go to bed."

"Oh, all right," Paolo says, his eyes nearly closed again. "If you're positive no one's packed anything." He takes three steps to the bed, then flops facedown and immediately begins snoring.

Okay then.

I walk the rest of the way down the hall, my stomach coiling into a ball as I pass my mom's bedroom, and up the stairs. I'm not exactly sure what Veronica's thinking, but it's possible that right now is the preamble to a reunion make-out session. And that is great.

Upstairs, Veronica is nestled into a corner of the chesterfield couch with her phone.

It occurs to me that if it turns out Veronica is acting as some kind of spy for her mother, then I am being ridiculously stupid right now. Essentially, I'm putting my mom's entire movement at risk because I'm horny.

"Hey," I say.

"Hey," she says, laying her phone facedown next to her on the couch.

"Um . . . I thought you had your phone turned off. So your mom wouldn't be able to track you?"

"Don't worry, Paranoid Pete." She lifts up the phone, flicks the screen on, and holds it up to my face. "It's on airplane mode. I was playing Feather Frenzy." Sure enough, the screen is filled with colorful feathers.

"Okay, cool." Maybe I am Paranoid Pete. "Well, thanks for waiting."

"No prob," she says, grabbing a piece of gum out of her purse. "Want a piece?"

"Sure," I say. This is good. Gum is good. It's what you chew when you think you're about to make out with somebody.

"I can't believe your mom's been alive all this time," she says.

"Yeah, I know. It's very weird."

"And you're alive, too. I can't believe that either." Veronica really looks at me for the first time today.

"Me neither, really."

"Do you seriously think P's going to live, too?"

"I don't know. My mom seems to think he might."

"Wow. Because of the splotch you gave him on your deathdate?"

"Yeah."

"Wait a second. You gave that to me, too. Does that mean I'm going to live through my deathdate when I'm eighty-eight? Or, shoot, does it mean I might die *before* my deathdate?"

These are very good questions. "Um, no, I don't think so. Because, well, based on what my mom has said, it seems like that wouldn't be what happens. I don't think."

"You have no idea, do you?"

"I really don't."

"Yeah, I figured." Veronica looks down at her hands. I'm contemplating whether now is the moment to reach out and grab one of them when she yawns and says, "I'm actually pretty tired. Can you show me where I'm sleeping?"

"Oh, all right, sure." I can't tell if she's hinting that it's time to get into my bed and make out or if she's actually wanting to go to sleep. "Um, okay, follow me." We head downstairs.

"So, Millie slept there," I say, pointing to the black leather couch at the bottom of the staircase, right near the room where I've been sleeping. "But—"

"That works," Veronica says. "Thanks, D."

"Oh, okay," I whisper. "The thing is, um, my mom said I can't have any more people from my old life here, so, uh, if you stay on this couch, you'll have to leave pretty early so you're gone before she sees you. But if you want to stay with—"

"That's cool," she says. "I have to leave early to make it back in time for work anyway." She's already unfolded the blanket that was sitting there from when Millie was here last night.

I'm not an idiot (well, I kind of am sometimes); she's clearly shutting down all hope of anything happening between us tonight. Or maybe any night. The gum was a total red herring.

I feel the disappointment deep in my gut. I want to say something, but without the helpful motivator of a death-date, I can't bring myself to do it. If she turns me down, I'll actually have to live with it; I don't get to die to escape the mortification.

"So, uh, all right," I say, lingering awkwardly near the door of my bedroom. "Good night, I guess. It's really awesome to see you."

"Good night, dude," Veronica says, flashing a quick smile as she tucks the blanket into the couch. I wince as she refers to me as *dude,* possibly the fastest and simplest way to indicate that nothing romantic will be happening between two humans. I'd almost prefer Frank.

"Yup. Okeydokey. Sleep well." If I could think of something else I could say to stall, I'd say it. But I can't, so I slowly back up into my bedroom, then very slowly close the door, allowing Veronica the time and space to shout, *Wait!*

Of course she doesn't, and the door closes with a definitive click, which triggers within me a garbled rush of anger, loneliness, and frustration. This is ridiculous. We've already hooked up; I don't know why this should be so hard. But it's like my deathdate has clean-slated everything, and now we have to start all over again. Was our entire fling contingent upon me dying? The more I think about it, the more furious I get.

I take a gray throw pillow off the bed and hurl it to the ground. It bounces once and lands on its side. I'm not sure what I was thinking, as the last thing I need right now is for my mom to wake up. I freeze and listen, but there's only silence. I lie back on the bed and look up at the ceiling.

I flip over onto my stomach for a minute, then again onto my back.

This is silly. I've been given the unheard-of gift of *more life,* and so far, I've mainly spent it holed up in apartments, doing absolutely nothing. Who cares if Veronica rejects me and it's mortifying? At least I'll feel *something.* I have no idea when I'm going to die, so I need to start, you know, grabbing life by the balls *now.*

I pop up from the bed and move toward the door with purpose. I'm going to tell Veronica that I like her more than I ever have. I am going to say this.

I swing open the door, but it quickly becomes clear that Veronica is asleep. She's still wearing her black hoodie and snoring lightly, a more delicate and refined version of what Paolo is doing. It's endearing.

Well. I'm not gonna wake her up just so I can pour my heart out. I go back into my room and lie down on the bed.

Why did Veronica even come into the city to meet up with us if she has to work early tomorrow? To take a walk, say hey, and then go? She didn't even seem that excited to see me.

Oh man. I really hope she's not a spy.

When I open my eyes, hours or minutes later, someone is at the foot of the bed, staring at me in the near darkness.

My whole body tenses. It's Paolo's mom, here to take me away. I need to run.

As my eyes adjust, though, I see it's not Paolo's mom, but her daughter.

"Hey," I say. "Are you okay?"

Veronica shrugs slightly. She's no longer wearing her black hoodie, just a T-shirt with the number seven on it. It's possible she might be sleepwalking.

"Are you awake?" I ask.

"Yeah," she says quietly. My body is coursing with adrenaline, even though I'm still not fully awake myself.

"Are you wondering where the bathroom is?"

Veronica shakes her head twice, without taking her eyes off me.

"So . . . ?" I say.

"Can I get in bed with you?" she asks.

Brain. Exploded.

"Um, of course, yeah," I say. This is happening.

She walks slowly toward the bed, I lift the covers, and she climbs in next to me, pressing her body against mine. She smells amazing.

This moment is suddenly rivaling my time with Veronica in the woods/bathroom for Hottest Thing That's Ever Happened to Me.

I put my arm around her. She seems okay with that.

"Is everything all right?" I ask. "I—"

Then her mouth is on mine.

Thank you, Universe, for allowing me to live.

I put my hands on Veronica's cheeks as we inhale each other's faces. Her lips are soft, her tongue is determined, her hands slide up and down my back. Our bodies are entangled, and I'm sure she can feel how turned on I am.

I'm so excited this is happening that it's almost taking me out of the moment. I like her so much.

"I missed you," I say, between kisses.

"Yeah," she says breathily. "Me, too."

"I really—"

But then her hands have slid down, touching me in new places, and I stop talking.

Veronica helps me take my shirt off, and I do the same for her. As unzipping and touching happen, it occurs to me that maybe this is all a dream, but I don't care if it is. It all feels so good.

I'm wondering if we should try to have sex, but that would mean stopping what's currently happening, even for a few seconds, and I don't want that. We're both breathing heavily, locked into a rhythm, using our hands on each other. Veronica quietly moans in this very genuine way that is so much better than the overly performative sounds Taryn used to make.

And then I have no room in my mind for anything except Veronica.

Her smell. Her body. Her.

Soon there's no room for even that as my entire body and mind are flooded with good feeling.

I'm glad to be alive. I'm so glad to be alive. I love being alive.

Then I'm disoriented, blissed out, feeling like I barely understand what has just happened. Veronica's eyes are still closed, though, so I keep moving my hand until it seems like her body and mind are flooded with good feeling, too.

We lie there and breathe in silence for a while.

"Wow," I say. "I was not expecting that."

"Mmm," Veronica says.

"I can go get a paper towel," I say. "To clean up." It's stupid, but I'm vaguely embarrassed by the sticky aftermath of what we've just done.

"Mmm," she says again.

I look down and see that Veronica's asleep already.

"Oh," I say.

Her head is leaning against my shoulder in a way that makes it challenging to get up, so I don't. I lie back, grinning at the ceiling, inhaling the scent of Veronica, and soon I'm asleep, too.

THIRTEEN

My eyes blink open, and I'm lying alone in bed.

Of course Veronica's gone already.

I search the nightstand, thinking maybe she's left a note.

She has not.

I rub my eyes and stare at the painting hanging on the wall opposite the bed. It's abstract, with thick, messy brushstrokes, but I think it's supposed to be a skeleton taking his dog for a walk, possibly in hell? (The background is a fiery orange and red.) It is not a comforting piece of art.

Oh geez. Is it possible my hookup with Veronica was a dream? Please, no.

My shirt's off, so that's something.

I sit up in bed, searching for clues that she's been here, some indication that our blissful, late-night rendezvous was not imaginary. There's nothing on the floor, nothing on the nightstand, and seemingly nothing in the bed. In a fit of frustration, I flap up the blanket like a parachute, then ball it up and chuck it to the ground.

It might be slightly problematic that whenever I hook up with Veronica, I'm never really sure if it happened. But assuming it did happen, it might have been part of some larger spy tactic on behalf of her mom. Which would also be problematic.

Defeated, I flop onto my stomach, my legs hanging off the side of the bed, my face buried in the sheet.

A powerful smell forces me to push up off the mattress. It is most assuredly the scent of my own bodily fluids. From last night. With Veronica.

I throw a triumphant fist into the air.

"Not a dream!" I say aloud to no one.

"Hey, bud, what's a five-letter word for apathy?" Paolo is sitting on the black couch Veronica slept on, holding a coffee in one hand and a pen in the other, the *New York Times* crossword puzzle splayed out over his crossed legs.

"Um, I don't know," I say. I'm a little surprised to see him so put together. After I showered and got dressed, the next item on my to-do list was *Tend to Paolo*. I assumed he'd be hungover.

"Also, you wouldn't perchance have a pencil on you, wouldja? It's very arrogant to do crosswords in pen."

"Yeah, uh, no. You've been outside already?"

"Oh, absolutely. The city is wonderful in the morning. People rushing to work, all the kids with their backpacks, the shopkeepers opening up for the day." He takes a delicate sip from his paper cup. "Ahhh. I got you an egg sandwich, by the way." He tosses it to me. "Reynaldo made it. He's got such a light touch."

"What are you talking about? Who's Reynaldo?"

"He works at that deli on the corner. You know Reynaldo."

"I really don't. And you do crosswords now?"

"When in Rome, my man. Oh, of course, it's *ennui,*" he says, excitedly filling in squares. "Duh!"

I feel irrationally jealous, like Paolo's getting the hang of life in New York City faster than me. He's always been better at rolling with whatever, taking each moment as it comes. That's never been me—I'm generally terrible with change—but maybe it should be. Maybe that's the way we're all supposed to be living.

I sit down next to him on the couch, where I detect a slight whiff of Veronica. It makes my stomach bounce. "Thanks for this," I say, gesturing with my sandwich. "I didn't mean to get all interrogatey."

"No prob, D," Paolo says. "It's cool. You're becoming more of an abrasive New Yorker." His pen bounces as he writes in another word.

"Um, can I ask you something?" I say.

"No, definitely not," Paolo says.

"All right, cool." I watch Paolo as he taps his pen against his chin and looks at the ceiling.

"Okay. Now you can ask," he says.

"Super," I say. We're idiots. "So, Veronica left and everything, right?"

"Yeah," Paolo says, reaching into his pocket and pulling out a crumpled-up receipt that he unfolds and looks at. "She said . . . *Going back to NJ for work.*"

"Oh man, you got a note?"

"I guess so."

"And that's all she said?"

Paolo looks closer at it. "There's also a little heart and the letter *V.* I think that stands for Veronica."

"You sure?"

"No, you're right," Paolo says. "This note could have been from Vince the plumber."

"That guy is great," I say.

"He's the best," Paolo says. "But, dude, sidenote: I can't believe you let Veronica stay here. I mean, if DRM saw her, she would have flipped the eff out."

"I know," I say. "It was pretty dumb of me."

"I hope y'all at least got your freak on."

"Oh. Well . . ." When Paolo first found out that Veronica and I had done stuff together, he was horrified. But now I guess he's become used to the idea. "I mean, yeah, we sorta did."

"Whoa!" Paolo puts down his coffee cup and sticks his fingers into his ears. "TMI, bro! That's my sister!"

"You're the one who said it!"

"Yeah, but that doesn't mean I want to hear all the messy details!"

"All I said was we sorta did! I mean, I think we did anyway."

"Are you kidding me? You were too drunk to remember? *Again?* Man, you can't only get down with my sister when you're wasted. She deserves better than that!"

"We weren't drunk. It happened in the middle of the night. But then she was gone when I woke up, so I thought maybe I had just . . . like, dreamed it."

Paolo eyes me suspiciously as he takes a long sip from his coffee.

"I know," I say, rubbing my face with my hands. "But, actually, I'm pretty sure it did happen, because this morning I . . . smelled something." Even as I'm speaking these words, I'm wishing I wasn't. "On the sheets. I, like, smelled proof. That it happened."

"Hold up," Paolo says, and I know I've said too much. "Are you saying what I think you're saying? Like . . . you smelled your own . . . proof?"

"Possibly."

"Wow," Paolo says, shaking his head at me. "I smell my proof, too! All the time!"

"Ew, wait, what? Seriously?"

"Of course seriously!" he shouts, jumping up onto his feet. "That's the smell of the circle of life!"

"So even though you didn't want to hear messy details, you're cool to discuss the smelling of one's own semen?"

"Hmm. A fair point," Paolo says, sitting back down. "I got excited, because hearing you say that you did that made me feel less alone in life. But check it—maybe you did dream that hookup with V. Maybe you *wet*-dreamed it."

"What?"

"Nocturnal emissions, yo!"

My mouth drops open. "Wow," I say. "Maybe you're right." Why can't Veronica and I have a hookup that I am one hundred percent certain happened?

"Well, whatever it is that went down, we're talking

about you proofing as a result of my sister, so let's change the subject."

"Yeah, actually, I still haven't even asked you my original question. I thought it was kinda weird that Veronica came into the city when she could only stay for, like, a total of eight hours. And then I started getting paranoid. Do you think it's possible that your sister is acting as a spy for your mom? Like, that she'd give up our location and everything?"

Paolo considers this thoughtfully. "V would make a good spy. She's very hard to read sometimes."

"Man! You're supposed to say there's no way V is on your mom's side, that you're sure she's aligned with us!"

"Whoa, calm it down, D," Paolo says, gently patting the air to pacify me. "V's probably cool. But I've barely seen her the past week, so there's no way I could know for sure."

"Sorry," I say.

"I just don't have any proof."

"That's all right."

"No, I was making another proof joke."

"Oh. Nice." It would have been better if Paolo could have assured me vehemently that Veronica would never work with their mom on this, that she would never betray me. The room is quiet except for the sound of Paolo's sipping. I unwrap my egg sandwich and take a bite. It's not warm, but it is delicious.

"You know, actually," he says, "your mom left a note on the counter upstairs. Said that when she comes home later, we all have 'lots of important things to talk about.' So maybe she does know Veronica's been here."

"Oh," I say, a rush of fear icing my veins. "Shoot."

"Don't worry, D. I got your back," Paolo says, his focus redirected to his crossword. "Ah, the answer is Pelé! They put him in, like, every puzzle!" In his excitement, Paolo knocks his coffee onto his lap. "Aw dippy, I spilled!"

I'm screwed.

FOURTEEN

"Where's Millie?" my mom asks, standing in front of us, both sleeves of her plaid button-down rolled up to her elbows.

"Oh," I say from my seat next to Paolo on the chesterfield. "She had to go home. Her parents were worried, and she couldn't miss any more school."

"Hmm," my mom says. She's not as pissed as I thought she'd be. "Okay. She knows she's not coming back here again, though, right?"

"For sure," I say.

"I'm trusting you on this one, Frank."

It's still hard to take that name seriously. "Of course."

"Judging by how late the two of you were out last night," my mom says, "I think it's fair to say you had a good time?"

I can't tell if she's saying this as some kind of test because she knows Veronica was here.

"Mos def, DRM," Paolo says.

"Yeah," I say. "I mean, it was pretty fun. Nothing crazy or unusual happened, if that's what you're wondering."

"That's what people generally say when something crazy or unusual *did* happen," Felix shouts from the kitchen, where he's pouring salsa into a bowl.

"Oh right," I say. "Well, not this time."

"Good," my mom says. "I'm assuming you were inconspicuous."

"Of course," I say, remembering how Paolo uttered a huge secret thing to a bearded douche, who I dramatically shoved minutes later.

"We were super-inconspituous," Paolo says.

"I'm glad you had fun," she says. "Because things are about to get a bit more serious."

"Yes," Dane says, sitting in a wooden chair, his long legs jutting out at peculiar angles. "Serious times now."

"Before I get into it," my mom says, "Paolo, if I find out anything from this room leaked to the DIA, I will blame you. And you definitely won't survive your deathdate, because I will kill you."

"Whoa," I say.

"I understand, DRM," Paolo says, eyes wide.

"She's just kidding around," Felix says, leaping in to defend her insane behavior.

"Am I, though?" My mom smiles. Very scary. "So, Frank." She is radiating excitement. "We finally have all the test results back."

I was just starting to find some joy in this new life, and now the game is about to change all over again. On the bright side, it seems like she doesn't know Veronica was here last night. Thank God.

"Many mice interact with your blood and saliva," Dane says. "You would not believe."

"Oh," I say, trying to ignore the atrocious imagery he's just conjured up. "What, um, what did the results say?"

For a moment, it occurs to me that maybe I'm not going to survive after all. But my mom seems so happy—smiling at me like a proud, crazy person with the world's best secret—so I know that can't be the case.

"Well," my mom continues while Felix puts down the bowl of salsa and a bowl tortilla chips and takes a seat in an orange puffy chair, "as Dane so elegantly put it, we did extensive testing with mice that we'd specifically procured because their deathdates were all in the week and a half after yours."

"It was not easy to find those mice, no way," Dane says. "Not cheap either."

"And so, we learned some new things," my mom says. "You already know the virus was injected into you when you were in the womb. The fact that you survived your deathdate is a huge victory in and of itself. It means the other three babies that were injected over the past eighteen years should live through their deathdates, too."

"Yes, Yuri, for example," Dane says.

"Right," my mom says. "Which is a big deal for our movement—it really is. Only a handful of women have been given the virus, but with your survival, so many more will want their fetuses injected." Those two words should never be used side by side in a sentence. "The babies will be born with deathdates that will prove to be incorrect, and the system will fall apart.

"But that will take time. Decades, really. We were

hoping that the movement could progress faster. And the tests confirmed that that is possible. They confirmed something I'd hardly dared to hope for."

"Dent is immortal, isn't he?" Paolo asks quietly.

"What? No, of course not." My mom is temporarily extracted from her dramatic reverie. "Please, just stay quiet a second."

"Okeydoke, sorry," Paolo says.

"What the tests confirmed is that your strain of the virus can *spread*. And not just on your deathdate."

"What?" I get light-headed for a few seconds, and I need to put a hand down on the couch to steady myself.

"Your saliva saved the lives of three different mice."

"Uh . . ." I don't know what to do with that.

"Fiona, Harold, and Jellyfish," Dane says. "They now live because of you."

"Wow," Paolo says. "Cute names."

"You're a very powerful person now, Denton," my mom says. She must be really excited, because she forgot to call me Frank.

"That's, uh, yeah," I say.

"Maybe *the* most powerful person in the world, even."

"Unreal, right?" Felix says, grinning proudly at me.

I'm having trouble processing this. "Are you saying that I can give anybody the virus through my saliva, and they'll . . . live through their deathdate?"

"Exactly!" my mom says.

I feel a volcano of joy erupt in my chest. Paolo's going to live!

"Granted," my mom continues, "they'll have no idea how much extra time they've been given—could be a few days, could be six decades—but it's everything we've been working toward! We've always had so many hopes riding on your return, Frank, and maybe that wasn't fair, but it turns out we were completely justified."

Paolo and I stare at each other, like we can't even believe this is really happening. My head's spinning, but I need to confirm what I've just heard. "So, are you saying Paolo will live because I already passed it to him?"

"Oh," my mom says, looking a little embarrassed, like she hadn't even been thinking of the way this news would relate to Paolo. "Well, it's . . ." She looks to Dane for a quick moment, then back to us. "The timing is critical. You have to pass someone the virus on their deathdate, or the day before. We've found that's when their DNA is open to accepting it. But if you do that, people will live past their deathdates, yes!"

"Oh, okay," I say, trying to quickly parse through what she's said. It seems like all I have to do is pass Paolo the virus again on the day of his funeral. Should be easy enough, considering I was able to do it once before, without even realizing it.

Which means my best friend is going to live.

I'm tearing up a little.

"Is more than okay," Dane says, standing up triumphantly. "Is DIA payback time." He points at me. "With our powerful weapon."

I don't love being referred to as a weapon, but I'm feeling too good to care.

"*Yes!*" my mom shouts for the second time in the past minute, doing nothing to regulate her volume at this point. "I'm so happy," she says, grabbing my hand. "I didn't know if I'd get to see this kind of change in my lifetime."

"Dude, you're a freaking superhero!" Paolo says, throwing an arm around me and pulling me close. "Who's gonna save my freaking life."

I *am* kind of a superhero. This is amazing. And nuts.

"Anybody mind if I break the seal on these chips?" Paolo says. "To celebrate the good news?"

"Do it," Felix says.

"Woo!" Paolo leans over the table to dip a chip into the salsa. We all follow suit and partake of some chips.

"So here's the deal," my mom says, rubbing her hands together to get rid of chip crumbs. "Our movement has been working for two decades to get to this moment. And now it's time to act."

"What is this salsa?" Dane asks the room.

"It's got peach in it," Felix says.

"It is magnificent! I usually am not a fruit person."

"Seriously, Dane?" my mom says, shooting eye daggers at him. "I'm about to lay out the most important part of our whole mission."

"I apologize," he says, his mouth filled with chips. "Please to continue."

She stares at him a moment longer before she does. "As I was about to say, this part of our mission obviously rests mostly on Frankie, at least at first. But—"

"I'm sorry," I say, doing my best to pretend she didn't just call me Frankie, "but when you constantly refer to this movement, do you mean there are more people involved than just us in this room?"

My mom looks offended. "Well, of *course*, Frank. There are dozens of people all over the country invested in our movement. I've been in New York City the past decade, but right after my deathdate, I spent many years in a number of other cities, finding like-minded individuals who wanted to live through their deathdates and who believed in people's right to choose whether or not to learn their deathdates in the first place. And all of those individuals are counting on you to bring this gift of extra life to people everywhere, while also bringing this wretched system of mandatory deathdates to its knees."

Well, that doesn't sound like a lot of pressure or anything. "Gotcha," I say. "Thanks for clarifying."

My mom picks up her messenger bag and digs out a newspaper, which she smacks down onto the coffee table near the couch. "Here," she says, licking a finger and flipping through pages until she finds what she's looking for, "is our plan."

There's a picture of an older, handsome, gray-haired man and his blond wife standing behind their teenage daughter, also blond.

"I don't get it," I say.

"Read the headline," my mom says.

"*Rep. Whitney and Teen Daughter Bond During Her Final Days*. Is he a member of Congress or something?"

"That's exactly what he is," my mother says.

I feel Dane and Felix staring at me, excited to see how I respond to this.

"And his daughter is going to die soon," I say.

"Well." A strange smile takes shape on my mom's face. "She's *supposed* to die soon."

Then I understand.

FIFTEEN

"Don't you see how powerful this could be?" my mother asks.

"Um," I say, my stomach flipping over and threatening to push the peach salsa out the way it came in.

"This is the perfect target. Congressman Whitney here has taken a shit ton of donations for his campaign from the pharmaceutical industry, specifically Epistemex, the company that makes the ATG kits. He's one of many politicians who make damn sure deathdates remain mandatory. So when his daughter somehow lives through her deathdate, oh man, it's gonna make a huge statement."

Paolo is looking back and forth from me to my mom to Dane to Felix, like he can't quite believe what he's hearing. "So, D's gonna waltz into this fancy funeral and find a way to secretly pass on his splotch to that plastic-lookin' girl? So everyone in the government will be all shocked when she doesn't die?"

"That's right," my mom says.

"Holy shit," Paolo says. "Dent, you're like an assassin. An *un*assassin."

That does sound pretty badass. "Will they know that"—I search the article for the girl's name—"Haley Whitney lived through her deathdate because of me?"

"No!" my mom says. "The whole point is that she's going to live through her deathdate and no one will have any idea why. It's the first step in making it seem like those horrendous ATG kits aren't one hundred percent effective after all. Like I said, it's a statement."

"So . . . how am I supposed to pass the virus to her?"

"Whoa, Dent," Paolo says, a lightbulb flickering on over his head. "You're gonna get to make out with that chick!"

"No, no," my mom says. "*Frank* is going to drink from a glass of water, making sure to deposit a big saliva sample—"

"Well, that sounds heinous," I say.

"And we'll make sure that glass of water gets into the Whitney girl's hands."

So I'm going to save a random girl's life by depositing my spit into her water glass. Not nearly as badass as I was thinking. But I can get behind that.

"The fact that she's a teenager makes it all so much easier. There's a much smaller chance anyone will question why you're at her funeral."

"Right," Paolo says, gesturing toward him and me. "Because *we're* both teenagers."

My mom narrows her eyes, unable to tell if he's joking. He isn't. "Right," she says, very slowly nodding her head. "Also, teen funerals usually get the biggest turnouts.

Because they're the saddest." The clinical way she talks about all this makes me uncomfortable. "So you'll have a generally easy time blending in."

"Yeah, okay," I say, propelling myself to my feet, filled with so much nervous energy I can't sit any longer. "We go in, we pass the spit, and we save this girl's life. But are we sure this isn't, like, playing God or something? Like, this girl and her family have been expecting one thing for her entire life, and now we're changing that?"

"Oh, this is absolutely playing God," my mother says. "But sometimes that's necessary. Sometimes people don't know what's best for them."

There's something not quite right about this, but it's hard to argue against saving someone's life.

"Honestly, dude," Paolo says. "Even though we all know deathdates are one hundred percent accurate—or, at least, used to be—every person probably still holds out a small slice of hope that they'll be the first to live through theirs. I definitely did. And now it's coming true. Booyah, mothafuzzers!"

"Well," I say. "I never held out that hope."

"Yeah, but you're weird. You love to follow the rules. You didn't even drink till the day before you were supposed to die."

This is true. I am big on rules. "But what happens to Haley Whitney when she lives?" I ask. "The government kidnaps and studies her? Like they want to do to me?"

"It's hard to say," my mother says. "The government only wants to study you because they know you're the first one to survive from a direct injection. And they've known about your potential to survive for years, way before your deathdate, which gave them plenty of time to prepare the cover-up. They had an agent tailing you most of your life, for God's sake. But with the Whitney girl, no one will see it coming; the government will be caught completely off guard. Especially her father."

"So . . . she'll be able to continue living her life like nothing ever happened? *Oops! Guess they got the date wrong!*"

"Well, I don't know about that. But people will find out she's lived. And it will be a huge news story."

"See, dude?" Paolo says. "She'll become famous. People love being famous."

Paolo's right about a lot of things today. And the more I think about it, the more this actually seems like an amazing gift to give someone. If it felt amazing to write nice things on people's Facebook Timelines, I can't imagine how much better it'd feel to bestow someone with more life.

"When's her funeral?" I ask.

"Wednesday," my mom says. "A week from now."

"Okay," I say, then pause, because I know it'll make it more dramatic. "I'm in."

"Yes!" my mom says, flinging her arms out and pulling me into a hug. "I'm so glad about this, Frank. You're incredible. Thank you."

Not gonna lie—it feels really good to hear my mom say that, even if she is kind of a nut.

Dane shakes a victorious fist in the air. "This make all the waiting for you worth it."

"Let's go change the world, li'l bro," Felix says, patting me on the back.

Their love and praise are intoxicating, and for the first

time since all this insanity began, I'm thinking maybe I'm on the right path after all. I'm going to save this girl Haley's life. And Paolo's life. And then maybe I'll start saving other people's lives, too. Maybe this truly is the natural extension of the kindness mission I started on my deathdate.

Maybe it's what I'm supposed to be doing with my life.

My mom releases me from the longest hug she's ever given me, and I catch eyes with Paolo.

"My boy's an unassassin!" he says, giving me a hug.

I still can't believe he's going to live. I'm about to say something to this effect when my mom puts a hand on my shoulder.

"Don't go anywhere, you two, okay?" she says, looking at Paolo and me with a decidedly less enthusiastic expression than she had a moment ago. "We need to have a quick talk."

"Um, sure," I say, glancing at Paolo to see that he's just as bewildered as I am.

My mom directs a loaded look at Dane and Felix. "Fellas," she says, "could you give me a moment alone with Frank and Paolo? Maybe go order some dinner for all of us or something."

"Oh yeah, absolutely," Felix says, heading toward the kitchen.

"Is there a surplus of that salsa?" Dane asks as he follows.

My mom sits in the orange chair just vacated by Felix. Her whole vibe is making me nervous.

"Hi," my mom says, as if by doing that, she's rebooting our time together.

"Uh, hi," I say.

"Hello," Paolo says.

"Um, I'm not sure how to say this," my mom continues, "but in the conversation we just had, I wasn't entirely straightforward about one, uh, more unfortunate aspect that the tests have brought to light." My heart is in my throat. "The past week, we've been working with the blood, hair, and saliva samples we took from Paolo, and we, uh, discovered something."

"Oh no," Paolo says, concerned. "Did my blood make the mice, like, explode or something?"

"Um, no, nothing like that," my mom says, confused but trying to be polite. "Frank, when you passed the activated virus to Paolo on your deathdate, it obviously wasn't Paolo's deathdate, too. So the virus operated differently on him."

"Differently how?" I ask, pressing my feet hard into the rug.

"It operated more like a vaccine."

"But . . . vaccines are good, right?"

"Not in this case, no," my mom says, shaking her head. "When you gave the virus to Paolo, his immune system formed antibodies to it. And now he's immune to the virus."

"Meaning . . . ?" I ask.

My mom turns to look right at my best friend. "Meaning the virus isn't going to save you, Paolo. I'm sorry."

SIXTEEN

"How can you be sure?" I ask.

"The mice keep dying," my mom says, sympathy in her eyes. "The antibodies that your body is creating, Paolo, mean that rather than incorporating the virus into your DNA, you've developed an immunity to it."

"But," I say, "I mean, you said you thought Paolo might survive."

"I know. That was before the tests. This is new to us, too. And it turns out the virus is like chicken pox. You can't get it twice. Paolo got the virus already, and his immune system defeated it. And created antibodies to fight it off in the future."

So, because I shared a bowl with Paolo, I ruined any chance he has of surviving past his deathdate?

"This is so wrong! I can save the life of some random blond girl, but I can't save my best friend?"

"Dude," Paolo says. "I appreciate the rage on my behalf, but it's really okay."

"No, it's not!" I say. "There has to be a way to figure this out." My mind is moving fast now, because if this logic is accurate, I won't only be losing Paolo. *Anyone* I make out with or share a glass with or, I don't know, whose mouth I accidentally sneeze into is going to become immune to the lifesaving powers of the virus. Unless it's their deathdate. I'm like a superhero who can only save people he's not close with.

"Look," my mom says, leaning in. "There are things we still don't understand about the virus. Maybe if you can successfully pass it to Tom Whitney's daughter, we'll figure out new ways that it works, pinpoint some kind of loophole that could save Paolo."

"Oh, so if I participate in your rebellion or whatever, maybe a fairy will miraculously emerge from the heavens to grant me my wish?" I've shifted into unreasonable-little-shit mode, but I can't help it.

"I'm trying to be helpful," my mom says quietly.

"Well, try harder," I say.

"I know this isn't your fault, DRM," Paolo says. "Thanks for being honest with me."

I ignore Paolo's polite words. "Ohmigod, this unassassin thing is why you were happy to have Pow around, isn't it? If we saved him, it would be the same thing as this Whitney girl, right? The son of a DIA agent survives. What a statement."

"Yes," my mom acknowledges, looking down at her lap. "I did hope for that."

"And now that he's immune," I say, "are you gonna kick him out of the movement?"

"Of course not," my mother says. "I've come to trust him. You're a sweet kid, Paolo. I know you wouldn't do anything to endanger Frank."

"Thanks," Paolo says.

I know there's nothing to be done, but I want to jump out of my skin.

Paolo takes a chip and scoops up the remainder of the peach salsa.

"This just sucks so bad," I say as Paolo and I roam the streets near my mom's apartment.

"I agree," Paolo says, dragging a stick he picked up along the slats of a random gate we're passing.

We took a few bites of the Colombian food Felix and Dane had ordered, then got the hell out of there. More for me than Paolo, I think. He's handling his renewed death sentence surprisingly well.

"So, dude," I say. A streetlight illuminates Paolo's face, and he looks kinda ghostly for a second. "You don't have to stick around here. You should spend your last weeks however you want. Maybe we should both ditch this place."

"Nah, man, you got your mom's mission. Which actually sounds kind of fun." Paolo taps his stick along the sidewalk.

"Well, you should come with me to that funeral, then. 'Cause I don't want to do it if you're not there. Look, you heard my mom. Maybe spreading the virus will teach us something that can help you."

"Ha, I wouldn't count on it, D. But, yeah, maybe I'll come to that and then go home." Paolo stops on the sidewalk and leans poetically on his stick, so I stop, too. "The way I see it, Dent," he says, "I wasn't ever supposed to have this time with you. Whenever I imagined the last few weeks of my life, you were already dead, and I was just moping around with my mom and V, and it was very sad.

"But this last week has been crazy awesome, and I have complete faith that the next two weeks will be, too. Because I'm gonna live life to the fullest. Like you did, Dent, but even better! No offense. And it starts *right now*." Paolo drops his stick under a tree and digs around in his jeans pocket. He pulls out what looks like a metal cigarette and a lighter.

"What's that?"

"Want some?" Paolo asks. He flashes the end of the metal cigarette at me. It's packed tight with pot.

"Whoa, where'd that come from?"

"Brought it with me that first day," Paolo says, lighting the end and inhaling deeply. "In my sneaker."

"That must have been uncomfortable."

"Yes. But highly worth it." He exhales a thick, narrow stream of white. "Been waiting for the right moment to whip it out. I believe I've found it." He says the last part in a fancy voice.

I can't help but be immensely paranoid. "Should you be smoking on the street like this? It smells really strong."

"It's NYC, baby," Paolo says. "Anything goes."

"I don't think that's true."

"Well, I'm gonna own this shit, and you should, too." He holds the pipe out to me. I haven't smoked since that time in the woods right before my deathdate, when everything was infused with the desperation and heightened stakes of dying soon.

Now I'll just be another teenager getting high with his friend. Well, his *dying* friend.

"All right," I say, taking a hit. It's possible we're smoking to run away from our problems, but I think that's actually okay right now.

"Yeah! You getting high is one of my most favorite things," Paolo says.

"I'm glad." I cough three times. "So you're definitely good to stick around, at least until the mission on Wednesday?"

"You know it, baby," Paolo says. "Let's save a dead girl!"

SEVENTEEN

My mom was right. There are tons of people at this funeral. Paolo and I are having no trouble blending in.

We stand in the back, behind dozens of rows of pews, fidgeting in our suits, borrowed from Felix's closet, neither of which fits correctly. Our pant legs are too long because Felix is taller than both of us, and Paolo's shirt and suit jacket are extremely tight. He's slightly wider than Felix.

"It should have occurred to me that we'd need suits," Paolo says, tugging on his jacket. "Could have gone to a thrift shop or something."

I don't respond, because, even though we're relatively camouflaged, the parents of the dying teenager—Congressman Tom Whitney and his wife—are in the middle of their joint eulogy.

"Oh, Haley," Mrs. Whitney says, her blond hair perfectly coiffed, her face a red mess. "You're our little darling, and you always will be."

"Yes," Congressman Whitney says. He has a full head of gray hair, and he looks pretty old to be the dad of a teenager; he's at least ten years older than my dad. "You'll always be Daddy's little angel."

Using the word *angel* in this context is perhaps a little misguided. A wave of sobs rises up around us in the audience, and the mother falls apart at the lectern.

"Oh, why?" she screams. "Why does it have to be our Haley who dies so young? It's not fair! IT'S NOT FAIR!"

"All right, Suzanne," Congressman Whitney says, patting his wife's back. "All right."

"It's been hanging over our heads since she was born, and you know what? Knowing hasn't helped. It hasn't! They say it will make it easier, but this has been HELL. For years!" Someone brings the congressman a martini glass, which he passes to his wife. "No! I don't want a drink right now! Can't shut me up with a cocktail. Not today!"

I feel a combination of sympathy and embarrassment for this woman. But for the first time, I really understand my mom's mission. Maybe deathdates bring more pain than they take away.

The funeral is happening in the chapel of an obscenely gigantic celebration home on the Upper East Side of Manhattan. Haley Whitney, the guest of honor, is a stereotypically pretty sixteen-year-old, all blond hair and cheekbones. So far, the main fact emphasized about her—mentioned in every single eulogy up to this point—is her passion for horses. Multiple friends have talked about how much they'll miss "going out riding together." I can't relate.

Haley's parents are now hugging Haley tightly.

Once the hug is done, the mother and father head back to their seats, and Haley takes their place behind the lectern. She wears a blue dress that sparkles in the light, and she carries herself like she's a princess.

Before she begins to speak, she picks up a glass of water and takes a sip.

"She likes to drink water," Paolo says. "We're set!"

"Yeah, totally," I say.

"Shhh," an older woman in the row ahead of us says, giving us a death stare.

Haley takes her time sipping the water, like she's unaware that hundreds of people are watching her. Maybe I should have taken that kind of ownership during my self-eulogy.

She stares out at everyone and begins to speak.

"Ohmigod, you guys!" she says, her voice high, childlike, and unpleasant to the ear.

You know how you can see a stranger one way, but then they say or do something that allows you to understand who they actually are, thereby instantly reframing their looks and making you wonder how you ever saw them as attractive? She's said only three words, but they were enough.

"Yeesh," Paolo says.

"I can't believe all of you are here for little old me," Haley continues, putting both hands on her cheeks, much to my mortification. I know this isn't fair. I'm trying to give her the benefit of the doubt, but her vibe is painfully self-aware and filled with self-love.

"My parents and I were trying to guess last night how

many people would be here. They thought three hundred. I thought at the very *least* four hundred. But now I'm looking out, and it's gotta be way more than that!"

"The usher said we're at six hundred seventy-nine," Haley's dad calls out from his seat.

"What? Ohmigod!" Haley says, looking around, mouth open wide. "That's even more than Violet Rosenstein had! Thank you soooo much, everybody!!"

Oh man. It seems like very poor form to compare funeral attendance. Though now I'm wondering how many people were at mine. It couldn't have been more than three hundred. But my dad's not a congressman.

Why am I seriously thinking about this?

"So, I love all of you beautiful specimens so much, but first I want to take this opportunity to settle some scores."

"Wow," I say.

"That is kinda what you did, too, though, right?" Paolo whispers.

"Yeah, but I didn't lead with that! It was totally different!" I say. But he's absolutely right. It is what I did. I want to crawl in a hole.

"Bella Turner," Haley says, one hand on her forehead as she looks out. "Is she here?"

"She's over here," another girl shouts.

"Good," Haley says. "Can we just admit once and for all that I'm the better rider? You're good at jumps, I'll give you that. But your overall form, otherwise? Please, girl."

"Sure, I agree, whatever," a voice that must be Bella's says from many rows ahead of us.

"Say it like you mean it!" Haley says, leaning forward over the lectern.

"I agree, okay?" Bella says again.

"Thank you," Haley says, a sneer still glued to her face, which now seems impossible to imagine as anything other than ugly.

"Next up: Tyler Mechlowicz. Where is he?"

"Charming gal, right?" Felix says, popping his head in between Paolo's and mine.

"Hey!" I whisper. "This is atrocious."

"You look so cool," Paolo says, admiring Felix's black-and-white waiter ensemble.

"I need to go—don't wanna arouse suspicion—but find me afterward."

Felix weaves himself through the crowd away from us. It'll be his job to serve my spit water to Haley somehow.

"So, Tyler, you see now," Haley is saying, "how you being confused about your sexual orientation makes *me* look bad? Why'd you agree to go out with me in the first place if you like guys? It's majorly offensive."

"That's enough, Hales," her father says.

"Fine!" Haley brushes her hair back.

"Okay, yeah," Paolo says. "This is different than what you did."

"Thank you for saying that," I say, genuinely relieved.

We watch as Haley berates and derides at least five other people. I keep waiting for her parents to stop her, but I don't think they want to ruin her moment. Every new bash session makes it harder for me to justify saving her life. She is not a nice person.

"I think that's everyone," Haley says, tapping her fingers on her lips. "Yes! Okay, so now I just want to say thank you to my parents, all my chicas, and, most of all,

FireFoot." She hangs her head and sniffs right into the microphone, letting all of us know how emotional she's feeling. "You're such a pure spirit, FireFoot. You're my best friend. You taught me so much. I don't want to leave you."

"Screw *Steve*," Paolo says. "I should be using *FireFoot* as my alias. So badass."

"I'm pretty sure *FireFoot* is the name of a horse," I whisper.

"Oh," Paolo says. "But still."

"So now," Haley says, wiping her face with a handkerchief that her mother has rushed up to her, "I want to sing a song for you, FireFoot." People in the crowd look around, like, *Is FireFoot actually here?* "Hit it, Frank," Haley says, and for the briefest of moments I think she's talking to me. Which is progress, I guess.

She's actually talking to the overweight, bearded man sitting at the big organ off to the side. He nods and starts to play. I recognize the music immediately, though it takes me about ten seconds to place the song.

"Good God," I say to Paolo. "It's 'I Dreamed a Dream.' She's about to sing 'I Dreamed a Dream.'"

"What is that?" he says.

"From *Les Mis*."

"What? Are you saying real words right now?"

"It's a musical," I say. "It doesn't matter."

If my ex-girlfriend Taryn were here, she'd appreciate how heinous this is. In the variety show we were both in last year, the one that successfully kick-started our romance, Rebecca Chorsky sang "I Dreamed a Dream," and we later bonded over how uneasy that performance made us feel. I don't even know musicals that well, but I know that song is way overdone. Like, past overdone.

I wonder how Taryn's doing.

In any case, Haley is giving ol' Rebecca Chorsky a run for her money. As she starts emoting into the microphone, I actually need to look down at my feet. It's that bad.

It's not even a question of talent—Haley has a decent enough voice, with vibrato aplenty—but she's singing as if she knows she's an amazing singer and it's her gift to all of us. Also, the lyrical connection to FireFoot seems tenuous at best. It's all pretty much the worst.

"Come on," I say, grabbing Paolo by the shoulder.

"Huh?" he says. Tears are streaming down his face.

"You all right?"

"Are you listening to the words? This is very moving." Of course Paolo's somehow made it through life without hearing this song. "It's making me think I should sing something at my funeral. Maybe that song from *The Breakfast Club*."

"Okay, that's great, but I need to step outside a minute or I'm gonna explode."

"Oh wow," Paolo says. "Say no more." He wordlessly follows me under the enormous stained-glass windows and through the heavy chapel doors. We stand on the sidewalk out front.

"It was too much emotions for you, huh?" Paolo says. "Bringing back memories of your own funeral and stuff?"

"Something like that," I say, sliding out of my jacket so my pits can breathe for a minute. "I don't know if I can go through with this, Pow."

"It's gonna be easy, bro-bro. All you have to do is spit in a glass of water."

"No, it's not that. It's this Haley girl. She's so mean. Out of all the people I could save, why does it have to be her? I don't want to erase her deathdate. She's just gonna continue to make the lives of Bella and Tyler and all those people terrible."

"Well, I mean, it's kinda too late to back out now, right?"

"Why?"

"Because," Paolo says, "you're gonna know for the rest of your life that she died because of you. She could have lived, but you chose to let her go."

"It wouldn't be my fault! There's probably tons of people having funerals today. Am I supposed to feel bad that I'm saving Haley and not them?"

"Come to think of it, maybe," Paolo says.

"I can't tell you how unhelpful this is," I say.

"You're welcome." Paolo digs around in his suit jacket, pulls out his metal cigarette, lights the end, and inhales deeply. "You want?"

"Yessir," I say, grabbing it and taking my own huge pull. My stance on weed has shifted dramatically in the past week. Maybe it's because I don't want my almost-dead best friend to have to smoke alone, or maybe I'm just grateful to have some kind of release. Whatever the reason, Paolo and I have gotten high as we've explored some of Brooklyn's finest destinations. High in Prospect Park? Check. High at Coney Island? Check. High at Grimaldi's Pizza? Yes, indeed! My mom doesn't seem to care; she's just happy I'm on board with this whole mission thing.

I exhale and then cough into my jacket as an elderly couple slowly walks by, arm in arm. The woman's overly made-up face is scrunched, giving Paolo and me a severe stink eye.

"Good afternoon, ma'am," he says.

"Meh," she says, looking away.

"And to you as well," I say, taking another hit. I'm definitely feeling it, which at this moment I appreciate. "This stuff always kicks in so fast."

"I know, right? It's Willis's superstrong stuff. So you don't have to smoke as much of it to get high."

"What the hell, man! Take it." I shove the pipe back into Paolo's face until he grabs it.

"Whoa, whoa, easy there, cowgirl."

"We've been smoking pot from Willis Ellis all week? Have you forgotten he's, like, my angel of death and almost killed me multiple times?"

"See, I didn't tell you because I knew you'd get all snippy. All of that stuff was on your deathdate, man. Almost two weeks ago. You're safe now, D. And anyway you can't die from mari-joo-ana."

"You can if it's laced with heroin or something."

"Well," Paolo says, taking another hearty pull. "That might be true. In which case, I should be the one freaking out."

The doors behind us open, and I jump. It's a skinny girl in a green dress. She walks past us toward the curb and lights up a cigarette.

I feel high, but not in the usual giggly way. It's more of a heart-stopping something-is-terribly-wrong way. We shouldn't have left the chapel. I have no idea what I was thinking.

But if we go back in, I'll have to save the life of that horrible horse girl.

"We're going to make Haley famous," I say. "You realize that, right?"

"What do you mean?" Paolo asks. "Like, be her agent or something? Her voice is pretty sick."

"No, man, I mean I'm going to pass her the virus, she's going to survive, and then, like my mom said, she's going to become a news story. The first person to ever live through her deathdate."

"But she's not the first."

"Yeah, but she's the first one the world will know about."

"Ohhhh, right. Famous, yeah. Like we talked about before. Man, you should have asked your mom if you could have been the one to get famous."

That's kind of a good point. "I just hope she doesn't get her own reality show," I say, massaging my forehead. "Because I would know it's entirely my fault."

The doors behind us open again, and this time waves of chatting people stream around us onto the sidewalk. Haley must have finished her song/speech, thus concluding the ceremony portion of the funeral.

"Come on," I say. We need to get inside and find Felix before the reception starts. I lead the way back into the chapel, where we dart around the clumps of milling people.

"I mean, I'm honestly concerned she might be murdered," a mousy lady says to a man in a bow tie as we walk by. "She said some terrible things in there."

My mom couldn't have picked a worse target for this mission. There are so many amazing teenagers out there destined to die young, never allowed to become the firefighters or Nobel Prize winners or life-changing teachers they could have been. But I'm saving Haley Whitney, destined to affect many people's lives by making them miserable. In a best-case scenario, maybe she'd make history by being the first human to marry a horse.

"Bacon macaroni and cheese?" Felix says, smirking as he holds a tray in our faces.

"H to the yizzle," Paolo says, grabbing two.

"Sure, thanks," I say, popping a tiny mac-and-cheese pie into my mouth and trying my best to act as if he's a waiter I've never met before.

"Meet me in the reception hall in ten minutes," Felix says under his breath. "In the corner of the room near the string orchestra."

"She's got a string orchestra for her funeral?" I say, but Felix has already moved on, offering food to another set of funeral guests.

"That was magically delicious," Paolo says. "I want to eat a hundred of those."

"Yeah, me, too— Holy shit holy shit," I say. Five feet away from us, my large uncle Andre, my shrill aunt Deana, and my condescending ten-year-old cousin Tiffany are in a somber conversation with Haley Whitney's mom. I take a sharp left and pull Paolo with me.

"Are you having a panic attack?" Paolo asks. "Want me to steal someone's inhaler?"

"No, dude," I say, looking over his shoulder to make sure my stepmom's brother and his family haven't spotted me.

Paolo follows my gaze. "Oh, look at that, yeah. Your annoying aunt and uncle and cousin. That's random."

"This should have occurred to me! They live in this neighborhood, and they always go to stupid events like this. Dammit."

"Okay, dude, you need to calm down. May I remind you that you look like a Hawaiian librarian right now, and I'm sure they don't remember me."

"But Felix . . ."

"You think rich people actually look at the faces of the waiters serving them? Yeah right, dude."

"Well, let's just be careful. And make this quick." We wander deeper into the packed chapel lobby, following an arrow on a placard that says, HALEY WHITNEY FUNERAL RECEPTION.

"Mini cheeseburger?" a tall waiter with sideburns asks, holding out another tray.

"Uh, *yeah,*" Paolo says, grabbing three. "This is ridiculous."

I take two. The tall waiter glides away.

"Why have we not been crashing funerals our whole life?" Paolo asks, his mouth bursting at the seams.

"I know. I didn't think it would be this easy. No one even cares that we're here."

"It's those guys," a voice says from behind us.

We turn to see the skinny smoking girl from outside standing with Haley Whitney, her parents, and a bunch of other disapproving people.

Haley looks us up and down.

"I've never seen either of you before in my life. What the hell are you doing at my funeral?"

"Um," I say, my arm frozen in the act of depositing another cheeseburger into my mouth.

EIGHTEEN

We're totally about to get thrown out of this funeral.

"I mean . . . ," I say. "I thought you were happy to have so many people show up here. So you could beat Violet or whatever."

"Shut up. I bet you didn't even know Violet." Getting thrown out might be a good thing. "I'm happy to have people I *know* here," Haley says as her mom strokes Haley's hair. "Not people in badly fitting suits, who are talking weird shit about me during my eulogy. Okay?"

I glance over at the green-dress skinny girl, who smirks back at me.

"Daddy," Haley says. "Would you please get Romo so he can throw these two out?"

Her dad stares Paolo and me down. I don't think he wants to have to go get this Romo guy.

"Please, Daddy! Now! I don't want them here!"

"All right, sweetheart," her father says, and he walks away.

"Look, Haley," I say. "You don't know us. I'm . . . Frank, and this is Pao . . . der." Damn. I realized too late I should be calling him Steve.

"Your names are Frank and Powder?" Haley says.

"Oh yeah, for sure," Paolo says.

"Right, and even though you don't know us, we absolutely know you. We're such huge fans of yours." I might as well go for it. "You're such an expert rider. It's breathtaking, really."

I can tell from Haley's face that she's hearing us. This is a girl who lives and dies on compliments. Well. That was supposed to be a figure of speech.

"And we also love that horse of yours," Paolo says. "FireFeet. Very majestic."

"Uh, yeah. Fire*Foot* really is great," I say, hoping Haley heard my pronunciation and not Paolo's. "So when we saw in the paper that this was happening, we were devastated. We had no idea you were an Early. It's horrible. We're so sorry. But we wanted to be here to celebrate you. And maybe . . . well, we hoped maybe we would get to meet you."

Haley blinks twice and licks her lips.

"These two, Romo," her dad says, reappearing with a muscular-looking man with a shaved head.

"All right, come on, yous," Romo says, placing a beefy hand on each of our backs and escorting us away through the crowd. I expect Haley to say something to stop him, but she doesn't. If only she knew how much was actually riding on her decision to throw us out. She starts to fade into the background behind us, and I have to say, I'm a little relieved. My mom can't be too upset; we gave it our best shot.

"Hold on, Romo," Haley says. Oh no. "Bring them back here for a second."

"This fucking kid," Romo says under his breath as he turns around and escorts us back the other way.

We're brought to Haley, who stares at us, expressionless, as she touches her neck. I wonder if she's like this every day or if it's a funeral-specific power trip.

"Which competition was your favorite?" Haley asks, a demonic twinkle in her eye.

"Excuse me?" I say.

"You said you're huge fans of me and FireFoot. So which competition was your favorite?"

So now we're definitively screwed. I can't even begin to fake an answer; I don't know dick about horse riding.

"All of them, really," I say. "You're just so impr—"

"Saratoga Springs," Paolo says. "That was our favorite. The shit you did there was legendary."

There's a shift in the air, and I can tell Paolo has somehow said something that might be passable as an actual answer. Hopefully Haley has stopped looking at me, because I'm quite sure I look absolutely shocked.

"Yeah," I say. "Totally legendary."

Haley looks at Paolo, then at me.

"Saratoga Springs?" she says. "Are you freaking kidding me? I was a mess at Saratoga. FireFoot had a cold."

Screwed again.

"Right," Paolo says. "But the way you bounced back

from that competition was the legendary part. After all, it's only our failures that give true meaning to our successes. Don't you think?"

Whatever reservations I had before about Paolo smoking pot are completely gone. In spite of the pot—or, hell, maybe because of it—he's locked into some other plane of existence, drawing upon wisdom and knowledge I had no idea he possessed.

Haley rolls her eyes, but she's smiling. "I think we should let them stay, Daddy," she says, as if it were anyone else's idea but hers to throw us out in the first place. "These guys are sweet. And that one's kinda cute." She points at me, like Paolo and I aren't standing five feet in front of her.

"Okay," her dad says, subtly shaking his head, like he's given up all hope of understanding the way his daughter's mind works. "Whatever you want, sweets."

"We've wasted too much time on this already. I want to go mingle with my real friends," Haley says, pushing forward, her entourage following her. "Find me inside later," she says loudly into my ear as she passes.

"Oh, um, okay," I say.

They disappear into the crowd.

I exhale. "That was incredible, Pow."

Paolo looks dazed, his eyes unfocused. "I think I just used all of my brain juice."

"Saratoga Springs? How did you know that?"

"Sometimes I watch the horse channel when I'm high."

Crowds of people start flowing around us toward the reception hall. We move along with the river of funeral guests, the tide pulling us toward large double doors. Live classical music streams out from the reception hall, under-scoring our migration to the other room.

"Man, I think that scary Haley chick has a crush on you, dude," Paolo says. "You should use that."

"Yeah, no thanks. I'll spit in her water, watch her drink it, and get the hell out of here."

"How will we know if the virus actually passes to her?" Paolo says.

"I have no idea," I say.

We cross into the reception hall, and I'm instantly in-timidated. It's a huge, ornate ballroom that reeks of wealth: thick red velvet curtains, crystal goblets on every table, impossibly large and shiny chandeliers. Not to mention the ten-piece string orchestra in the corner.

"Damn, this girl's family must be loaded," Paolo says.

He clearly has used up all his brain juice if he's just clueing in to that now.

We head toward Felix, who's standing alone near the orchestra, holding a tray of waters. "Hey," I say, speaking loud enough so it will carry over the sound of the violins.

"Care for a water?" Felix asks.

"Yes, absolutely." I take one off the tray.

"I would also like one," Paolo says, winking at me as he grabs one.

"So, Feel, can we talk normally for a second," I say, shifting my volume into a lower register, "or do we have to keep up this pretend thing?"

"Just drink the water and put it back on the tray," Felix says. "Quickly."

"Should I take it out in the hall or something so no one sees me do it?"

"Come on!" Felix says, his eyes darting around.

"Okay, geez." I collect a pool of saliva in my mouth, take a sip of the water, then send it all back into the glass.

"Should I do it, too?" Paolo says, matching our frantic energy.

"What?" Felix says. "No."

I pop my glass back onto the tray. You can see the saliva bubbles in there (it's gross), so Felix sticks his pinkie in and does a quick stir of the ice cubes. He gives us a nod and walks away.

But not even ten steps later, he's stopped by that tall waiter with the sideburns. "Hey, hey, hold up, man. Hold up."

"Yeah, what's up?" Felix says, so smooth it seems like he cater-waiters all the time.

"So, look, here's the deal," Sideburns Waiter says, quietly enough that Paolo and I need to take a few steps closer to hear. "Some lady over there saw you let that dude spit in one of the glasses of water. I happen to be in full support of that, as this party is full of assholes—especially that chick who's dying—but you just got spotted, so I gotta send you home."

This is not good.

"Ah, no," Felix says. "That guy took a sip and thought something tasted weird in the water, so I was taking this back to the kitchen. Gonna drop it off with the dirties."

"Nice try, bro," Sideburns Waiter says. "But you know how much money the family is paying us to cater this thing? You got spotted—it's time to go." Sideburns Waiter sees me hovering nearby and throws me a dirty look.

"How's your night going?" I ask Paolo, trying to make it seem like we're having small talk and not eavesdropping.

"Not good, dude," he says. "Don't you hear what's happening over there?"

"Yes," I say, "that's why I'm . . . Never mind."

"Come on, man, I need the money from this job!" Felix says, switching to a new tack. "For my kids!"

"Don't worry. We're not firing you. I just can't let you work this one event."

"Well, I need to," Felix says, clearly panicking now. "All right? Please, just let this slide."

"Bro, let me get real with you," Sideburns says, starting to lose his cool. "That lady wanted to call the cops on you. I talked her down, said we would handle it, but she's staring at us right now, and I'm sure she's three seconds away from getting authorities involved. Or at least ratting you out to that girl's parents, so—"

"All right, I get it," Felix says, knowing when it's time to fold. "I'll go."

"Good," Sideburns says. "Give me your tray, and I'll watch you leave."

Felix looks at us for a brief moment. He hands Sideburns his waters, then heads across the room and out the double doors.

"So," Paolo says. "What the hell do we do now?"

NINETEEN

Felix's absence might not be a total deal breaker, but it definitely means there's going to be more heavy lifting for Paolo and me. I'm tempted to walk right out the door after him. But then my mom's going to think I'm a coward or that I don't believe in her movement, and it's going to be more trouble than it's worth.

"Should we follow Felix outside?" Paolo asks. "Maybe he can suggest an alternate plan for us?"

Screw Felix. He should have listened when I said I should leave the room to spit in the glass. Paolo and I can handle this alone. "No, I already have an alternate plan."

"Really?"

"Sorta." Another waiter walks by with a bunch of waters, and I grab one. I take a swig from my glass, adding less saliva this time so you can't see any bubbles. I do a quick scan of the room, which has now entirely filled up with people. Haley is easy to spot, though, surrounded as she is by her huge entourage. I start walking in her direction, keeping my head down to avoid being spotted by my aunt and uncle.

"Wait, so what exactly is the plan?" Paolo asks as he tries his best to keep up with me.

"I'm gonna give her the water myself."

"That's the whole plan?"

"Pretty much," I say.

The string orchestra has been playing very dramatic downer music all night, and it echoes in my ears as we approach Haley's table. I can make this work. I know I can.

Paolo and I plant ourselves in front of Haley and her crew. "But what do I care if she didn't show up?" Haley is saying. "She's a total butter face! After I die, everyone let her know I said that."

"Last chance to change your mind," Paolo says quietly.

"Um, hey, Haley," I say.

Her head snaps toward us, her nostrils flaring, like, *Who dares interrupt me at my own funeral?* "Oh, it's just you two," she says, her face relaxing into an only slightly less scary expression. "Everyone, this is Anne Frank and Baby Powder."

It takes me a few seconds to understand where she's gotten these strange nicknames for us.

"Hey," I say.

"What's up," Paolo says.

Every member of her crew is watching us with delighted anticipation, like they can't wait to see what cruel thing Haley will say to us next.

"So, what the hell do you want?" Haley asks.

"Oh, nothing, really. I brought you this water," I say, holding out the glass.

Haley scrunches her face up and looks at her friends incredulously. "You brought me a *water*? Like that's some big gift or something? What, are you trying to poison me?"

She's surprisingly sharp. I can tell Paolo's freaking out.

"Ha, yeah," I say. "I'm trying to poison you."

"Ooh, scandalous." Haley likes that I've played along, even though I'm really just telling her the truth. "What kind of poison?"

"Cyanide, mainly," I say. "A pinch of arsenic."

"Sexy," she says, followed by a little feline growl and chomp. Her friends laugh. It's all extraordinarily mortifying. "Give it to me."

I pass over the glass. This is going to work. I'm astounded at my own abilities. I think I'm just really good at reading people.

Haley sniffs the glass. "Hmm," she says.

A few sips should be enough, and then we're out of here.

Haley splashes the entire glass of water into my face.

I gasp. I am soaked with ice-cold saliva water.

"I've always wanted to do that," she says.

"OMG, you are so mean," the skinny girl in the green dress says, laughing in shock and glee along with the rest of Haley's friends.

That's it. There's no way we're saving her.

I look to Paolo. His face is frozen into a stunned smile. "You okay, Frankie?" he asks.

"We're leaving," I say.

"Hold on a second," Haley says. "Hold on, poor little

baby. That wasn't personal. I just couldn't resist. I'm going to die tomorrow, so I get to do things like that."

"I guess," I say.

She grabs a cloth napkin off the table behind her and starts rubbing at my face and hair. "Let's get you dried off, little poopsie-doo."

I back away from her. "No. Thank you, but no. You're not nice, Haley."

"No shit, Sherlock," Haley says. "Nice is boring. Who wants to be nice when you can be memorable instead?"

One of her terrible friends says, "Amen!"

"I think that's actually the official motto of the Serial Killers Club," I say, wiping a drop of water out of my eye. "So, congratulations: you're a psychopath."

"Fuck you, Frank!" Haley says, getting right up in my proverbial grille. I've hit a nerve. "You don't know what it's like to die young, so shut the hell up! People with long lives can afford to be nice. Good for them! But I don't have time for that."

"Oh, I don't know what it's like to die young?" I say, realizing as it's coming out of my mouth that I shouldn't be saying it. "Well . . . maybe not, but I do know you can die young and still be a nice person. Your argument is bullshit." This girl is the opposite of everything I stand for. She's making me question my life choices once again, which makes me feel self-conscious and horrible.

Haley stares at me, her blue eyes unreadable. "You've got some fire in you, Frank," she says. "I like that."

But I'm done trying to make this happen. "Why do you talk like you're a powerful queen in a fantasy movie? Speak like a normal person."

"You have any more advice for me?" Haley says, making a heinous sexy face at me.

"We have to go. Come on, Pao . . . der."

I start to walk away, and Paolo follows, but as he does, he's giving me a look that says, *Dude, the door is completely open for you to go make out with her and pass her the virus.* And I know that he's right. I turn back.

"Actually," I say, gesturing to the string orchestra, which is currently playing an infinitely undanceable song, "I don't have any advice, but . . . do you want to dance or something?"

All of Haley's friends again wait in suspense for her response.

"I thought you'd never ask." Haley smiles in a way that seems evil, though I don't think she's going for that. "I don't want to dance. But I could definitely go for some 'or something.' "

"Ooh, yeah, girl!" Skinny Green-Dress Friend says.

"Come on." Haley holds out her hand to me. I look to Paolo. He nods. Internally I sigh as externally I grab Haley's hand. It's very soft, which might be her only positive characteristic.

As Haley leads us toward the double doors of the reception hall, we receive a series of surprised looks and wolf whistles. Just before we walk out the doors, we pass Haley's father. "Oh," he says.

"Are we good to leave your party like this?" I ask.

"It's my funeral," Haley says. "And I'll leave if I want to. Besides, we won't be gone long."

I'm glad to hear that. I want this make-out to be quick.

We walk down an empty hallway of the huge celebration

home. The air-conditioning is blasting, and since my hair and shirt are still wet, I'm shivering. Haley pushes on various doors as we pass them to see if any are open. Finally one swings inward. Haley peeks in. "This works," she says, pulling me into the room.

It's some kind of chapel office, with a big desk, a few bookshelves, and lots of crosses and candles everywhere. I'm suddenly nervous. I've never made out with someone I barely know, let alone someone I actively dislike.

Haley pushes me up against the desk. Here we go.

"So, am I making one of your dreams come true right now?" she asks.

"Yeah," I say, in spite of the screaming desire to leave emanating from every bone in my body.

"I know you're such a big fan of mine." She strokes her fingers down my chest, and it gives me chills. The bad kind. "Bet you never thought you'd be touched by me like this."

"Totally, yeah. Never thought it."

"Oh, you're shivering like a little puppy dog." She strokes my hair. "I love that."

I don't. I hate all of this. Why am I about to make out with this girl? For my mom? How messed up is that?

"Hey," I say, putting one hand on Haley's cheek.

"Be careful of my makeup," she says.

"Sorry." I move in to kiss her.

"No," she says, putting her hand over my mouth. "No kissing."

"Huh?" I say through her hand.

"Let's just touch, okay?" She takes her hand off my mouth and moves it down toward my belly. It's the tiniest bit arousing—just because—but mainly it's not. Because she is a demon lady.

"I really want to kiss you, Haley," I say, not sounding all that convincing to my own ears.

"Sorry," she says, shrugging like she's trying to be all cute. "This is something else I've always wanted to do. Doesn't it make it so much hotter?" She caresses my shoulders.

"Not really," I say.

"You don't know; you're just a dumb boy. Have you ever seen this old movie called *Pretty Woman*?"

Oh man, this is where she's going with this? "Yeah, parts of it."

"Well, me and my best friend, Hayley, watched it once during a sleepover back when we were in middle school, and—"

"Your best friend is also named Haley?"

"Yeah, but she's Hayley with a *y* in the middle. Let me finish my story, Frank." Now she's touching my thighs. "So, there's this one scene in the movie where Julia Roberts won't let Richard Gere kiss her, and it was . . . the sexiest . . . thing . . . either of us had ever seen." She'd been touching my back, and now she's moved her hands down to my butt. "It still is. And I've never gotten to do that with anyone. Touch me, Frank."

"Um, okay . . ."

I put my hands on her waist, but she grabs them. "No, *here*," she says, placing them on her chest. "Yes, that's soooo good," she says. "Don't you think I deserve this before I die, Frank?"

"Absolutely you do. But it's worth mentioning that, in

the movie you're talking about, Julia Roberts was playing a prostitute."

Haley takes my hands off her. "What's your point? You think I'm some kind of slut for being here with you?"

"No, not at all, not in the slightest," I say, realizing this whole thing could fall apart at any moment. "Just that that's why she didn't want to kiss him. Because she didn't want to develop, like, an emotional connection to her clients."

"What the fuck are you talking about, Frank?" Haley takes a step back toward a bookshelf and puts her hands on her waist. "Do you want to mess around with me or not? I'm doing you a favor here."

"Yes, of course I do. Totally. But, please, I get nervous, so can we just make out a little first before we do the no-kissing thing?"

"We can't make out and *then* not kiss. Are you stupid or something?"

"Yeah, no, I mean, I realize that." I'm running out of options. But I know I can't stay in this office touching someone I'm repulsed by for much longer. "I'm a really good kisser, though."

"I don't give a shit how you kiss, asshole. Have you listened to a word I've said? I'm asking to touch you, okay? Most guys would kill to have these hands on their dick."

I don't think that's true. And did she seriously just say that?

I don't have time to contemplate any further because Haley reaches down and grabs my crotch. Naturally I'm soft down there, and Haley is not pleased.

"Ohmigod," she says, her face stone cold. "I should have known."

"Known what?" I say, panic rising. "There's nothing to know."

"You're not turned on at all!"

"I was, I totally was, but then we were going on and on about movie logistics—"

"You like boys, don't you?" And then, much to my surprise, Haley's eyes start to get teary. This is not going well. "You're just another closeted loser trying to use me as a beard. How could you waste my time like this? I'm going to die. This was supposed to be special. . . ." She begins to sob.

"This *is* special, Haley," I say, putting a hand on her face. "I like you. You're one of the most beautiful people I've ever seen." I can almost sell that lie.

"Really?" Haley says through tears. She's showing vulnerability for the first time all day, and it actually does make her look prettier.

"Really," I say.

"Thanks, Frank." Her mouth slightly opens, her lower lip quivering. Somehow I've righted the ship. This is my moment.

I lean in, my hand still gently stroking her pronounced cheekbone. Her eyes close, still wet with tears. Our mouths are millimeters away from each other, and my tongue is prepped and ready to invade.

Just as we're about to make contact, though, Haley's knee slams into my crotch like a wrecking ball.

I'm seeing stars and swirls as I fall back against the desk.

"Suck it, Frank!" she shouts in my face. "You're still not even hard. That hurts my feelings, okay?"

The pain radiates up to my stomach, an all-encompassing

throb. I slide down against the desk and find my way into the fetal position on the floor. "I'm just . . . trying to . . . save . . . your . . . life," I grunt.

"Oh, get over yourself," Haley says from the doorway. "Romo will be in shortly to escort you out. Hope the rest of your life is brief and terrible."

I try to say, *You, too,* but it comes out as a moan. Her footsteps click away down the hall.

TWENTY

"I don't understand. How hard is it to deliver a glass of water?"

As expected, my mother is not pleased that our operation this afternoon was a complete bust.

The usual crew is gathered once again in the living room of her apartment: me, Paolo, my mom, Felix, Dane, and Yuri, whose head is buried in a book about a well-dressed robot. The coffee table is covered with bags filled with our dinner, delicious-smelling Indian food that we're not allowed to eat until we've discussed what happened today.

"It's my fault," Felix says. "I should have had Dent—I mean, Frank—drink the water outside the main reception hall. I got careless."

A few minutes after Haley left me huddled on the floor of the chapel office, Romo did indeed show up, gripping Paolo by the arm. He lifted me up to my feet, and within moments, Paolo and I were out on the street. I peeked back into the lobby and almost made direct eye contact with my cousin Tiffany, who was sitting on a fancy chair, looking at her phone, at which point I made the executive decision that our mission was concluded.

"Sure, it's not like you to goof up like that," my mom says. "But Frank and Paolo were still inside. It seems like, between the two of them, they should have been able to figure out a way to get the dying girl some water."

"There really wasn't," I say.

"This is not to be believed," Dane says.

"We tried everything," Paolo says. "Dent was even ready to get nasty with this girl, but she kicked him in the nuts."

"What?" my mom says. "Did you try replacing her glass of water on the table with a new glass of water that you had spit into? While she wasn't looking?"

Not sure why that didn't occur to me. "It was hard to tell which seat was hers . . . ," I say, trailing off.

"Well," my mom says, tapping her nose as she stands up to pace around us. "I'm gonna be honest: I'm disappointed. I expected more from the three of you."

"I'm sorry," I say, even though I'm totally pissed off. We're the ones out there in this impossible situation, while she gets to stay here and then judge us when we get home.

"No, *I'm* sorry," she says. "I feel like I haven't really told you why all this means so much to me." She continues pacing around, then takes an overly theatrical pause to look out the window. "Frank, did I ever tell you why I didn't want to know my deathdate?"

I can't deal with another lesson or story or sermon from

this woman. "I think so," I say, trying my best to be curt. "Because you felt it was unfair that it was a government decision based purely on money."

"That's not what I'm talking about." She turns away from the window and perches on the arm of the couch. "When I was sixteen, my mom had a heart attack and died. She was thirty-nine."

"Oh," I say. "I didn't know that. I'm sorry." I guess that woman was my grandmother.

"Of course you didn't; Lyle barely even told you my name."

"Dad's ridiculous," Felix says.

"You don't get to speak right now," my mom says. Felix looks down, clearly embarrassed. I feel bad for him. "So I lost my mother. She was the best—so funny, so loving—and then one day she was just gone." My mom shakes her head. "The worst part is, I'd grown up hearing how *her* father had died of a heart attack at age thirty-seven, when she was just seventeen."

"That blows," Paolo says.

"So you might understand why it was always in my head that maybe I, too, would be dead sometime in my thirties. Then, not even two years after my mom died, I was a freshman in college, and the government was suddenly saying that it was mandatory for us all to learn our deathdates. I panicked. It was bad enough imagining I might die young, but I didn't want definitive proof."

Even if I am still kinda pissed, I can't help but be completely captivated.

"Brian and I organized a series of protests, but in the end, it didn't matter. We were forced to get ATG kits and learn our deathdates. Brian was undated—the lucky bastard—but I was going to die at thirty-two, even earlier than my mom and grandfather." My mom hangs her head, as if she's just found out the news all over again.

"I was so depressed. For years. I mean, what was the point of anything? I didn't want a career, I didn't want to date anyone, and I definitely didn't want to have kids. I would just die and abandon them, the way my mom did me."

I am feeling so many things as I listen to this story, but the predominant one is sadness that I never knew any of this until now.

"Brian was the one who finally snapped me out of it. He'd done research on what it was that made people undated, and he was pretty sure it had to do with a specific gene that factored hugely in the ATG kit readings. I'd never given two shits about chemistry before, but suddenly it was the only thing getting me through the day. I thought, *Screw it, what do I have to lose? Maybe I can find a way to live.* That's how I ended up in grad school for pharmaceutical science. Where I fell in love with my professor. Lyle Little."

"Whoa, cool twist," Paolo says quietly.

"I told Lyle I didn't want kids, and he was fine with that. But then, well, things happened, and three months after we started dating, I was pregnant." She's talking about Felix. "I didn't want to keep him, but Lyle wore me down, convinced me that nine years with a child would be better than no years. And I'm so glad he did." My mom looks at Felix, and she's tearing up. It's the first time I've seen her cry. "I'm sorry I snapped at you before, Feel. You know I love you." She walks behind the couch to where Felix is sitting.

"I do, Ma," Felix says.

She leans over and kisses him on the forehead. It's the most she's seemed like a mom since I got here. "Once I had him in my life," she says, draping her arms on Felix's shoulders, "then I really didn't want to die. That's why Brian and I, and some others we enlisted from my grad school class, worked to create the virus."

"For this, we will always thank you," Dane says.

"Yes, thank you," Yuri says, briefly lifting his attention from his book.

"And, yes, I lived, but that means it's my responsibility to see this thing through," my mother says, pacing again. "To make the world how it once was, a place where we can choose to not know when our days will end, where we can live each day to the fullest without being driven mad by knowledge we never asked for in the first place.

"Frank knows what I mean, right?" She turns to me.

"Uh, yeah," I say. "Totally." But the thing is, as moved as I am by all this, I'm also confused, because if I'm going to be honest, I was never driven mad. I mean, it was always a complete bummer that I was going to die at seventeen, but it also just was what it was. I never knew anything different.

"And *that* is why we do this," my mother says. "*That* is why today was so important."

"Absolutely," Felix says.

"Now, I'm tempted to send you back out to have another go at saving that girl's life, but it's also fine if we move on. Because today's funeral was just a warm-up for the main event. You're going to have quite the chance to redeem yourselves."

I'm one part excited, eight parts uneasy.

My mom again smacks a folded newspaper onto the coffee table. This time, there's a photo of an older woman wearing glasses and a pantsuit. It seems like she's at a press conference or something. The headline above her reads, *Corrigan Funeral to Be Held at Plaza Hotel.*

"Who's Corrigan?" I ask.

"Karen Corrigan," my mom says with a wicked grin. "She's the head of the USDLC. Do you know what that is?"

"The United States Department of . . ."

"Lady Cougars?" Paolo asks earnestly.

"Life Conclusions," I say.

"Correct," my mom says as I start to put the pieces together. "The USDLC is the organization responsible for everything deathdate-related in this country. The DIA is a part of the USDLC."

"Oh wow. Are you saying you want me to save her next?"

"It's too perfect, right?" my mother says, her eyes shining maniacally. "I mean, you couldn't pick a better person to help make a statement than the very face of what you're fighting against. And the funeral is *this Monday.*" That's the day before Paolo's funeral. "It's fate, Frank."

"Truly," Dane says. "This has made me to believe in fate."

"Huh," I say. On the plus side: I get a chance to redeem myself. On the negative, though: is secretly delivering my spit to powerful government officials and/or their kids really my fate?

"The Plaza Hotel," Paolo says. "Now *that's* the way to do an unassassination!"

TWENTY-ONE

I wake up thinking about Haley. Today is her deathdate. She is not going to survive. She might have, but I failed. So she'll die.

I know a billion things got in my way, and if my cousin had identified me, it would have been very bad, but those still don't feel like solid reasons to let a human being die. Even someone as cold-blooded as Haley Whitney. My mom said we should move on, but why couldn't Paolo and I go find Haley today? The virus should still pass, on her actual deathdate. We just need to find out where she lives. Immediately.

I hop out of bed and throw on a shirt and some shorts, adrenaline coursing through me. It's 9:44 a.m., still many hours left in the day.

"Oh," I say as I climb the stairs and find Paolo and Millie huddling together over a crossword puzzle. "What's up, Millie?"

"Chillin', villain," Millie says. She's wearing a yellow blouse with oranges and pineapples all over it. "How's the living thing going?"

"Uh, fine," I say, nervously looking around the apartment, knowing that my mom will explode if she sees that Millie's here. "What, um, what are you doing here?"

"It's all good, D," Paolo says, tapping a pencil on his cheek. "After the funeral flop yesterday, I emailed Mildew. From the *library*." He flicks his eyebrows up and down proudly. "I told her to come by now, because it's always the time when your mom goes running. We thought we'd wait for you to wake up, then hit up lunch somewhere. No harm, no fail."

"I don't think that's the expression."

"I can go if it's making you bug out," Millie says.

"No, that's . . . it's fine," I say, barely able to keep still. "But I mean, maybe before lunch, you could come along to do this other thing with us. I don't know if Paolo brought you up to speed on this Haley situation, but I've decided we're not going to let her die. She sucks, and there's every reason to let her deathdate proceed according to plan, but I have to try. So I say we get the subway to the Upper East Side and I'll make out with her, whether she wants to or not."

Paolo and Millie stare up at me.

"I know that kind of thing is normally frowned upon. This is the only case in which I would force a human to make out with me."

"Yeah, bud, it's not that," Paolo says. "It's just, uh . . ."

"Here," Millie says, picking up what I guess is her laptop from the couch and putting it into my hands. I stare down at the screen. It's Haley's Facebook page. "Paolo did just bring me up to speed, and I wanted to see her picture. But then, when we found her page . . ."

It'd been updated with a new post an hour ago.

Thank you to all those who attended Haley's funeral. It was a huge success, and she couldn't have been happier with it. Haley died at 1:12 a.m. Thursday, surrounded by friends and family. She was very calm and peaceful at the end, and we think that's in no small part because of all the love she'd received. Thank you.—Tom Whitney

I audibly gasp.

She died. Haley died.

I just saw her yesterday, felt her hands on my body. Granted, she was making me feel very uncomfortable at the time, but she was alive. So alive. And now she isn't.

Maybe it's silly, but it's possible I'd begun to think death wouldn't actually happen anymore. I was supposed to die, and I didn't. Then my mom, dead for years, turned out to be alive. In the same way that deaths have a traumatic impact, maybe there's something traumatic about nondeaths, too.

But still. Haley died. What happened? I wish the message went into more detail, but it hovers at the level of generic facts.

"I'm sorry, dude," Paolo says.

"It's okay," I say, not realizing I'm crying until I hear the thickness of my voice. Haley was horrible, but she was also memorable, the way she wanted to be. And this vanilla death memo from her father captures none of that. What an injustice.

"People die," Paolo says. "She always knew she was going to die."

"It sounds like there's nothing you could have done," Millie says.

"That's not true!" I hear myself shout. "I could have made her kiss me. Or, better, I could have told Haley the situation. I could have explained what I was doing."

"That would have been a terrible idea," Paolo says. "Not only would she not have believed you, but the whole point is that no one can know how it happened. Plus, she definitely would've told her dad. And that big Romo dude."

"You don't know that," I say, trying desperately to keep an image of Haley's lifeless body, arms crossed, lying on a bed surrounded by her family, out of my mind. "It might have worked."

"No," Millie says, an arm on my shoulder.

Paolo comes around me and puts an arm on my other shoulder. "Really, no, buddy."

I bury my face in my hands. "She could have gone on to do so much," I say, straight-up sobbing now. "She could've been, like, the no-nonsense head of some company or something. You know, when men act all forceful, we respect them, but when women act like that, we call them bitchy. It's such a double standard. . . ."

I catch Paolo and Millie exchanging a look like, *Huh?*

"Look, duder," Paolo says. "Whatever she was going to go on to do, it ain't happening now. And that's not your fault."

I wipe my face dry and grab their crossword up off the table, along with the rest of the newspaper. "Saving this Karen Corrigan woman at the Plaza, or whatever, is fine, but I need to try to save more teenagers. No one should have to die young if I have this ability. Why should anyone ever die young?"

"I think you're confused," Millie says, putting her hands into the pockets of her denim skirt.

"You're not God, bro," Paolo says.

"But I kind of *am*," I say, which immediately sounds, even to my own ears, like an insane thing to say. "I mean, it's in my power to do something about this."

Paolo's rocking some super-raised eyebrows. "Well, okay, God, but even before deathdates, people died young. Only difference is they didn't see it coming."

I ignore them and crouch down in front of the table, licking my finger and flipping pages like a madman. Finally I arrive at the obituaries.

A sea of older faces stare up at me.

I scan them all, but the youngest person on the page is dying at age seventy-four. Most are dying in their eighties.

"Is this today's paper?" I ask.

" 'Tis," Paolo says. "You gonna try and make out with one of those old ladies?"

I don't respond. None of these people needs me. They've lived full, long lives.

"Maybe bring that smokin' old lady on the top right a glass of water?" Paolo asks.

"I mean . . . maybe not," I say.

"I think you and your mom are both confused," Millie says.

"What? Why? Because we want to save people's lives?"

"Because your mom says she's anti-deathdates. But I think she's really just anti-death."

Her words immediately make some kind of sense, but I sweep them aside like crumbs.

"That's not true," I say. "You didn't hear what she said last night."

"Think about it," Millie says.

I don't want to.

"It's like," Millie continues, "her so-called movement is just a club for people who are unhappy because they drew the short end of the stick. I don't blame them. If I knew I was going to die young, I'd want to find a way out of it, too."

"It's bigger than that," I say. "The movement is about allowing people the freedom to not know, no matter when they're dying. Giving them the choice."

Millie purses her lips and moves her mouth to the side of her face. "I don't know. Seems like that's just a way to justify what they're doing. 'Cause no one wants to say, *I'm really afraid to die, and I want to find a way out of it.*"

"I get what Mills is saying," Paolo says. "Like, even in that story your mama told, I got the sense that if she'd found out her deathdate wasn't until she was old, she wouldn't have cared about any of this."

"Well, maybe not, but that's true with anything," I say. "You get inspired to fight for a specific cause when it personally affects you. Like, for example"—I stare directly into Paolo's eyes—"my best friend, Paolo, is supposed to die in six days, and even though my mom said there's no hope that the virus can save him, what if she's wrong? What if I successfully pass the virus to some teenager and then, like my mom said, I learn about, like, a loophole or something that could also save him?"

"D," Paolo says. "We're not trying to gang up on you."

"It wasn't supposed to be like this, Pow." I'm fighting to speak through my body's urge to sob. "I was supposed to go first. So I would never have to live life without you. But now it's gotten all reversed and screwed up, and now *I'm* gonna be alive and you're gonna be lying lifeless in the ground somewhere."

"Not to interrupt," Paolo says, "but I actually decided I'm goin' cremo all the way. And don't get too excited, but I want you to have twenty-five percent of my ashes."

This is probably true, but I know he's also saying it to make me laugh, which I sort of do. Even though I had a nice momentum going with the point I was trying to make, I can't help but ask, "Why twenty-five percent?"

"Figured I'd go splitsies between you, V, and my mom," Paolo says. "And then the last twenty-five will be a hodge-podge: Dave Chu, Mrs. Costa, Alexei at 7-Eleven, Lorette, who delivers our mail. You're gettin' some, too, Mills. If you want."

"That's sweet," Millie says.

"You're giving some of your ashes to Alexei at 7-Eleven?" I ask. "Is that the ponytail guy?"

"Yeah, dude, he's the man!"

I laugh and sob simultaneously. "See?" I say. "What the hell am I gonna do once you die? I seriously don't care if my mom's movement is really about living past your deathdate, because that seems pretty worthwhile to me right about now."

"Thanks, Dent," Paolo says, looking down and wiping his eyes. "But can I just say something?"

"Okay," I say, staring at my bare feet.

"I'm not, like, making any exumptions about what's going to happen here."

"Assumptions," I say.

"What did I say?"

"*Ex*umptions."

"Oh yeah, I did, didn't I?"

"Ha, yeah."

"Classic me. Anyways, I'm not going to, um, bank on surviving my deathdate. Because, dude, really, my whole life, this was the plan, so why should it change now?"

"Because now all the rules have changed," I say.

"Yeah, but . . . I mean, the way you're feeling about Haley, this girl you actively disliked . . . If things don't work out, I would hate for you to feel responsible for my death that way, too, you know?" Paolo rubs at a piece of food that got on his jeans. "If I die, I want you to be thinking about how awesome I was. Not how guilty you feel."

Millie stands between us. She looks down and chews on a strand of her hair.

"Well," I say after a few long seconds. "You're not going to die."

"Dude, you're not listening to me. I probably will die."

"Stop saying that," I say. "You won't. You sound suicidal."

"This isn't suicidal. This is realistic! All this movement talk is a real beautiful fairy tale, and it's almost got me sold on the idea that I'm gonna live, but then the whole Haley thing happened yesterday, and I thought, *What if I don't? Then I've wasted the last days of my life.* Well, that ends now." Paolo takes a deep breath and gets down on one knee. "This is the reason I wanted you to come here today, Milladelphia. I was gonna wait to do it later, but now feels right."

"Wait, what's happening?" I ask.

"Millicent Pfefferkorn," Paolo says, taking a stunned Millie's hand.

"Oh," I say.

"I'm not sure if you know this," Paolo continues, "but before you and me, I'd been around the block a bit with the females." He looks to me for confirmation. "Dent knows."

"Uh, sorta, sure," I say, shocked and also thinking he's off to a strange start.

"But there was always something missing. And in the past couple of weeks, you have stolen my heart like no human girl has ever before." I guess a number of nonhuman girls have stolen his heart before. "You are charming and hilarious and beautiful, and you smell like basil, and even though I always thought marriage sounded stupid and suffocating, now that I've met you, I'm thinking it could be cool to get a small sampling of what it's like. I know this is all happening so fast," Paolo says, taking something crinkly out of his pocket and biting off the wrapping with his teeth. "But, Miss Millie, will you marry me?"

Paolo holds out a red Ring Pop.

I can't tell what the look in Millie's eyes is, but I'm pretty sure it's panic.

TWENTY-TWO

There's silence, and then a car horn outside blares for a solid five seconds. "Move!" a voice on the street shouts.

"Um," Millie says. "Please stand up, Mr. Diaz."

The car horn blares again. "Come on!" the same voice says.

"You can take as much time as you need to think about it," Paolo says, still on the ground. "Well, maybe not more than two days, because time is a pretty key component of this situation, but, you know, no need to rush the decision."

"No, I don't . . . um, I don't need time, Paolo. You're great, but I can't marry you."

"Oh. Because . . . of your parents?" Paolo says.

"It is not because of my parents, no." Millie is unable to make eye contact with Paolo. I am very uncomfortable. I feel like I shouldn't be here watching this.

"Okay . . . so then . . . ?"

"I don't believe in marriage."

"Oh."

"And even if I did, we've never even kissed," Millie says.

"But we could," Paolo says. "I'd be totally open to that."

"That's nice, but . . . I'm not ready to get married. What if you don't die? Then we'll be married for no reason."

"If I don't die, you can divorce me," Paolo says. "I promise."

"I'm sorry," Millie says. "I don't . . . I can't."

"Oh," Paolo says. "All right." You can almost hear the sound of his heart deflating.

"It's not you," Millie says. "You're a very spectacular person."

"Right, yeah. Guess I'll, uh, stand up now." He does. "I just . . ." He gestures emphatically, the Ring Pop still in his hand. "If we like each other, and I'm going to die . . ."

"Yeah, I know. But I . . ."

"You what?" Paolo asks.

It's almost as if the words came out of Millie's mouth involuntarily, and now she has to backpedal to account for them. This isn't going well.

"Oh, nothing," Millie says.

"Marriage is overrated anyway, Pow," I say, trying my best to wrangle the conversation back onto smooth terrain. "It's like, what does—"

"Let Millie finish what she was saying," Paolo says, suddenly possessed by a different kind of energy entirely.

"I wasn't going to say anything," Millie says.

"Is anybody else hungry?" I ask.

"You definitely were, babe," Paolo says. "Just say it."

Millie looks to me like she's drowning and I'm the one closest to the anchor.

"I don't think she was going to say anything, Pow," I say. "She just feels bad. This is awkward."

"Oh, am I making you feel awkward?" Paolo asks. "Because you had to watch me get rejected—"

"I'm sorry!" Millie says. "It doesn't feel honest to me."

"It doesn't feel *honest*?" Paolo says, inadvertently flinging his Ring Pop across the room, where it plings off a framed portrait of two naked people and lands on the hardwood floor. "Since the prom, we've been having so many deep conversations and making each other laugh all the time about stupid things, so I just thought—"

"I know. You're so fun, Paolo, but it's not—"

"It's not what?" Paolo says, both hands on the back of his neck. "Please! Talk to me! I'm a dying man. I deserve to know!"

"I like Denton, okay?" Millie blurts.

Ohmyfuckinggod.

"What?" Paolo says, the man in the western who just got unexpectedly shot in the gut.

Really, though, I probably don't look too different.

The world has halted on its axis.

"I've liked Denton for a long time now," Millie says, the words spooling out at a measured pace. "So it's nothing personal. I like you, too, Paolo. But I'm slow. My feelings take a while. So, with Denton, they've had—"

"Are you messing with me right now?" Paolo says. "Please say this is some bizarre Millie joke. Please. I might even laugh. Because I'll be so relieved."

But all three of us know it's no joke.

"I'm sorry," Millie says. "You said you wanted me to be honest."

Paolo stares at Millie, then at me, but, really, he isn't looking at anything. He is a lost human being. It demolishes my heart.

"Pow," I say, but he's already taking unhurried steps toward the staircase. "Where are you going?"

He doesn't respond. I race after him. "If you hold up, I can come with you."

Paolo stops and slowly turns his head to look at me. "Just let me go, all right?"

I wish he'd used a nickname. It would make me feel less like he hates me. "Um, sure, but if you want to talk about any—"

"What, you don't have enough already?" Paolo asks.

"What?"

"You get to live," he says. "And now you get Millie's love, too. Anything else you need? How many more hearts do you have to win to feel good about yourself?"

"I'm sorry. I—"

"Taryn, my sister, the girl I love. Maybe give it a rest."

"I wasn't trying to win Millie's heart!"

Paolo shakes his head, his eyes tearing up. "Forget it, man." He descends the spiral staircase, and then we hear the front door downstairs open and close.

I turn back to Millie, who's looking distraught and vulnerable, her hands still in her pockets. "Why did you say that?" I ask in disbelief.

"It's how I feel."

"I know, but—"

"You know?"

"No, I mean, I didn't know until now, and I'm flattered, but why did you have to say that to Paolo?"

"He wanted to know the truth."

"Right." I wipe a layer of sweat off my forehead. It's gotten incredibly hot in this apartment.

"I see you staring at me sometimes," Millie says, her eyes glued to her Vans. "I thought you already knew how I felt."

"No," I say. "I didn't."

"That's why I was biking around on the night of your deathdate. I went by your house to try and see you one last time, but then I saw your stepmom on the porch waiting for you, so I figured you might be at Paolo's. I started biking to his house. And then you hit me with Danza."

"Wow," I say. All of this is news to me.

"I thought it was fate. Like, bringing us together. It's dumb."

"Yeah." I'd be lying if I said Millie hadn't grown on me a ton in the past weeks, and I'd also be lying if I said I hadn't found her attractive and adorable on more than one occasion. But I know how Paolo feels about her. And I know how I feel about Veronica. "Millie, you're fantastic, but—"

"Please don't give me the same spiel I gave Paolo. You love who you love. It's not your fault."

"Right. Okay."

Millie stares at the portrait of the two naked people, as if she's newly intrigued by its artistic merit.

"I think I'm gonna go try and find him," I say. "Do you wanna come?"

"I don't think that's a good idea." She doesn't take her eyes off the painting.

"All right. Um, you should probably leave when I do, though. Just, you know, because of my mom."

Millie nods, still not looking at me.

I grab my sneakers from my room and put them on, and we both leave the apartment. I'm about to say something about how great Millie is and how, if circumstances were different, I might be into her. But then that feels like a dick move on at least four different levels.

So I just stand there on the sidewalk like an idiot before we head off in different directions.

TWENTY-THREE

I start my search at the somewhat redundantly named Brooklyn Deli and Sandwiches, just a block away. I think it's where Paolo always goes for his egg sandwiches, so I'm hoping he'll be here. But there's only one customer inside besides me, a short, older lady with swoopy white hair.

"Thank you, dear," she says to a mustachioed man at the deli counter as he hands her a wrapped-up sandwich.

"Of course, honey. Have a great weekend," he says. I'm impressed by the apparent richness of their relationship.

"What can I get ya?" the mustachioed man says to me, all business now. He has two stud earrings in his left ear.

"Um . . . are you by any chance Reynaldo?"

"Yeah. Why?" Reynaldo is very intimidating.

"Oh, just 'cause my friend Paolo comes in here a lot, and I was—"

"Paolo!" A gigantic smile blossoms on Reynaldo's face. "That's my boy, right there. You must be his buddy Frank."

"Yeah," I say, stunned. Reynaldo extends a hand over the counter, and we shake. I've never met anyone as skilled as Paolo at making friends and garnering goodwill from people he barely knows.

"Yo, what can I make for you, Frank? Anything you want. It's on me."

He wants to give me a free sandwich? Because of how much he respects Paolo? Wow. It reminds me yet again how lucky I am to have Paolo as a friend. And also that he's off walking the streets, feeling awful right now.

"Um, actually, I'm here looking for Paolo. He wasn't just in here, was he?"

"Nah," Reynaldo says. "Sorry. But come on, let me make you a sandwich. I'm rapid-fire, bro."

I don't turn him down. I know I'm terrible, but I'm really hungry, and I figure I'll search much better on a full stomach. Seven minutes later, I'm devouring a bacon, egg, and Swiss as I walk the streets looking for Paolo, who was right: Reynaldo does have a light touch. This is a subtly crafted gem of a sandwich.

But I don't think I'm going to find Paolo. And I don't think he wants to be found.

Oh man. His funeral is in five days. What if he goes back to New Jersey and I can't see him again until then, the day before he dies? Or what if I can't even make it to his funeral because there're too many DIA agents lurking around?

What if just now—that brutal, heartrending moment—was the last time I'm ever going to see Paolo?

No.

I refuse to let that be the case. I will be at his funeral. And I will figure out a way to pass him the virus. Maybe I couldn't save Haley Whitney, but I will absogoddamnlutely be saving Paolo Diaz.

I work myself into an impassioned huff, and I keep walking, not sure if I'm even searching for Paolo anymore. I pass women with strollers, kids with scooters, old people with walkers. I keep walking.

At a certain point, I realize that all the people passing me are conversing in Spanish. As I look around to get a better sense of where I am, I notice I'm standing right next to a celebration home. The R. G. Martinez Celebration Home, to be specific, as its red-and-black sign gaudily proclaims.

There are two men in suits standing in front, smoking cigarettes and speaking rapidly about something. I've been taking Spanish since middle school, so you'd think I'd know exactly what they're saying. I don't. The only words I can pick out are *hungry* and *sad* and *beautiful*.

I'm pretty sure there's a funeral going on inside as we speak.

I slide past the hungry, sad, beautiful men, open the white door, and enter.

On any other day, I'd be incredibly self-conscious that I'm not dressed well enough for this event; I'm wearing cargo shorts and a green T-shirt that says, *JUST BE YOURSELF . . . AS LONG AS YOU'RE NOT ANNOYING*. But today I don't care.

I step into a small foyer area and immediately encounter a huge painting of Jesus. His hands are spread out, welcoming. His smile is knowing.

There's a tall woman in a black dress standing next to the painting, her eyes closed as she speaks into a small cross held close to her face.

I try to sneak by her, but she looks up, angry and disoriented to have been jarred out of her prayer session. She takes in me and my wardrobe and gives me some serious stink eye.

"Hi," I say.

She shakes her head at me. I creak open the door beneath a sign that says CHAPEL/CAPILLA and peek inside. There is indeed a funeral going on, and it's a much smaller one than Haley Whitney's: probably about seventy-five people spread out amongst a hundred or so folding chairs.

There's a teenage girl standing up at the lectern, crying as she speaks in Spanish.

Bingo.

I didn't even have to try. A teen funeral just fell into my lap.

This is fate.

(*Like when you crashed into Millie's bike with your car? That kind of fate?* a voice in my head asks.)

This whole time I've been trusting my mother, believing her words about what the virus can or cannot do. Yes, she and I both survived because of it, and apparently so did a few mice, but I haven't actually seen proof that I'm actually this Important Vessel or whatever it is they have me pegged as.

Well, screw that. I'm tired of putting my trust in others.

I need to know for myself.

And then maybe I'll be one step closer to saving Paolo.

I let the chapel door slowly close as I step backward, and then I barrel past Tall Praying Woman onto the street. I look left and right, and find what I'm looking for two doors down.

I stride into the bodega, head straight to the refrigerated beverages section, and grab a bottle of Poland Spring. I pay for it at the counter, exchanging nice smiles with the dark-haired man who takes my money.

I also buy a couple of Peanut Chews from a plastic jar on the counter. For later.

Bells on the door ring out as I leave the bodega in my wake. I'm already feeling the satisfying crack of the plastic seal as I open up the bottle and raise it to my lips. I never stop moving, swigging water into my mouth and sloshing it around as I glide into the small celebration home foyer, then spitting it back into the bottle as I head through the chapel door.

I take a seat in the back. A couple of heads snap toward me—one of which belongs to Tall Praying Woman, who's made her way to her seat—but most remain focused on the teenage girl at the lectern. She's finishing up her self-eulogy, which, of course, I can't fully understand. She seems less sad now and more hopeful. I figure I'll wait until she wraps up. Even if I am going to save her life, that doesn't mean I should interrupt what she believes to be her final words.

My heart is rat-a-tatting at a rapid pace.

The teenage girl takes a moment and stares out at some people in the front row, then says some words up to the ceiling, then says words to everyone. This is the end of her speech.

I grab on to the seat in front of me and brace myself, ready to pop up and make some magic.

But as the girl leaves the podium, she's intercepted by a large man, who gives her a huge hug and three kisses on her cheek and then walks up to the podium.

Wait a second. Someone else is speaking after the self-eulogy? That doesn't make sense. Whose funeral is this anyway?

Oh.

The large man carries himself with dignity and grace, and as he looks out at the room of people, it's instantly obvious that the funeral is for him. The teenage girl must be his daughter.

I slide back into my seat.

This is a curveball, but, honestly, it changes nothing. The only advantage of passing the virus to a teenager was that I could more easily blend into the crowd. Clearly I let go of that when I waltzed in here in my summer wear. And why shouldn't this man survive? I already know he's got at least one kid who's going to miss the hell out of him.

I'm doing this. For Paolo. And for my mom, who'll see that I didn't mess it up this time.

The man begins his self-eulogy with a line that gets a huge laugh. Something in me pings, and I know, even though he's just starting to speak, I have to act now. Before I understand what's happening, I've ridden the laugh up onto my feet.

"Hey there," I say from the back of the chapel. *"Hola."*

The man stares at me, along with everyone else in the room.

"Lo siento," I say, "but I, uh, come bearing a gift for you, sir. Um . . . in order to live. To, uh . . . *vivir! Tú vives si bebes esta agua."* I am so proud of myself right now for digging that sentence up out of my brain.

"I'll live if I drink your water?" the man says. "Is that what you're saying?"

"Oh. You speak English." Whatever, I'm still proud of myself. "Yes, that's totally what I'm saying."

"You are aware this is my funeral, right?" He speaks with a poise and calm I instantly admire.

"Yes, absolutely. And I'm truly sorry I'm underdressed."

"Do I know you?"

"No, sir."

"Does anyone here know you?" He looks out to the audience. *"¿Alguien sabe este chico?"* People vigorously shake their heads.

"No, sir," I say. "No one does. But—"

"Do we have to call the police to escort you out of here?"

Okay, time for a new tactic.

"I know this seems crazy, like a stupid prank or something, but I swear: if you drink this water in my hand, you will live through your deathdate."

The man says something in Spanish to people in the front row. The only word I understand is *policía.*

"¡Por favor!" I say. "Don't call the police yet. Please." Come on, Powers of Persuasion, don't fail me now. "Look, I think it will work because it did for me. I lived through my deathdate."

The man makes a hold-on gesture to his front-row posse, and they do. "By drinking that water?" he asks.

"No, well, for me it was different." I can't tell this man that I'm a carrier and so I spit in the water and now he has to drink it. That has to be the absolute worst way to convince him. "I mean, it was a different bottle of water. But, yes. I survived by drinking it. There's something mixed in the water that erases your deathdate."

"Get out of here!" an old woman shouts. "This boy has been sent by the devil! Leave, Devil Boy!"

A chorus of voices rises up in support of the old woman, including the voice of Tall Woman, who I'm realizing might be the soon-to-be-dead man's sister; they have the same eyes.

"I promise I have not been sent by the devil!" I raise my voice to be heard over the din. "I know this sounds insane, but, seriously, what do you have to lose? If you don't drink the water, then you'll definitely die, right?" The voices simmer down. "What's the worst that could happen if you do?"

The room falls silent as the man looks down at his thick hands. I like him. This is a life I can really get behind saving.

"¡Podría ser veneno, Miguel!" Tall Woman shouts. The man, who I now know to be Miguel, lifts one hand to quiet her.

Finally he looks up. "Why have you chosen me?" he asks.

There's a billion things I could say here, but rather than doing a lightning-fast comprehensive analysis of which of those things has the odds of being most convincing, I'm just going with the truth.

"It's kinda random, really. I was just passing by, and you seem like a nice man. But, the thing is, I need to know if this works. We think it will, but we're not completely sure. And my best friend, Paolo, is supposed to die in six days, so I need to know before then."

"How old is your best friend?"

"Eighteen, sir."

"So you thought you would just crash my funeral and use me as a guinea pig?"

"Well, when you put it like that, it doesn't sound very—"

"Okay."

The crowd gasps. It's possible I do, too.

"Miguel, no! Please!" Tall Woman begs.

"Okay?" I ask.

"I want to get on with the ceremony, so, yes, okay. If me sipping that water will get you to leave."

"It will," I say, already moving down the aisle, the water bottle shaking in my hand.

Almost every face that greets me is suspicious and distrustful, and for the first time since I walked through that chapel door, I'm wondering if maybe this is the completely wrong thing. Maybe I've gone too far. I didn't mention my name, did I?

Lost in thought as I am, I'm not paying close enough attention to my surroundings, and I trip over a loose tile. I'm flying forward, desperately trying to keep the open water bottle upright, when two arms catch my torso and lift me back to my feet, without letting even a drop of the water spill. It's Miguel's daughter. She's surprisingly strong.

"Thank you," I say, shaking.

She looks me straight in the eyes. "Please don't hurt my father," she says.

"Of course not," I say.

I step up to the lectern next to Miguel. I hold out the bottle of water. He nods and takes it from me.

This virus pass is actually going to happen.

"I hope someone comes to your funeral one day and

ruins it for you just like you have done here!" Tall Woman says.

You're too late for that, sweetheart.

"Salud," Miguel says, lifting the bottle. I watch warily, half expecting him to splash it in my face like Haley did. But he takes a huge chug.

"Salud," I say.

It's happened. If it is going to spread, that should do it.

Miguel's face twists up as he forces the bottle back into my hand.

"Mierda," he says. "You little shit, did you spit in that water?"

"Uh," I say.

TWENTY-FOUR

I don't stop running until I'm at least twenty blocks away from the R. G. Martinez Celebration Home.

That did not end well.

I unwrap one of my Peanut Chews and pop it into my mouth. I catch my breath as I chew and try to get my bearings. A woman in her twenties walks by with a huge yellow dog, which growls at me.

I think I convinced Miguel and his family not to call the cops on me, but I can't be completely sure, since I was running as I shouted, "Please don't call the cops on me!"

As he ran after me, Miguel said I wasn't the devil, just a disrespectful little punk. I honestly think he wanted to strangle me, Homer and Bart–style. But he didn't, because I'm a pretty good runner and, as I've mentioned, Miguel is a large man.

I start walking again. I pass a series of outdoor restaurants, where people only slightly older than me are enjoying burgers and sunshine, talking and laughing loudly at each other.

I keep remembering the look in Miguel's eyes the moment after he chugged, how sad and angry he was to have been duped in front of all his friends and family on the day before he's going to die.

Well, that's life, right? Sometimes it's hard to do the right thing.

Which brings me to a bigger question: have I done the right thing? Ten minutes ago, my body flooded with adrenaline, my feet pounding the sidewalk, my answer would have been an unqualified yes. I felt triumphant.

But now I'm feeling extreme doubt. For one thing, I wasn't under the radar *at all*. Putting aside the fact that I already stuck out as one of the few white people there, I was also the only person wearing a T-shirt and shorts. And the only one standing up and saying things in the middle of the self-eulogy. I think it's safe to say many of the funeral attendees will remember me.

Which I don't think my mom would be so into, no matter how excited she is that I've successfully passed on the virus.

The entire strategy at Haley's funeral involved passing her the virus in such a way that it would be impossible to trace it back to us. At Miguel's funeral, I employed pretty much the exact opposite strategy. My forehead is sweating, and my hands are trembling. I think I really messed up.

"Hey," a voice says from behind me.

"Huh?" I turn around.

It's Veronica.

"You okay?" she asks. You just walked right by me."

"I did? Oh man. Sorry, yeah, I'm fine. What are you doing on a random street in Brooklyn?"

Veronica gives me her are-you-messing-with-me look and points to the building next to us. "This is where you're staying, isn't it? With your mom?"

Yes, she is correct. I was about to walk right by not only Veronica but also my mom's apartment. Wonderful.

"It totally is," I say. "Yes. Right."

"No one answered the buzzer, so I've been sitting and waiting."

"Whoa, whoa, you should not be buzzing. Look, my mom assumes everyone is a spy. Especially you. The daughter of the spy trying to get me."

"Fine, but you said she usually works during the day anyway, so."

"Yeah, I'm just saying. In the future, don't just show up here. If my mom saw you, she would be crazy pissed at me."

"All right, all right," Veronica says, raising her hands and backing up a couple steps. "Sounds like you don't exactly trust me either." She's wearing a light blue V-neck T-shirt and jean shorts, and, man, I really do want to trust her.

"I mean," I say, wiping sweat off the back of my neck. "I don't know what to think, honestly. You show up for one night, then disappear the next morning."

"*Disappear?* I told you I had work."

"I know, but then I felt, like, why did you even bother coming at all?"

"Okay, forget this." Veronica's turned in an instant and is already walking away.

"Hey, hey, wait," I say, running to catch up with her and getting a whiff of potent déjà vu from my funeral reception. I cross in front of her. "Look, I didn't mean that to be insulting. It just seemed weird."

"I came to see you," Veronica says. "Because P said he knew where you were and I got excited, all right? I can't stick around long this afternoon either. But I wanted to come in and say hey."

"Oh," I say, feeling relieved and ecstatic. "Of course that's all right." I also feel like a paranoid dick.

"Where is P anyway?"

"I don't know. He left. We got in a sort-of fight."

"Whoa," Veronica says. "You guys don't fight."

"I know. It sucked."

"What were you fighting about?"

"Oh, you know, death stuff."

"Man, that's intense. P doesn't have much time left. You guys gotta get it together. Guess that explains why you look like even more of a mess than usual right now."

"Thanks," I say. "Look, do you want to maybe take a walk with me in the park? It's only a few blocks from here. Just in case my mom comes home early or something."

She stares past me in thought as she does that thing where she rubs one finger back and forth over her lips. "Yeah, okay."

We start walking. A couple of construction workers sitting on a stoop stare very obviously at Veronica as we pass. "Oh yeah, miss, what's *your* name?" one of them says. The other one whistles. It's uncomfortable.

I figure we'll just keep walking, but Veronica stops and holds up a black rectangular thing she took out of her bag. "My name is Stun Gun. Would you like to know what I feel like pressed up against your body?"

They look as shocked as I am.

"Crazy bitch," one of them says as we walk away.

"Wow," I say.

"I don't know why men think that's a good way to connect with women," Veronica says, clearly shaken up. "Assholes."

"Yeah," I say, the mere presence of a stun gun apparently all it takes to stun me. "For sure."

She turns to me, like she's just remembered I'm there. "Don't worry. I've never actually used it. My mom gave it to me when I left for college."

Veronica might be the most intimidating person I know.

We walk toward the park, silent and, in my case, in complete awe. I finally gather enough courage to speak.

"So, the other night," I say. "When we . . ."

"When we what?"

It's heartbreaking, but I'm pretty sure my hookup with Veronica was actually me having a wet dream. "Never mind," I say.

"Are you talking about when I got into bed with you?"

"Yes!" It did happen. "Yes, I was. Oh, thank God."

"Do you not remember that or something?"

"No, I do, very well. I just . . . you know, it was the middle of the night, and it was so . . . good, you know? I thought I might have dreamed it."

"You seriously have a problem, D. It's not normal to never know if you've actually hooked up with someone or not."

"I agree," I say. We walk into Prospect Park and onto the wide cement path that loops around it. "But can I just say: that was very awesome. I haven't stopped thinking about it."

"Yeah," Veronica says. "Cool."

"All right, wait," I say. I put my hand on Veronica's arm so she'll stop walking. We're underneath some huge trees.

"What?"

"I mean, what's the deal with us? I really like you. And I mean, I'm alive, I've been given a second chance to, like, I don't know, be with you. And I think you like me, too. But it's like you can never admit it. You had to creep into my bed in the shadows, like you're embarrassed to be with me in the light of day or something."

Birds flutter by us. Veronica follows them with her eyes.

"At the hospital, right before I ran away, you told me that you felt all the same things for me. Didn't you? Am I making that up?"

Veronica looks out into the trees. "No, you're not making it up. I did say that."

Three bikers whiz by us in quick succession.

"And did you mean it?" I ask.

"I did," Veronica says, finally looking at me.

"So what the hell?"

"Can we keep walking? Standing still makes me nervous."

"Okay." We walk.

"D, look," she says. "I care about you, but it's not . . . I'm weird with guys, okay?"

"If you're going to explain this, at least try to make it specific to me."

Veronica gently kicks a stone in her path, and it rolls to the side. "It's like, you're my little brother's best friend, you know?"

"Your little brother is only a year younger than you!"

"I know, I know, but when all this started, I thought you were going to die, so that changes the whole, like, context for everything."

"You mean those were pity hookups?"

"No, it's not like that," Veronica says. "But sometimes . . ."

"What?"

"Sometimes I think I'm, like, too tough for you."

I'm genuinely offended. Maybe in part because this thought has occurred to me, too. "Screw you!" I shout, a little harsher than intended.

"Excuse me?" Veronica says. Now she's the one who stops walking.

"I said, screw you."

"No, screw *you*," she says, and gives me a shove.

I'm about to shove her back, but then I stop myself. "You know what? No, I don't have to prove to you how tough I am so you'll like me. We're supposed to keep shoving each other until our energy is so fiery and passionate that we end up making out, right? Is that how this goes?"

"Ew, no," Veronica says. "I was just shoving you because you pissed me off."

"All right, whatever. I'm not saying we should go steady or something, I just want to be able to be in a room with you and not wonder if you hate me."

"Seriously, Dent. Even having this conversation is

making me feel sort of suffocated, like you're getting all commitment-y. I'm telling you, I have issues."

"Oh," I say. I notice we've stopped next to a big lake. "Like, you care enough about me to want to come to the city to see me, but you don't want to have any sort of label for what this is?"

"Yeah," Veronica says. "Something like that. You actually said that really well."

"Well. Okay, then." None of this is particularly satisfying to hear, but at least I told her how I feel. That's something.

A couple of ducks quack and splash at each other in the water.

Veronica takes my hand and intertwines her fingers with mine.

"You think too much," Veronica says.

We stand and stare at the ducks.

She is a very confusing person.

TWENTY-FIVE

"Seriously, you have nothing to worry about," I tell my mom for the eighteenth time. We're having some rare one-on-one time, as Felix and Dane aren't here this morning. "Paolo left because he's going to die soon. He wanted to be at home with his family."

"Yes, and again," my mom says, madly chopping onions for the omelets she's making us, "when you say *his family*, you're referring to a key DIA agent, who soon will be told by Paolo exactly where we're both located."

I hate having to defend my friends over and over to her, especially because it only serves to remind me that they're not here. And that soon Paolo's going to be permanently not here.

It sucks, and I don't know what to do. I've gone on my mom's laptop at least a dozen times this morning, searching for some sign that my supposedly magical spit worked and that Miguel from the celebration home lived through his deathdate. Since I don't even know his last name, this has mainly consisted of me Googling variations on the phrase *Miguel survives*. I haven't found anything, but I have learned a lot about a basketball team in the Philippines called the San Miguel Beermen, who have survived a lot of close games.

It doesn't help that the last time I saw Paolo, he stormed out of here crying. Because of me. *Awful* doesn't begin to describe what I'm feeling. I need to get to his funeral, but I have no idea how that's going to happen. It's making me so anxious. The Karen Corrigan funeral is the day before Paolo's, so I guess I could do the whole spit pass and then, I don't know, try to escape from my mom again? That doesn't sound very realistic. Plus, what with Paolo's mom being a definite attendee at Paolo's funeral, there's no way I can go without being caught.

It's pretty much the most horrible scenario I can imagine. Not only can't I save Paolo's life, but it's looking more and more like I might never see him again.

"Please," I say to my mom, "just trust me on this one."

She stops chopping onions, looks at me, and sighs. "Okay," she says. "I will."

It almost seems like a joke, but then she keeps talking.

"You know," she says, "it's been great getting to know you these past weeks. I mean that."

"Oh," I say.

"You have a sweetness that your brother doesn't. I think I used to have more of that sweetness myself. At one time or other. It's nice to be around."

I can't help but be touched. "Thanks, Mom," I say. I finally feel inspired to try calling her that. Still doesn't feel quite right, but I'm glad I did. "For what it's worth, you have a strength that I really admire. Your, you know, passion and drive are really amazing."

"Huh," she says, like she's never thought of herself that way before. "Thanks, Frank." Her staunch commitment to using my alias has moved from annoying to endearing. "That's exactly the sweetness I'm talking about." She goes back to chopping, and as I sit at the table grating cheddar cheese, I realize that, maybe for the first time, it feels easy to be in a room with her.

My mom's phone buzzes, and she stops chopping to answer it.

"Hey there, Feel," she says. "You coming over? Oh. What?" She looks right at me. Not in a fun way. "Okay. Oh, I will." She puts the phone down. "Do you have something to tell me?"

Oh no. "Um, what— I mean, what are you talking about?" The fun bonding moment is definitely over.

"You know what."

She's right. I do. Felix must have somehow found out that Veronica and I were together the other day. "Okay, yeah . . . I'm sorry. I just really like her. Like, a lot, and, honestly, I don't think she's going to—"

"Stop messing around! This is very serious."

"I'm not!" I say. "Yes, I saw Veronica, but I didn't tell her anything!"

My mom's emerald eyes burn into me before she breaks away and heads into the family room. "Come," she says.

What if Veronica is a spy? What if she blew our cover?

I'm trembling as I follow my mom, who pushes a button on the family room wall, which rotates the painting of two naked people like it's on a carousel, leaving a flat-screen TV in its place.

"Wow, that's awesome!" I say, completely forgetting myself. "Why haven't you shown me that before?"

My mom ignores me. She reaches underneath the flat screen's lower edge and rips the remote free from a strip of Velcro. She extends her arm fully, like the remote is a torch with which she's trying to light the television. The channels blip by, and I honestly have no idea what she's looking for.

Until she stops on a channel with a banner across the bottom reading, *BREAKING NEWS*.

Then I am flooded with a dozen feelings at once, unmitigated joy and nausea leading the pack.

Because there, on the screen, is what I'd been searching for all morning. Miguel, the large man from the R. G. Martinez Celebration Home, is speaking with a reporter.

He is very much alive.

TWENTY-SIX

"Who knows how long this will last," Miguel is saying, "but I feel very blessed and thankful to God that I can still be here for my daughter and my wife. I'm just stunned."

At the bottom of the screen, right next to *BREAK-ING NEWS,* the banner reads, *MAN LIVES THROUGH DEATHDATE.*

It worked. My mom was totally right.

"Miguel, do you have any idea how this could have happened?" the reporter asks.

Please give God all the credit, Miguel. Chalk it up to God.

"Well, actually, you know, a young man showed up to my funeral." No, Miguel! "At the time, we thought he was there to make some mischief, but I think he may have saved my life."

My mom turns to look at me, her eyes wide, then snaps

back to the screen as the news report cuts to the old woman who called me the devil.

"We were visited by an angel. No other way to explain it. I say, when I see him come in, *That boy is an angel.* And he was." Tears stream down the old woman's cheeks. "He saved my son. He give my son more life."

My mom shoots me a look. "You did this," she says.

"Um," I say. "There are lots of young men out there. It could have been anybody." In my panic, I'm trying to be funny, but I'm also hoping she might actually believe that.

The report cuts back to Miguel. "The young man gave me some water to drink, said it would save my life. I didn't know what to think, but he seemed honest, so I said, *What the heck,* and drank it. It tasted like he'd spit in it, so I was furious. We all thought it was a prank."

"Let me get this straight," the reporter says. "You drank this man's saliva?"

"You told him it would save his life?" my mom says. "Denton, what were you thinking?"

"I . . ." My plan seems reckless and ridiculous now, but at the time, it seemed like the only thing to do. "I wanted to see if it would actually work," I say as I watch Miguel's daughter appear on-screen, breathless and grateful, explaining how scared they'd been when her father had turned purple with red dots and how astounded they'd been when he'd lived through the entire day. "There's been so much talk about it, and all those mice. But we've never tried it on a person, and I wanted to know. . . . I'm sorry."

"You realize our whole mission is blown if everyone in the world knows who you are," my mom says.

"Yeah, but they still don't. All they know is that it was a young man. Nobody has any idea what I look like."

"Based on the various eyewitness accounts at the R. G. Martinez Celebration Home that day," the reporter's voice intones over an image of the building's exterior, "our artist has drawn up this sketch of the young man who saved Miguel's life." A full-body drawing pops up on-screen. It looks almost exactly like me.

"Holy shit," I say. "That's pretty good." They slightly mangled the catchphrase on my T-shirt to say *You Are Annoying. I Am Not,* thereby making an already lame T-shirt even lamer. Still, that eyewitness-drawing thing actually works. Who knew?

"Oh God," my mom says, holding her head in her hands. "Oh God."

"Okay, okay, so people might know who I am," I say. "But this is still a huge step forward for the movement, isn't it?"

"This is very bad," my mom says, both hands covering her face.

"Miguel," the reporter says. "If you could say something to this young man, what would it be?"

"First of all," Miguel says, speaking directly into the camera. "Please forgive me for not immediately trusting you." Miguel is such a good guy. "But more importantly, thank you, wherever you are. Thank you for choosing me." He starts to get a little choked up. I do, too. "Even if today is the only extra day I get, it is such a gift."

I'm tingling all over. I saved this man. I have done something good for another human being, and it feels amazing.

My heart felt flipped inside out in this exact same way

when I made it my deathdate mission to tell all my classmates why they're so great.

But, just as I thought, this is even better. Compliments are one thing, but giving life to someone who was certain they were going to die is astonishing.

Even though my mom's freaking out beside me, I suddenly know that I've done the right thing by saving Miguel. What could be wrong about giving people more time to enjoy the beautiful mess that is being human?

"I want to save more people," I say aloud before thinking about it. First up is Paolo. There has to be a way.

"What?" my mom says. "No! Out of the question! Our plan was to secretly infiltrate the system, not just walk around saving people."

"Think about it," I say. "I go from funeral to funeral, saving people one by one, until deathdates are proven to be wrong time and time again. Isn't that what you want?"

"I can't even think straight. This compromises what we're doing in so many ways."

The three-note jingle of the doorbell rings out into the apartment. My mom and I stare at each other.

"Oh shit," she says, completely still.

I'm having trouble forming words. "What is— Why are— Isn't it possible that's just the FedEx guy or something?"

"They've found us," my mom whispers. "It's all unraveling, Denton."

"You mean *Frank*."

"It doesn't matter now." My mom ducks into a closet to get a duffel bag, then scurries around the apartment, filling it with random things.

"I think you're overreacting," I say. "Remember that night I arrived at the safe house and Dane was freaking out about the buzzer? That turned out to be absolutely nothing."

The doorbell rings again.

"I'm gonna see who it is." I move toward the intercom. "I just push the talk button, right?"

"DON'T!" my mom says. "I don't care if it's a delivery person. Just let it ring! Please!"

But I'm experiencing an odd form of denial, like I need to know that I haven't drawn the DIA to us, that I'm not responsible for this.

"Hello?" I say.

"Happy dinosaur," Dane's voice says through the speaker.

I exhale. "See?" I've never been so relieved in my life. "Speak of the devil."

"Oh sweet Jesus, I was seriously about to have a heart attack," my mom says, letting her duffel bag flop to the ground. "Well, what're you waiting for? Buzz him in!"

I do. Moments later, Dane walks in.

"You should have seen how scared I—" my mom starts saying, but then abruptly stops.

Because behind Dane is a DIA agent with a gun trained to Dane's head.

"I am sorry, Nadia," Dane says.

Paolo's mom bursts past them into the room, both hands on a gun trained directly on my mother.

"DIA!" she shouts. "Put your hands up. Both of you."

"God*dammit*, Denton," my mom says, raising her hands into the air.

TWENTY-SEVEN

"So you're the infamous Cheryl Little," Paolo's mom says, gun still held high. The DIA agent holding Dane has stepped into the room, joined by another DIA agent, who also has his gun raised. I recognize both of them from the chase through Manhattan. "Pleasure to finally meet you. Been on your scent for more than a decade now."

My mom, so panicky sixty seconds ago, is now stony, calm, and composed. She doesn't respond.

"You've got a genuinely great kid," Paolo's mom says, one of the floorboards creaking below her as she takes a step closer. "I love Denton very much. Not that you had anything to do with raising him."

"Thanks," my mom says. "Congrats to you on spending so many years of your life spying on a child. You know that's disgusting, right?"

Paolo's mom ignores my mom and turns to me. "Hi, Dent. I'm sorry that we have to keep meeting like this."

I don't know what to say. Whether they're here because of my appearance on the news or because Veronica is a spy who gave up our location, it's my fault.

"I messed up," Dane says, embarrassingly near tears. "I come here when I see the news. And these three were waiting in front."

"Pull it together, Dane," my mom says. "You did the right thing." She moves her arm in a way that's either a twitch or some kind of very subtle signal.

"Well, anyway," Paolo's mom continues. "This will be the last time we have to do this. There will be no clever escapes with the help of Big Brother Felix. This ends here.

"Lin, get Denton in cuffs and bring him over here. I'll get Cheryl."

"On what grounds are you going to take us away?" my mom says. "We haven't done anything."

"Oh?" Paolo's mom says, taking one hand off the gun to reach into her back pocket. She pulls out a piece of paper, awkwardly unfolds it against her hip, and holds it up. It's a copy of the sketch of me from the news. "Not that we didn't already have plenty of grounds, what with Denton being the subject of your grand experiment, but I believe as of this morning, we have eyewitness proof that Denton tampered with another man's life on your orders. Giving that man the vaccine or virus, or whatever it is you people are calling it these days."

"Tampered with another man's life?" my mom says. "He *saved* that man's life, is what he did. How is that wrong?"

Agent Lin—the short Asian one—gets my arms behind me and puts the handcuffs on. "No," I hear my mom whisper. As the cuffs click into place and I can no longer do things with half of my limbs, the reality of our situation sinks in. This is not good.

My mom chuckles to herself. Again, I think I see her hand subtly gesturing, maybe pointing behind us? I feel like I'm supposed to understand whatever plan she's trying to communicate.

"What's so funny over there?" Paolo's mom asks.

"Do you honestly think you're on some sort of noble mission? Valiantly protecting the interests of huge pharmaceutical companies who want to keep making billions of dollars on deathdate kits?"

"Ha!" Paolo's mom says. "Like you're one to talk."

"What the hell is that supposed to mean?"

"Don't play dumb, Cheryl," Paolo's mom says, stepping closer to my mother, pulling the handcuffs off her belt. "You act like your mission is purely for the good of mankind, and not influenced at all by the life insurance industry and the hundreds of thousands of dollars they're funneling your way."

Beg your pardon?

"Oh, give me a break," my mom says.

"Do you deny taking handouts from them?" Paolo's mom asks.

Is that the benefactor my mom once referred to? The life insurance industry?

My mom looks at me, then back to Paolo's mom.

"I don't, but . . . ," my mom says. "It's more complicated than that. Don't listen to her, Denton."

"Seems pretty simple to me," Paolo's mom says, now mere feet away from my mom. "The life insurance people support what you do, in the hopes that we'll return to an un-dated system and they'll become relevant—and wealthy—once again. But that experiment is over."

I see my mom's eyes darting around the room, sizing up the situation. "So if I resist right now, you seriously have permission to shoot a woman who hasn't really done any-thing wrong?"

"Sweetie, as far as the government is concerned, you already died eighteen years ago. I don't think they're all that worried about what happens to a dead woman."

"Maybe not," my mom says, lunging down into the duf-fel bag.

"Whoa, whoa!" Agent Lin shouts from behind me, his gun following my mom as she picks something up and wings it down onto the floor. A billowing cloud of smoke fills the room.

"Stop her!" Paolo's mom says, coughing. "Shoot for her legs, Lin!"

"I can't shoot if I can't see my target!" Agent Lin shouts right next to my ear.

"FRANK!" my mom shouts. "Come on!" But I'm handcuffed, not to mention I'm close enough to Agent Lin to be considered a seen target.

"Aaagh!" the other agent shouts.

"Fields, are you all right?" Paolo's mom says.

"I lost him," Fields says, low-voiced and grunty, like he's just taken a punch to the gut.

There are footsteps scampering and more coughing. I close my eyes, keep my head down, and try to hold my breath as much as I can.

"No!" Paolo's mom says. "Are you kidding me?" When

I open my eyes again, the smoke has begun to dissipate. The back window leading out to the fire escape is open.

Dane and my mom are gone.

Paolo's mom climbs out the window and looks down. "Where the hell did they go?"

"I'll go after them, Diaz," Fields says, joining her at the window.

"Don't bother," Paolo's mom says, coming back in from the fire escape. "Denton's the one we came for. Their whole mission rests on him. Those two are harmless on their own. Not to mention pathetic."

I can't believe they left.

"Let's go," Paolo's mom says.

Lin's strong hands land on my shoulders and guide me toward the door. He's surprisingly gentle. I'd always thought once you're in handcuffs, getting roughly pushed around is part of the deal.

Outside, the day has gotten gray. It smells like rain.

A huge black Escalade waits out front. Paolo's mom opens the back door, and Lin helps me in, doing that thing where he pushes my head down so it doesn't hit the top of the car. I feel vaguely out of body, like I'm watching all of this happen to me.

"Buckle him up, Lin," Paolo's mom says. "Learned that lesson the hard way."

He does, then gets into the backseat with me. Paolo's mom slams the door and gets into the front seat. Fields is driving.

The Escalade navigates through the streets of Brooklyn, and all I can think is that I've fucked up royally. First with the Miguel thing, and again just now. Why didn't I try to run? Or knock down the agent who had the gun trained on my mom? What happened to all the knowledge I absorbed from Netflixing *Danger People*? It's like, no matter how much I try, I can't be the rebel I want to be. I think about my mom telling me this morning how great it's been spending time with me. I'm sure she's not feeling that way now.

I know there's a version of this where I should be furious that my mom and Dane ditched me—not to mention that my mom's movement is likely funded by the life insurance industry, which I can't even begin to process right now—but, honestly, I'm happy they got away. This is my screwup. I should be the one to pay for it.

The Escalade cruises across a bridge. I think it's the Brooklyn. I let my eyes blur as I stare at the webbing leading up, up, up to the bridge's tower.

Then we're speeding along another one of those city highways, green water to our right. No one—not Fields, not Lin, not Paolo's mom—has said a single word since we got in the car.

"So, Cynthia, you don't talk anymore?" I finally ask.

"Hmm?" she says, like she was so deep in her own thoughts I barely matter. "No, I talk, but considering that the first two times I attempted to apprehend you, I effed it up by blabbing, I figured I'd keep quiet this time."

My arms are tired from the handcuffs, my elbows contorted uncomfortably. "You know, I still don't really get it," I say. "It was your job to watch me for *thirteen years*? Like, you got a salary just to spy on your son's boring, normal best friend?"

Paolo's mom looks out her window for a few moments. She sighs. "You're not boring, Denton. And you're definitely not normal."

I guess I *can't* really pull off normal anymore. Not normal, not a rebel . . . What am I?

"Trust me," she says. "The money they paid me was pennies for them, considering how much is at stake. Now, that's it for the talking."

I adjust my butt back and forth on the leather seat. It's sweaty and itchy.

"One more thing," I say. "Was it Veronica who gave you my mom's address?"

Paolo's mom looks at me over her shoulder for a few seconds, then shakes her head. "No. It wasn't." I can't help but smile, I'm so relieved. It's like I've won the lottery or something. "Which isn't to say I didn't try to get it out of her. But you know V. She's stubborn."

Maybe Paolo's mom is lying to defend her daughter, but it doesn't seem like that. Of course Veronica didn't betray me. Though—how *did* they find our location? We turn off at a sign that says East Thirty-Fourth Street.

"Just one last thing, Cynthia: now that you've seen this man Miguel alive and well the day after he was supposed to die, doesn't even part of you wonder if we could use this virus on your son? I know you don't want Paolo to die."

"I said, no more talking," Paolo's mom says after a very long pause.

Fields weaves the Escalade through traffic way more carefully than Paolo's mom did the last time we were in a car together.

"Be quiet, kid," Lin says.

"Paolo is going to die if we don't do something!" I shout. "And that's all right with you?"

The car comes to an abrupt halt. My torso snaps forward, then back.

"We're here," Paolo's mom says, already opening her door.

"What? I thought you were taking me to Washington, DC."

"Change of plans." My door swings open. Paolo's mom leans over me to unbuckle my seat belt. She smells like sweat and flowers. "Come on."

I slide out of the car, my hands still cuffed behind me. It's embarrassing to step out into the world like this.

Raindrops land on my neck seconds after I exit the Escalade.

Lin follows me out. As soon as he shuts the door, Fields speeds the Escalade down the street and around the corner. Everything is strange.

We're standing in front of a large building with huge columns and an American flag sticking out of it. "We're going to the post office?" I ask.

"Yep," Paolo's mom says.

We stride inside, and I'm immediately the focus of the seven people waiting in line. Can't say I blame them; if a handcuffed dude, accompanied by two federal agents, came into the post office while I was waiting to mail a package, I'd stare at him, too.

"Whoa, the post office can arrest people?" a teenager says as I follow Paolo's mom past the line. "Whatchoo do, man?"

"I ate somebody's mail," I say without thinking.

"Yooooooo!" the teenager says. "That's crazy. Dude said he ate somebody's *mail.*"

"Don't talk anymore," Paolo's mom says as she walks us to a door right next to two big mail slots. It's marked *Employees Only.* She knocks on it twice, and another agent opens the door, this one a short woman in a black blouse and slacks.

"Agent Diaz," she says. "Agent Lin."

"Agent Merrill," Paolo's mom says.

"Do you always have to greet each other like that?" I ask.

"I don't know," Paolo's mom says. "It's just something we do. I don't think we *have* to. I mean, do any of us in the world really *have* to say hello to anyone else?"

I didn't think she'd be so defensive about it.

We walk by stacks and towers of different-size packages, then down some dusty steps covered with metal bumps that look like big sprinkles. In spite of being terrified, I can somehow also recognize that this is very cool. I've always wanted to walk through an *Employees Only* door.

"Do you always work out of this post office?"

"No," Agent Lin says. "This is new."

Once we're down the stairs, we reach a T-shaped juncture, and Paolo's mom and Lin clearly have no idea which way to go. "Hello?" Paolo's mom calls out.

"Over here," a woman's voice answers from the right.

Agent Lin stays near the bottom of the stairs as Paolo's mom and I head down a cramped hallway with a low ceiling until we reach a door that's slightly ajar. "Yes, come on in," the woman says.

Paolo's mom pushes the door open to reveal a couple of chairs and a big desk in a tiny, cluttered office. Behind the big desk is an older woman who looks familiar, though I'm not sure why.

She angles her head to the right, and then I figure it out.

It's Karen Corrigan, the woman whose photograph I saw in the *New York Times*.

Also known as: the woman I'm supposed to unassassinate on Monday.

TWENTY-EIGHT

"Good Lord, Cynthia, why do you still have him in the handcuffs?" Karen Corrigan asks. She has a slight Southern drawl.

"I just wanted to make sure I got him here this time," Paolo's mom says.

"Well, fair enough, but now he's here. Get the damn cuffs off. Boy hasn't even really done anything wrong."

Paolo's mom fiddles with the handcuffs behind me as Mrs. Corrigan stares at me across the desk, white rectangles reflecting onto her glasses from the room's strange fluorescent lighting. "So, my name is Karen Corrigan," she says, as if I'm her kindergarten student. "I head up the USDLC. You know what that is?"

"The United States Department of Life Conclusions."

"Very good!" She bangs the desk once with both hands. "Well, I am sorry we have to meet in this pitiful excuse for an office. Once we saw the news today, the urgency of our operation ratcheted up quite a bit. When we get you to DC, everything will be much nicer." The cuffs come off behind me, and it's the greatest relief. I stretch my arms up over my head. "But that's how it goes sometimes. You know what I mean, Dinton?"

Her pronunciation of my name is like nails on a chalkboard. I'm not even sure why; everything else about the way she talks is strangely comforting.

"So," she continues, not seeming to mind that I didn't respond. "You can both take a seat." We do. "You've sure had an eventful couple of weeks, haven't you?"

"I have," I say.

"And I'd say you've handled it all very well. I know you didn't ask for any of this. It's that mama of yours who's to blame."

"I guess," I say.

"Oh, it is. Make no mistake about it, Dinton!"

I know why it's so grating. She says my name exactly the way HorribleCop did. He's that policeman who was on my ass from the day of my funeral until the very end of my deathdate, and in case it's not self-explanatory, I started calling him HorribleCop because he's horrible.

"Though," Mrs. Corrigan continues, fishing around through papers on her desk, "this little stunt you pulled Thursday with that man"—she looks over her glasses at a document in her hand—"Miguel Gutierrez. Now, in that case, it seems the blame rests solely with you. Because I'm thinking your mom didn't instruct you to walk right into a celebration home and start proclaiming yourself some kind of lifesaver. That was . . . well, it was downright ballsy. Am I correct in thinking that you were acting of your own volition?"

"You are," I say quietly.

"Why'd you go and do that, Dinton?"

I ignore the chills shooting down my spine. "I, uh, I wanted to see if it would work."

"Ha!" Mrs. Corrigan says, laughing and looking at Paolo's mom. "Ain't that a hoot? You went and blew the doors off your mom's entire mission just so you could *see*?"

When she puts it like that, I feel very bad.

"My friend Paolo's deathdate is in four days," I say.

"Hmm," Mrs. Corrigan says, chewing on her bottom lip thoughtfully before tilting her head and smirking at me like I'm a moron. "You think I don't know that, Dinton? You're talking about the son of one of my best agents, who happens to be seated right next to you! And may I remind you that this Paolo is the reason Agent Diaz was assigned to your case in the first place."

"You may," I say. I can't help myself.

"Well, ain't you a sassy one," Mrs. Corrigan says with a twinkle in her eye, like she's always enjoyed a good smart-ass comment. "I like you, Dinton. In fact, Agent Diaz, if you wouldn't mind giving us a moment alone, I would greatly appreciate it."

Paolo's mom looks up, surprised. "You want to be alone with Denton?"

"That's what I just said, isn't it?"

"Right, of course, sure." Paolo's mom pushes back her chair and stands up. "I'll wait outside with Lin."

"Wait wherever the hell you want, my love. Just give us a minute."

"Sure." Paolo's mom and I make eye contact before she leaves. If she's trying to convey something nonverbally,

I have no idea what it is. She walks out of the room and shuts the door.

The mood instantly shifts with the departure of Paolo's mom. I examine Mrs. Corrigan's desk as I wait for her to speak. I can feel her staring at me, but I don't want to look back until she starts talking.

"So we have a bit of a situation here," she finally says, most—if not all—of her levity gone.

"Yeah . . . ," I agree, even though I don't exactly know what she's talking about.

"This virus your mom and her crew created, you know, as part of their little plan to eliminate mandatory death-dating in this country . . ."

She pauses, as if waiting for me to affirm what she's just said. I don't. "Well," she says with a mirthless smile, "you seem to be the first activated carrier of it. And as you demonstrated on that Gutierrez fellow, you have the ability to nullify other people's deathdates. We were afraid this might happen."

I don't say anything. Something about this room, all harmless clutter at first, now feels dangerous. If I were to shout, if I were to scream, no one would hear me.

"Because, you know, Dinton, knowledge is power, and deathdates are the ultimate knowledge. We need them." The more I stare at Mrs. Corrigan, the more I realize she and HorribleCop actually look alike; they have the same facial structure. If it turns out they're related, then I'm legally required to hate her. "They give this country a sense of order and organization that it simply didn't have decades ago."

"Plus," I say, feeling some probably misguided sense of

courage, "if we got rid of them, the government would lose out on all those millions of dollars from the pharmaceutical company that makes the ATG kits, right? All those senators and congresspeople whose campaigns are paid for by Epistemex."

"No, no, no," Mrs. Corrigan says, vigorously shaking her head. "Your mom's been feeding you propaganda, and it's simply not true."

I give a slow shrug. I try to do it in a way that seems badass, but it ends up looking more like my shoulders are twitching.

"Don't be foolish, boy," Mrs. Corrigan says, giving me a look like, *What's wrong with your shoulders?* "This ain't about money. It's about the well-being of all Americans."

I don't believe that. In fact, her words are making my mom's mission seem more justified than ever. If I can somehow get out of here, I'm going to unassassinate the crap out of this woman on Monday.

"That's why we had Agent Diaz assigned to you so many years ago," Mrs. Corrigan continues, "to put everything we had into understanding this thing inside you and to see if she could dig up any leads on your lunatic mom. We were trying to anticipate any problems before they happened, stamp 'em out. 'Course, you know it all got bungled the night you were supposed to die . . . but it's worked out in the end. Agent Diaz had the brilliant idea to tail her son's little girlfriend. Led us straight to your mom's apartment." My heart sinks. They followed Millie. "We got a team combing through that place as we speak, looking for information." My mom should never have trusted me. I've ruined this for her. I want to barf. "And we're gonna take you down to DC, deal with this virus. Get you back to healthy again."

She smiles in a way that's trying a little too hard, and my bullshit detector blares. I'm not sure what's going to happen to me in DC, but I don't think it's going to be a positive experience.

"Is that what you guys did to Matilda, too?"

"Huh?"

"A woman named Matilda was taken by the government a couple of years ago, because she'd lived through her deathdate."

"Oh," Mrs. Corrigan says, tapping her fingers on her desk. "Sure, I remember her. She's been relocated. Got a whole new life in a whole new city. She's doing quite well." She says it in this way that makes it sound like a lie, but it's hard to know for sure.

Regardless, it creeps me out. I stand up.

"Come on, Dinton. No need to get uppity. Please, take a seat."

I could make a dash for the door, but Paolo's mom and Agent Lin, not to mention that third agent upstairs, will be there to stop me. I'm a rat in a maze. I sit back down.

"Thank you," Mrs. Corrigan says. She grabs a tissue from a cardboard cube in front of her and blows her nose loudly for seven or eight seconds. "You know," she says, sniffling and wriggling her nose, "I believe you met my brother. On your deathdate."

And there it is. HorribleCop is her brother. Of course he is. And she's HorribleLady.

"He said you fancied yourself to be a real rebel, but I frankly don't know what he's talking about. You seem like a pretty considerate fella to me." HorribleLady leans forward over the desk. I'm pretty sure I hear some of her bones crack. "See, I've got a bit of a personal conundrum, Dinton. And I'd like to share it with you, and only you. That's why I made Agent Diaz excuse herself."

I clutch the wooden arms of my chair. What the hell is she about to say?

"I'm sure you're not aware of this, but my deathdate is in three days."

I was not expecting her to go there. "Oh yeah, no," I say, calling on any minimal acting chops I have. "I'm sorry to hear that."

"Well, thank you. Now, technically, I retired from being head of the USDLC a week ago. But everyone knows I love my work, my work is my life, blah blah, which is why they think I got you meeting me in some post office basement instead of an actual government building. 'Cause I'm retired."

"Oh," I say. "But that's . . . not the reason?"

"Hell no, Dinton! I'm about to die. It's time to leave this work shit behind me. You think I want to be in here, threatening some teenage boy? Anyone who tells you their work is their life is really just scared and alone. I want you to remember that."

"Okay . . ."

"The fact of the matter is, Dinton . . ." HorribleLady takes off her glasses for a moment, closes her eyes, and rubs her skinny fingers against them. Then, in a flash, the glasses are back on her face, her eyes once again boring into me. "I don't want to die."

"Oh," I say.

"I want you to pass me that virus."

TWENTY-NINE

I try to say *What?* but I'm speechless.

"You heard me," HorribleLady says. "Whatever you need to do to get that virus into me, I want you to do it."

Ew, gross. After three tries, I'm able to spit out the word: "But—"

"But what? You can save some random guy in the ass crack of Brooklyn, but not me?"

"But you . . ." I run my tongue around my very dry mouth in an attempt to loosen my speaking muscles. "You just spent all this time saying how you need the deathdate system in place and how you're going to stamp the virus out. So asking for me to pass it to you seems kinda . . . hypocritical?"

HorribleLady stares at me like I've just asked if we could continue our conversation with our pants off. "Dinton," she says. "I *do* believe in the deathdate system. I think it's vitally important for society that we all know when we'll die, and I *have* devoted most of my life to making sure that system runs smoothly. But that doesn't mean I'm ready to die *now*."

She's making my brain hurt. She and my mother want the *exact same thing:* for HorribleLady to live through her deathdate.

"But . . . you don't see how you're completely contradicting yourself?"

"Oh boy," HorribleLady says, staring at the ceiling and shaking her head. "You're not one of those semantics guys, are you? Nitpicking over the meaning of every word? Look, there's the entire system, right?" She holds out one of her long-fingernailed hands. "And then there's one person." She holds out a finger of her other spindly hand. "What I want for myself can sometimes be different than what I want for the whole system." She sticks the finger out over the desk toward me. "Can you understand that?"

"Yeah, you're saying that you believe in the system as long as it doesn't apply to you."

"You're just a kid, all right, Dinton?" HorribleLady stands up, her volume rising. "You're not gonna be able to understand this, and you don't need to. All you need to know is that your life will be made way easier if you do this for me."

This is happening faster than my mind can process. I'm sure there's an opportunity here, but I don't know what it is yet.

"How?" I ask.

"What?"

"How will my life be made easier?"

HorribleLady slinks back down into the cracked black

leather rolling chair behind the desk. "Well, for a start," she says, "the government will get off your back. Let you live your life in peace."

"So you won't take me to DC?"

"Hwell, that's the one thing I can't do for you, unfortunately. We have to nip this situation in the bud, nullify that virus in you, make sure everyone's actually dying on their deathdates from this point forward."

"I thought you didn't care about your job anymore," I say. "Just staying alive."

"There you go with those semantics again, see?"

I don't think she actually knows what *semantics* means.

HorribleLady steamrolls onward. "But *after* we stamp the virus out, you can live your life."

"As Denton Little?" I ask. "I can go back to New Jersey?"

"Oh God, no," HorribleLady says. "Nobody can know you lived. Even I don't get a free pass as far as that's concerned; I've got a whole new identity planned for myself for after you help me out, once the world thinks I've croaked. But I promise: we'll make sure you're taken care of. Get you a new name, new life, set you up somewhere nice. Just like that woman Matilda. Hell, maybe even give you a free ride to college if you play your cards right."

"Would I be able to go to Paolo's funeral? On Tuesday?"

"Hmm." HorribleLady bends behind the desk and comes back up with a bottle of Pellegrino in her hand. She takes a long sip; the glugging sound makes my skin crawl. "I don't think so, no. Didn't you already pass him the virus anyway? We're gonna have a ton of agents stationed there in case he survives his deathdate, too. Make sure we don't have a repeat of what happened with you."

"Don't worry," I say, seething. "He's not going to survive."

"Good. 'Cause we really can't afford to let anyone else live through their deathdate."

I can't believe the contradictions coming out of this woman's mouth.

"Other than you," I say.

"I know this seems unfair to you," she continues. "But that's how everything seems when you're a teenager. You'll get over it."

I chew my thumbnail. I want to explode.

I come up with a plan. It's a long shot, but it's all I have.

"All right," I say. "I'll give you the virus."

"Yes!" HorribleLady says. "Now, that's the spirit." She clasps her hands together and tucks them under her chin. "So how does this work?" She's a kid in a candy store. "It transfers through saliva, right? Do you want to spit into my bottle?" She holds it out for me. Gross.

"No, I can't do it yet."

"What do you mean?"

"It won't work right now."

HorribleLady continues to hold out the Pellegrino bottle. "Don't lie to me, Dinton."

"I'm not," I say. "It won't work until it's within forty-eight hours of your deathdate. That's the window of time when your DNA will accept it."

"Then how'd you pass it to your little friends? It wasn't their deathdates."

"I passed it, but their bodies didn't accept it. They're

immune now. I'm telling you, the virus will only work to cancel a deathdate if it times out the way I'm saying. That's why I had to go to a random funeral to test it out."

"Okay, you can give me your spit now, and I won't drink it until I get to the forty-eight-hour mark."

I cannot believe I'm having a conversation about my spit with a high-ranking government official. "That *might* work. But I don't know how long the virus will stay active in my saliva once it comes into contact with air." I've stolen this biological idea from something I heard about sperm once, but maybe it's true with the virus, too. Who the hell really knows? "We could try that, if you want to risk it." I shrug, and this time I'm more successfully badass. "It's your funeral." Zing!

HorribleLady leans back against the cracked leather of her chair and slowly taps her fingers against the desk. "All right, then. We'll set something up for Monday morning, before my funeral. You'll pass me this virus, and we'll send you down to DC, and then off to your new life. That sound about right?"

"I guess so," I say.

"We'll obviously be keeping you in our custody until then. I didn't know about these time conditions, so I'll have the USDLC get you set up somewhere nice in the meantime. Agent Diaz will be with you. But given her low success rate when it comes to keeping you in her care, Agent Lin will be there, too. Just to make sure this goes as planned. Incidentally, not a word of this to either of them. Or anyone else, for that matter. If I do find out you've said anything, that virus won't be the only thing getting stamped out. You know what I mean by that?"

I nod, too furious and terrified to speak.

HorribleLady nods back and looks down at her papers, like she has important business to attend to in this post office basement. "Agent Diaz!" she barks.

The door opens, and Paolo's mom pops her head in. "Yes, ma'am?"

"We're done here. Slight adjustment to our plans: we're gonna keep the boy in the city a couple of more days. With you and Agent Lin."

"Oh," Paolo's mom says, clearly confused. "But, uh, my son's going to die on Wednesday, so I'd like to get back to spend time with him."

No. My long-shot plan becomes a zero-shot plan without Paolo's mom.

"You'll be with Dinton till Monday morning. Then you can take all the time with your boy that you want. Sound good?"

Paolo's mom looks at me, and I try my best to make my eyes convey desperation.

"All right," she says, after a few moments.

"Here," HorribleLady says, scribbling on a piece of paper and passing it over to Paolo's mom. "You and Lin take him to this address, get settled in. I'll be in touch with updates. Go on, then." HorribleLady flips a hand at us and looks back down at her work. Paolo's mom ushers me out ahead of her.

"Oh, and, Diaz?" HorribleLady says.

"Yeah?"

"Better put those handcuffs on him after all."

THIRTY

"See what movies they have on pay-per-view," Agent Lin says from his position by the door.

"I don't particularly care," Paolo's mom says. "You can see yourself when it's your turn."

We're in some nice Manhattan hotel where everything is red. I am sharing a room with Paolo's mom and Agent Lin. It is very weird.

"Geez, Diaz," Agent Lin says. "Lighten up."

I'm on one of the double beds, my arms behind my back, handcuffs chewing into my wrists. I've found an awkward way to contort my body so that I can lie down and sleep. I give it a comfort rating of one star out of five.

Paolo's mom is on the other bed, while Agent Lin stands guard by the door. They're taking shifts.

None of us have talked much. We had a silent car ride from the post office, an audience of raised eyebrows as I was paraded through the hotel lobby, and now an almost entirely silent stretch of hours in this hotel room. Paolo's mom and Agent Lin were not expecting this. They were thinking they'd escort me down to DC, and that would be the end of their responsibilities. I can tell they don't understand what the point of keeping me here is.

Which is why I am going to tell them.

Well, not Agent Lin. Just Paolo's mom. If I can get her alone for a minute.

"If they have something starring The Rock, we're watching it," Agent Lin says.

It doesn't look like it's happening tonight.

I close my eyes.

When I open them again, sun is streaming through the window, my body feels like it's been pulverized, and Paolo's mom is sitting up against the headboard, looking at her phone. It's a new day, and Agent Lin is not in the room.

"Where'd he go?" I ask, my voice thick with sleep.

"To get some ice," Paolo's mom says, without looking at me.

"She wants me to give her the virus," I say, shaking my head like a dog drying itself and feeling my body scream as I try to adjust myself into something that more closely resembles a sitting position.

"What? Who?" Paolo's mom says, looking up now.

"Corrigan. That's why she's keeping me here." I'm trying to speak quickly and clearly. Everything hinges on right now. "Because the virus won't work until we're within forty-eight hours of her deathdate. She wants to stay alive, so she's using me for that before she sends me to DC, where who the hell knows what they'll do with me."

I have Paolo's mom's attention, but she's skeptical. "Don't toy with me, Denton. That's not funny."

"I'm not joking," I say. "She wanted it to happen in that office, but I told her it wouldn't work yet."

She scoots closer to my bed and leans her head in. "Denton," she says. "I know things between us have been a little strange ever since your deathdate." Understatement of ever. "And I know you have every reason to want to manipulate your way out of this situation. But I need you to tell me the God's honest truth here. Did my boss, Karen Corrigan, foremost proponent of deathdates, truly ask you to help nullify her deathdate?"

I make my face look as trustworthy as possible. "She did."

"You're serious?"

"I am."

Paolo's mom stares at me for a solid five seconds. "No," she says. "I don't believe you."

I barrel forward, speaking faster now. "She said that what she wants for herself can be different than what she wants for the whole system. And she asked how I could save a random guy in the ass crack of Brooklyn and not her. And she said we couldn't save Paolo because we could only afford to save one person: her."

"What?"

I thought that might be an effective point to make. "I'm not lying. I promise. Why do you think she wanted to talk to me *alone*?"

Paolo's mom turns away from me, one hand on her forehead as she stares down at the maroon carpet. Then she grabs her hair till the blood drains out of her knuckles, her face turning red as she shouts, "FUUUUCK!"

She believes me.

"What happened?" Agent Lin says, blasting back into the room with an ice bucket in his hand.

Paolo's mom whips toward him, and she takes a deep breath. "Nothing, nothing. Sorry." She picks her phone up off the bed and holds it up. "Someone got my credit card info. Through PayPal. Charged a bunch of stuff to my account. Sorry."

"Holy hell, Diaz, you should be sorry," Agent Lin says, closing the door behind him. "I thought the world was ending."

"I'm sorry about that. Everything's fine."

I look at Paolo's mom, hoping to acknowledge that we have some kind of new understanding, but she avoids my eyes.

Room service arrives with breakfast—fruit and old pastries—and we return to business as usual. But I can tell Paolo's mom is thinking about what I said.

"Do either of you want ice in your orange juice?" Agent Lin asks, plopping two cubes into his.

"No thanks," I say.

"Absolutely not," Paolo's mom says.

The hours tick by. I stay on one bed; Paolo's mom stays on the other; Agent Lin sits in a chair near the door. We watch a movie starring The Rock. We eat lunch. Agent Lin is channel-surfing when I see Miguel Gutierrez's photo.

"Wait, hold up," I say.

The banner below Miguel reads: *DEATH OF BROOK-LYN MAN WHO LIVED A DAY PAST DEATHDATE.*

"No," I say quietly.

"Just yesterday," the reporter says, standing in front of

a light blue row house, "Miguel Gutierrez, forty-nine, was being hailed as a medical miracle, the first person to live through a deathdate. But this morning, his family was saddened to discover that Miguel had died in his sleep."

Holy. Effing. Shit.

"What seemed at first to be a miracle," he continues, "now seems to be nothing more than a glitch, most likely a typo on his original death certificate."

"Guess that virus of your mom's isn't quite as effective as you thought, huh?" Agent Lin says.

"Guess not," I say. But I know that's not true. "Or the DIA killed him."

Paolo's mom looks at me for the first time since Agent Lin walked back in, and I can see that she knows. Her eyes are saying something along the lines of *Goddamn Karen Corrigan.*

But she says, "Oh sure, that's likely. You can change the channel, Lin."

The report cuts to Miguel's daughter, her face a glistening mess. "After the news broke yesterday," the daughter says, "my dad got really tired, so he went to sleep around two p.m. He had been sleeping for almost eighteen hours, so I went in to check on him and—"

The channel is flipped to a show featuring people in helmets jumping onto huge inflated things.

"Ha!" Agent Lin says. "Have you guys ever seen this show? It's fantastic."

I can see Paolo's mom's brain spinning. She gives me the tiniest of nods.

I don't know exactly what the nod means, but it doesn't

matter, because a second later, she's grabbing Agent Lin by the shoulders and straight-up head-butting him in the nose. He slumps down in his chair, unconscious.

"Dude . . . ," I say. "You and Veronica are so hardcore."

"Letting you get away seems to be my greatest talent. Might as well embrace it," Paolo's mom says, fumbling around in Agent Lin's pocket until she finds a tiny key. "Get over here."

I try to quickly clamber over and end up falling off the bed with a thump. "Shit, sorry," I say, using the side of the mattress to shinny myself back up to a standing position.

"Come on," she whispers. I walk over and turn around, and she quickly undoes the handcuffs. "Here, help me get his arms back, handcuff him to the chair."

"Okay," I say, in complete disbelief that this is actually happening. "Wait. Maybe we should handcuff him to one of the legs of the bed so it'll be even harder to leave the room."

Paolo's mom looks at me a moment. "Yeah, that's a good idea." We pull Agent Lin off the chair, gravity dragging his full body weight down to the ground. We slowly slide him up against the bed, and I pull his arms back around its leg. Paolo's mom strains and reddens as she reaches under the bed to click the handcuffs into place.

"All right," she says, exhaling and putting the tiny key into her pocket. "Time to go."

"Shouldn't we gag him with something? So no one can hear him and we'll buy some more time?"

Paolo's mom gives me a nonverbal *Hey, look at you,*

then grabs a pillow from the bed and deftly slides off the pillowcase. She pulls the case taut and shoves it into Agent Lin's mouth, tying it around his head.

Agent Lin wakes back up, his eyes full of questions. "HuhhuhHUH?" he says, trying to say, I believe, *What the FUCK?*

"I'm really sorry, Matt," Paolo's mom says, crouching in front of him. "But I need to try and save my son."

Agent Lin starts kicking wildly and nails me in the shin. I pretend it doesn't hurt, even though it really does.

"Let's go," Paolo's mom says.

I stand up and take one last look at Agent Lin. "Sorry, dude," I say. "It's not personal."

We open the door a crack and slide out into the hallway.

Agent Lin is shouting into his pillowcase gag as we close the door and run.

THIRTY-ONE

"What in God's name am I doing?" Paolo's mom says as the Escalade bounds out of the parking garage into the flow of New York City traffic. "I just head-butted and tied up a fellow agent, and enabled your escape."

"I know. I was there, and it was awesome," I say, making damn sure to buckle my seat belt.

"If that Karen Corrigan story turns out to be something you made up to—"

"It isn't."

Paolo's mom grips the steering wheel and gets furious all over again. "Fucking KAREN CORRIGAN! *She* wants to be saved? My son is going to die the day after her! Don't you think it's crossed my mind that maybe I should try to save *him*? But I didn't, because I *believed* in this crap."

"Yeah," I say, mildly terrified.

"If we're saving anyone, it's gonna be my eighteen-year-old son, not that ancient bag of bones. She's, like, seventy-something. She doesn't need any more life."

It slowly dawns on me that Paolo's mom thinks I'll be able to save Paolo. That's why she busted me out. Oh shit.

"So, here's the deal: we're gonna figure out a way to get you back to New Jersey so you can give Paolo this virus and allow him to live. And once you do, you, me, and Paolo will get the hell outta there."

"Um, yes, I agree," I say. "But, well . . ."

"What?"

"No, it's just that—"

"Spit it out, Denton."

"I can't actually give Paolo the virus. Because he's immune to it. From when I gave it to him on my deathdate."

The car is disturbingly silent.

"Is that a joke?" Paolo's mom asks quietly.

"No," I say. "It is not a joke."

Paolo's mom screams, completely unhinged.

"I'm sorry," I say.

"What the hell are we doing this for, if we can't save Pow? Are you insane? Why did you bait me into this?"

"I didn't think I was baiting you!" I stammer back at her. "I mean, I am still trying to find a way to save Paolo. Together we can do this! And either way, I thought you'd want to help me get to Paolo's funeral so I could see him before he dies. And also just help me, because you care about me."

"Get to Paolo's funeral? We can't go to Paolo's funeral, Denton! We're on the run now! Not only have I just lost my job, but I'll probably be arrested and put in prison for the shit I just pulled. And Paolo's going to die anyway!

OhmiGOD!" She inadvertently bangs on the horn as she says *GOD,* and it startles both of us.

"I'm really sorry," I say.

"Why did you say those things to me in the car on the way to the post office? About wondering if you could save Paolo?"

"Because I *am* still wondering! I didn't mean to leave out the part about him being immune to it."

"Oh, Denton, we are so fucked."

My eyebrows are riding up to the top of my skull. Adults dropping the f-bomb will never not surprise me.

"Look," I say. "Let's think. Maybe there are still more options." I think about my mom, where she might be right now. At Dane's apartment? Felix's? Maybe a new place altogether? Maybe a new state altogether? Even if I wanted to call her, I don't have her number. And she probably hates me anyway for ruining her entire movement.

"Yeah, good luck there, D," Paolo's mom says. "Maybe look up *splotch virus specialists* in the Yellow Pages?"

Brian Blum. That's who I need to call. I know he and my mom had some kind of falling-out or whatever, and she said he wouldn't know anything, but I don't have any other options.

"Can I have your phone?" I ask.

"You're not actually going to find that in the Yellow Pages. I was being sarcastic."

"Cynthia, just please give me the phone."

She hands it over to me without looking as she turns onto a street that cuts through Central Park. I dig out my wallet and find the business card Brian Blum gave me a lifetime ago. I punch in the number.

The phone rings four times, and I'm just giving up hope when he picks up.

"Hello?" Brian says warily, sounding tired. I'm so glad to hear his voice.

"Brian, hey, it's Denton."

"Denton! Are you all right? Where does the DIA have you?" I'm confused as to how he knows I was taken by the DIA. I guess he has been in touch with my mother after all.

"It's, uh, it's kind of complicated, but I'm all right. I need your help, though."

Paolo's mom looks over at me and exhales through her nose, like, *Speed it up.*

"Of course, Dent, but I'm actually really glad you called. We've obviously had no way to get a hold of you. And, uh, I hate to share this over the phone. But. Well. Yeah. I guess I have to."

The one-eighty is disorienting. I called *him,* and now he's throwing me off balance with something to share with *me?* "Okay," I say.

"It's your mom, Dent. . . . Cheryl passed away."

My brain short-circuits, sparking as my past and present collide. My mom passed away when I was born, right? No, she's alive. She's alive now.

"Wait, what?" I ask.

"She's dead, Denton. Your mom, Cheryl, is dead. I'm so sorry."

"No, Brian, I just saw her yesterday," I say, wanting to clear this up as quickly as possible. "She's not dead. She's on the run with Dane. The DIA came. They escaped, but I didn't." It's irritating to have to explain this. Just because *he* doesn't know where she is doesn't mean she's *dead.*

"Dent," Brian says. "I know all that. I'm with Dane now. And Felix."

What? I can't make words. I'm confused. Paolo's mom looks over at me, irritated.

"Your mom and Dane did get away," Brian says, "and they were on the subway together, heading to Dane's apartment, and . . . her heart gave out, Denton. It happened so fast."

"Are you joking?" I ask. I feel tears on my cheeks. "Is this one of my mom's jokes?"

"No," Brian says. "I wish it was."

"My mom was throwing down smoke bombs and jumping onto fire escapes yesterday. She's totally fine."

"That's how it happens, Dent. There was a history of this in Cheryl's family."

"NO," I say. I can feel Paolo's mom looking at me, no longer annoyed. "It must have been the DIA." I stare back at Paolo's mom as I say this. "They poisoned her or something."

"Dent, we know for sure that wasn't the case. It was a heart attack. Plain and simple."

I choke back a sob. I think about my last conversation with my mom, when she told me how much sweetness there was in me. I take off my glasses and cover my eyes with my free hand.

"Is everything okay?" Paolo's mom asks.

"My mom . . . ," I say. "She had a heart attack. She's dead. So you must be really happy." And suddenly I'm not choking back anything.

"Denton, who's with you?" Brian says.

I'm crying too hard to speak.

"Oh God, Denton," Paolo's mom says. "I'm so sorry. That's . . . awful. That's really awful." She pulls the car over to the curb. Out the window, there's a park bench and trees.

"This is really important," Brian continues. "Where are you right now? Please."

"This is my fault," I say. "I'm the one who forced my mom to invite Millie into her apartment, and Millie's the one who was tailed. And I'm the one who gave that man the virus in a completely conspicuous way."

"Denton, stop, okay?" Brian says. "You are not responsible for your mother's heart attack."

"She was so stressed when the DIA showed up. I'm sure that brought it on."

"Whatever stress your mother had was not your fault. Because of you, she lived almost eighteen extra years. You gave her that gift. So you can feel sad that she's gone, but you are not allowed to feel responsible. Do you hear me?"

A pigeon is perched on the park bench outside my window.

"I said, *Do you hear me?*"

I don't say anything.

"Where does the DIA have you?" Brian says.

"I'm with Cynthia," I say, my nose packed with snot. "She attacked another DIA agent and helped me escape, so I think she's on our side now."

Paolo's mom is taking a deep breath and looking out the windshield.

"Whoa," Brian says. "Can she take you to my place in Jersey? I live about thirty minutes from your dad and stepmother's house."

I'm in shock, so it's taking me longer than usual to respond.

"We should all be together, Dent," he continues. "To honor your mother."

I'd like to do that, but I need to see Paolo before his deathdate.

Which reminds me: the only person left with even the tiniest hope of knowing how to save Paolo is Brian.

I look to Paolo's mom.

"Change of plans," I say.

THIRTY-TWO

"I keep expecting this to be one of her jokes," Felix says, sitting next to me on the gray couch. His eyes are red and puffy. "I just, you know . . . I keep waiting for her to call and laugh that I fell for it so hard."

I'm at the house Brian shares with his husband, Langston, in Westfield, New Jersey, in a cozy room that has framed photographs on the wall of dancers in all these crazy positions. I arrived here last night, but it was late, so everyone was already asleep, except Brian, who showed me to the guest room. I was out within minutes. Now it's morning. Dane's zoning out on the other end of the huge U-shaped couch, while Yuri sits next to him, reading a book that has an elephant on the cover. Brian and Langston are making tea in the kitchen.

Paolo's mom and I figured that, in an ideal world, we had until this morning before Karen Corrigan would show up at the hotel to receive the virus, discover we were gone, and flood the greater tristate area with federal agents looking for us. So, before that happened, we decided to split up, Paolo's mom going to see Paolo, probably for the last time, and me heading here to mourn my mother and talk to Brian.

I assumed Paolo's mom would drive us to New Jersey, but she said that if by any chance the DIA was already after us, they'd be tracking the car. And since she figured the DIA's next thought would be the train, we went to the nastastic Port Authority instead. And took buses.

But before that happened, Paolo's mom called someone to come drive her car upstate as a diversion. The woman who showed up to drive seemed incredibly familiar to me, and then I saw the three-year-old girl with her. It was the mother of Dylan, who I'd seen on the train the night of my deathdate and again when I escaped from my mom's safe house. "Holy crap, you work for the DIA?" I asked her.

"No," she answered, pointing to Paolo's mom. "I work for her."

"Single moms get the real dirty work done," Paolo's mom said.

Then we split up. I realized people might recognize me from that drawing on the news, so I went into an overpriced souvenir shop and bought a green trucker cap that featured the Statue of Liberty's face. The bus I was supposed to take was delayed for two hours—it had broken down in New Jersey somewhere—so I spent way too much time drifting through the Port Authority, the brim of my flimsy cap shadowing my eyes, the phrase *My mother is dead* looping in my brain. By the time I got on a bus, traveled the seventy minutes to Westfield, and hopped in a cab to Brian's, it was past eleven.

"I was just getting used to the idea of her being alive," I say to Felix.

"This sucks so much," he says, putting his hand over his eyes. "And you want to know what the funniest part is?" he asks, wiping his cheeks and blinking a lot. "Part of me kind of wishes I *had* known her deathdate. Because this is too shocking."

I know what he means. My mom's death still doesn't seem real. How can people be here one day and then gone the next, with no warning at all? Maybe it's what my mom always wanted, but it feels unfair to the people she's left behind.

"I already miss her so much," Felix says. It's followed by another set of sobs.

I wish I were crying about my mom, too. I'm definitely feeling the tragic loss of this woman I was just beginning to understand, but I'm also feeling a strange disconnect.

As Felix wails, it hits me: Cheryl is Felix's mom, not mine. That may sound obvious, but it feels like a revelation. They loved each other so much. I don't think it's an exaggeration to say that her whole movement existed because she wanted to stay alive for her son Felix.

"Are you okay?" Yuri asks Felix, looking up from his book.

"All good, Yuri," he says, blowing his nose.

"Don't say that," Dane says, suddenly choosing to engage in our conversation. "It is not all good. Nothing is good."

Brian walks in, holding a teapot, followed by Langston,

who's carrying at least five mugs. Everything gets placed on something that looks more like a sculpture than a table.

"Here you go, Denton," Langston says. For all of my mom's resentment toward Langston, in person there's nothing that offensive about him. He seems like a gentle guy, and I can see how he and Brian make a good couple. I nod and thank him as he passes me a mug.

"It will be good again, though," Felix says. "We'll continue forward with the movement, the way she would have wanted to. You're down, right, Dent?"

I'm not sure what to say, so I just stammer for a few seconds.

"Please," Brian says, "as I've already said, Felix, let's take time to honor Cheryl and her life before we start, you know, making new plans to do . . . whatever it is you're doing these days."

"We *are* honoring our mom's life," Felix says. He glares at his tea. "This is what she would have wanted. Just because you got married and your husband—no offense, Langston—doesn't approve of what we do doesn't mean you have to shit all over it."

"I agree, but please watch language," Dane says, gesturing to Yuri.

"All right," Brian says, standing in front of us. "This has got to stop. Felix, I didn't leave the movement because of things Langston said. I mean, maybe Cheryl had to tell herself that to feel better about it, but it's not true. I left the movement because . . . there is no movement. Not anymore."

It's shocking to hear him say that, mainly because I know right away that it's probably true.

The room is silent except for the ticking of an ornate grandfather clock in the corner.

"Oh, there's no movement, Brian?" Felix finally says. "Then how the hell is Denton alive right now? Tell me that!"

"Yes, okay, sure, there once was a movement," Brian says. "And we worked on a virus, and it was actually effective. And we did inject a few other women with it, women who have started new lives across the country. But those women never cared about Cheryl's political agenda. They just wanted to *keep living*!"

"Not true!" Dane says. "Matilda cared about more than that. And I want still to find her. And also to get revenge for what the government has done."

I remember what Karen Corrigan said about Matilda starting a new life in a new city. But given what happened with Miguel, who even knows if that's true? I decide not to mention it.

"Now that Denton has lived," Felix says, "we can do things. Life-changing things!"

"Look, that may be, and I don't blame either of you for still caring about it," Brian says. "I just can't do it anymore."

Felix stands up, practically vibrating with anger. "Fuck you, Brian," he says, and walks out of the room.

"Language, please!" Dane shouts after him. He turns back to Brian. "Why you have to say these things?"

"I'm sorry, man," Brian says. "But it's how I feel."

Dane sighs. "I think Yuri and I will take walk now."

"I want to do some jumping, too," Yuri says as they head out the front door.

Now it's just Brian, Langston, and me. I drink my tea.

"How you doing, Dent?" Brian asks. "You've really been put through the wringer this month."

"Is that true?" I say. "What you just said about the movement?"

Brian looks to Langston, then back to me. "Well, truth is subjective, but, yeah, it's true as far as I'm concerned. Your mother hasn't really been herself for at least ten years, Denton."

It's so sad to hear him say that. "What do you mean?"

"I mean, that intensity you probably experienced these past weeks, that was always there to some extent, but it'd gotten way more extreme. She was consumed by this movement stuff, and for what? Money from the life insurance industry? I mean, she was so reluctant to take their money at first, but once she did, I feel like it changed her. I wanted her to start a new life, you know? She had this new identity as Nadia Forrester; she could have been out in the world instead of plotting in the lab all the time."

"But maybe that was the life that made her happiest," I say.

Brian thinks a second, then nods. "Maybe," he says. "Who even knows. It just seemed to me that she never really lived after she, you know, lived."

I take another sip of my tea. I remember that whether the movement is real or not, Karen Corrigan is definitely still going to be after me. And Paolo is still going to die.

"Brian," I say. "This may not be the best time for this, but the reason I called you yesterday—before I learned about my mom—was that, um, well, you remember my best friend, Paolo, right? His deathdate is Wednesday. I'm trying to save his life, but my mom did tests and said he's immune to the virus because I passed it to him on my deathdate. I thought maybe you would know some way . . . something we could do?" Brian has this pained look on his face that doesn't seem very promising. "Do you?"

Brian stares down into his teacup for at least fifteen clock ticks.

I'm desperate. "I mean, when *your* best friend was dying, you helped her. . . ."

He sighs. "There is . . . something," he says, looking up. "Nobody knows about this, Denton. Like, nobody." He turns to Langston, who shrugs. "You know what, screw it."

I put my tea down.

"Your mom and I knew so little about the virus," Brian says, "because we weren't the ones who created it."

My breath catches in my chest.

"What? Who did, then?"

Three more clock ticks go by.

"Your dad," Brian says. "The virus was created by your dad."

THIRTY-THREE

I'm in my backyard, staring at the house where I grew up.

It's almost dark. I breathe in the familiar smell of grass and dirt. A firefly circles my head.

I can't believe I'm here.

I'm not entirely convinced that the quiet man who rarely wants to discuss anything deeper than the Knicks' insistence on shooting so many three-pointers is the person who might be able to save Paolo's life.

But for lack of any better options, here I am.

In light of the high probability that Karen Corrigan would be waiting for me here with scores of DIA agents, Brian convinced me it'd be better to come after dark. He also convinced me that, since my likeness was recently featured on every major network, I should probably change up my look again. So I ditched the glasses and shaved my head. Ridiculous.

As we approached my parents' house in Brian's green

Honda Civic, there was, sure enough, a lineup of three black Escalades and a police car in front of the house. Brian took a quick right turn to the next block over, where, my hands shaking, I thanked him for everything and proceeded to stealth-walk through the Ritters' backyard, remembering the exact spot in the chain-link fence where Felix and his onetime friend Ian Ritter said you could bend it up and sneak underneath.

So now I'm standing here at the back door, my heart beating in my throat, trying to imagine how this will all play out. It's almost 9 p.m. on a Monday night. Both of my parents should be home.

Here we go. I hope my dad can help.

I turn the knob. It's locked. I can't even see inside, because of the curtain covering the door's window.

I knock. My whole body is vibrating.

A mosquito buzzes in my ear, and I trip over myself as I wildly smack it away. I collide into the covered barbecue grill my dad rarely uses. It doesn't make much noise, but I do when one of its corners slams into my hip. I clench my teeth and hop around, producing a low *Ah!* sound. I see the curtain on the door lift up to the side, and part of my dad's bespectacled face peers out at me.

He opens the door. "Denton?" he asks. "Are you okay?"

"I am," I say as the hip stabbing starts to subside. "I ran into the barbecue."

"Oh wow," he says. "Yeah, gotta watch out for that."

My dad already knew that I wasn't dead, but you'd still think he might express a tiny bit more surprise at finding me in his backyard. We stare at each other in the fading light. I can't quite see this soft-spoken, befuddled man as the person who created the splotch virus and incited all of this insanity.

"Is it safe for you to be here, Denton?" he asks.

"No, not really. Not at all."

"What'd you do to your hair?"

"You're really asking me that right now? Can I come in? So it's more safe?"

"Oh. Um." My dad looks back into the house. "Of course, yeah. Come on in." He steps outside and ushers me forward. I stop on my way past and give him a hug. "Ah," he says, surprised.

"It's really good to see you, Dad."

"You, too, Dent." His arms wrap around me, strong and fatherly. I had no idea how much I missed him. We hold the hug for at least ten seconds, a new record for us.

I walk inside. My dad lingers a moment longer in the yard, looking both ways, before coming in and closing the door. He walks with a limp.

"Oh man, that's right. Is your leg okay from the car accident?"

"It's healing," he says, lifting his pant leg to reveal a brace. "Slowly but surely. Just got out of the cast two days ago."

"I'm so sorry. Is Mom all right?" I ask, and it feels good to use that word for my stepmom, in a way it never did when I used it for my actual mom. Though I feel bad thinking that so soon after her death.

"She's okay. Her bruises have mainly healed. She's been going to a chiropractor for her neck."

"That's good. Is she here?"

"No," my dad says, leading the way to the family room.

"She's at book club." I'm disappointed, though this means it will probably be easier to get down to business. "But there's lots of leftovers in the fridge, if you're hungry."

"Dad, that was really sexist, the way your mind just worked."

"Huh?"

"As if Mom's sole purpose in being here is to provide us food."

"Oh . . . I see what you mean. Yeah, I should work on that." He pauses. "That said, *do* you want any leftovers?"

"Um, no, not right now," I say, even though I'm hungry. Being with my dad, I find it easy to get lulled into our usual slow, easygoing rhythms, to forget that I'm on a very specific, very urgent mission. "Let's sit down, Dad."

"All right," my dad says, joining me on the couch. The last time I was in here was for my Sitting.

"I mean, I don't know if you're putting on an act right now or what, but I *know* about you."

"What . . . what're you talking about, Dent?"

"I know that you know about all this."

"Uh . . ." My dad sticks a finger under his glasses and scratches his eye.

"Did you create the virus?" I ask.

"Huh?"

"Come on, Dad. The virus that saved me. The virus that saved my mother. Did you create it?"

My father stares at me. He blinks and shrugs, his head subtly nodding, a bobblehead seconds away from stillness.

"Ohmigod," I say.

"It was a different time," he says.

"You saw how terrified I was on my deathdate as this

purple splotch slowly crept over my entire body, and you didn't say anything?"

My dad looks up at the ceiling for a moment. "I thought I was protecting you. And, honestly, I didn't know if it would work. Nobody did."

"Sidenote," I say. "Did you ever consider letting me know that MOM WAS ALIVE?"

"Please, lower your voice," my dad says.

"You're a total bigamist, Dad!"

"It's . . . not bigamy. In the eyes of the law, your mother has been dead all these years."

"Yes, but in the eyes of, like, reality, she was alive. And that didn't seem like worthwhile information to share?"

"Denton," my father says. "You know I couldn't tell you that. You're being irrational."

"Well, shit, Dad, if the way you behave is rational, I'll choose irrational every time!" I'm up on my feet. It's like somebody's accidentally bumped the rack during a game of Connect Four: all the chips are pouring out of me.

"Please calm down." My dad gets to his feet, too.

"You want me to be like you? Like, I don't know, like a statue or something? You want me to never show emotion and never be honest with people so that we can all be perfect, rational creatures living our lies together? Screw that!"

As if struck by a gust of wind that stirs up out of nowhere, I find myself slammed down by the shoulders onto the couch. My dad hovers over me, leaning into my face. "You need to be quiet, Denton," he says. It scares the shit out of me. "I'm sorry for the choices I've made that haven't been to your liking, but it's always you I've been thinking of. Always." His eyes are calm but shimmering with moisture. That scares the shit out of me even more. My dad almost never cries.

"Oh," I say.

"Do you think I wanted to lose your mother? Or to live without her once she lived?"

He pauses, as if he's waiting for an answer to his seemingly rhetorical questions. "Uh . . . ," I say.

"Of course I didn't. That was the hardest thing I've ever done. But I knew it was also the *right* thing. And once I learned you had such an early deathdate, I was even more sure. Was I going to have you spend your short life on the run with me, your brother, and your undead mother? Absolutely not."

I've never seen my dad exhibit this much passion. The only moment that's come close was when he scared Mrs. Donovan into letting us into prom.

"I figured if you really did end up surviving," my dad continues, sitting down next to me, "you'd have plenty of time to be on the run as an adult."

"Oh," I say, still stunned. "That makes sense." I never had any clue that my dad had thoughts like these.

"Trust me," he says. "There were many times when I considered telling you. But I couldn't do it. You always wanted your life to be normal, Denton. And letting you in on all this, well, it felt like the opposite of normal."

He's got a point there.

For the first time, I'm seeing my father as a man who's been stuck in an incredibly weird situation.

"I worked tirelessly, for *years,* on a serum that would save your mother. When I finally thought I'd done it, it turned out it couldn't alter a human's DNA once they were born. You needed to inject it into a fetus *before* birth. But there was a loophole: when you injected the virus into a fetus, it would transfer to the mother-to-be, too.

"So your mother wanted to get pregnant again. Even though she'd spent our whole relationship saying she didn't want kids, because she would abandon them when she died. Felix was an accident, a surprise, and I fought tooth and nail to convince your mother we should keep him. But then, when she learned having another child could help *her,* she suddenly wanted another baby, and I just couldn't do it, Denton. Creating another person—a person she would immediately abandon along with me and Felix—just so she could survive?"

The person he's talking about is me. I wouldn't have existed if he'd won that argument.

"That's what I was trying to explain to you in the kitchen at your Sitting, how your mother went off birth control without telling me and we conceived you. I was furious. Because she'd gone and made a huge decision without me, a decision that impacted my life maybe even more than hers."

I have never heard my father talk this much. Ever.

"I refused to inject you, and, by extension, her, with the virus, but she convinced Brian. The two of them had been helping me in the lab, so they knew enough to be able to do it without me. At a certain point, it wasn't about a movement for them at all. It was about Cheryl looking out for herself, even to the detriment of the people she'd leave behind. I wanted no part of it." My father sniffs and takes off his glasses. "So you ask why I never told you about your mother? It's because as far as I was concerned, she *was* dead. It was the only way I could go on, Denton. Most of me started to believe it."

"Dad," I say, wiping at my face with my T-shirt. "She just died yesterday. For real."

"What?"

"Cheryl. She had a heart attack. She's dead."

"Oh," my dad says, looking down at his glasses, still in his hand. "My God. That's what she was always scared of."

"I know," I say. "But I got to meet her and everything. So, you know, that's something." I let go entirely. I am a messy, tremoring pile of mush. My dad moves down the couch and wraps his arms around me.

"Oh, Dent," he says. "I'm so sorry."

"I'm sorry to you, too. Are you sad?"

"I think I'm more shocked right now, but, yes, this is very sad news. God, I hope Felix is okay."

We sit there for a while. It's the longest my father and I have ever sat together without doing anything. All kinds of records are being set tonight.

"Dad," I say, feeling a renewed sense of purpose. "I need to save Paolo. And you're the only one who can help me."

"Denton," my dad says, retracting his arms.

"He can't die! And he has the virus in him! I passed it to him on my deathdate. So there has to be a way to save him."

My dad rubs his forehead. "I'm afraid it doesn't work like that, Denton. From what I remember of my research, I think you passing him the virus that long before his deathdate would be almost like an inoculation, which means that Paolo—"

"—is immune to the virus. Yeah, I know. But you created it; I thought maybe there would be, like, another loophole or something."

My dad purses his lips and shakes his head.

"That's it? That's all you have?"

My dad shrugs. "Once you start trying to play God like this, things can get very sticky. There's a difference between not wanting to know your deathdate and just not wanting to die. I think that was something your mother lost sight of. Whether we like our deathdates or not, that's the hand we're dealt. Who are we to think it could be otherwise?"

"Well, clearly, at one point, you *did* think otherwise. You just told me you spent years working on this! I mean, Dad, *please,* just think, for a moment, of all your research. Time is running out, and all those government people parked in front of the house are probably going to get me sooner rather than later. So it's now or never." I shakily stand up from the couch. "I know you thought Cheryl was being selfish, and I'm sure I am, too, wanting to save my best friend, but I also know you didn't want to abandon me. And right now, well, I am alone and on the run, and having Paolo by my side would mean everything."

"All right," he says, standing. "Come with me."

"What?" I say. My dad is already heading up the stairs, taking them two at a time.

I do, too, and I'm out of breath when I reach the top and see my dad ducking into his bedroom.

"Dad, what?" I say, following him inside and seeing that he's in his mess of a closet, the same one from which he dug out the long-withheld letter my mom had written me on the day of my birth. He's crouched down, his head brushing against a couple of clear plastic suit bags.

"Come down here," he says.

I crouch next to him. He pushes aside a congregation of shoes and reveals a metal box with a panel of numbers in front.

"After your mother left," my dad says, "I didn't actually stop the work I'd been doing."

"What? But you just said—"

"I know, I know. But I'd gotten so close to cracking it that I couldn't stop there. It was a side project. A challenge. It took me a few more years, but I did it. I created a new strain of the virus."

"Dad, what are you saying?"

"In this safe is a vial of a superstrain of the virus. If you inject it into somebody, it nullifies their deathdate instantly."

I gasp. "So, Paolo—"

"But it's powerful, Denton. Maybe too powerful. It wipes out the part of your DNA that gets read by the ATG kit, instantly making you undated. And it also makes you an active carrier for the rest of your life. So anyone who comes in contact with your saliva would become undated as well, no matter when you pass it to them. And they might die after their predicted deathdate, but they also might die before it. Plus, there's a good chance that anyone with this virus would go on to have undated children; it alters the gene in a much more powerful way than the strain you have."

"Wow. I mean, this—this is huge. But why did you make it? I mean, why did you even keep it if you feel so wary of all this? You know, all the playing-God stuff."

My dad sighs. "Trust me, I've thought about chucking it into the trash every single day. But nobody wants to die, Denton. Even if we know it's coming. I'm supposed to die sixteen years before Raquel."

"You were thinking you would inject *yourself* with this?"

My dad shrugs. "I didn't know. Maybe."

"Jesus, Dad."

"We're all full of surprises, right?" Well, that's a fucking understatement. "Of course, if I did use it on myself, I'd quickly pass it to Raquel as soon as I kissed her, so then we'd both be undated. Meaning maybe we'd both die *before* our expected deathdates, which would make me feel pretty damn stupid. So, yeah, there's a lot to think about, Dent."

My dad rubs his hand over the top of the safe, then pats it twice. "But, look," he says, "if you feel prepared to take on the responsibility of sending this thing out into the world . . . I won't stop you."

"I . . ." He's phrased that in a really terrifying way. But this is the solution I've been desperately searching for the past two weeks; I can't back down. "Yes, I feel prepared. Thank you, Dad."

"Well," he says. "All right. Now, if only I could remember the code to open this safe."

"What? Seriously?"

My dad smiles.

"You pick the strangest moments to be funny."

"I'd never forget this code," he says. "Definitely not the first three digits anyway." I watch him punch in a seven, then a one, then a two. He turns to me and smiles again.

"Oh," I say, after a moment. Seven twelve. July twelfth. My birthday. It's a small thing, but it also feels like proof that he cares about me, and I turn my head away as my eyes fill with tears. My dad punches in a bunch more numbers, and the safe clicks open. He takes out a syringe and a tiny vial filled with a clear liquid.

"So here you go. You *cannot* let this vial fall into anyone else's hands. Do you understand me?"

The rumble of the garage door reverberates up to us before I have a chance to answer.

"Oh shoot," my dad says. "She's early."

My stepmom is back from book club.

THIRTY-FOUR

"Do you think you can get out the back door before she comes in?" my dad says.

"What? Why would I—? No, Dad, I'd like to see her."

"But . . . I don't think that's wise, Denton. At least not right now."

"Oh man." I suddenly realize what's going on. "Don't tell me Mom thinks I'm actually dead."

"Well." My dad stares down at the beige carpet of the closet floor. "Yes."

"What the hell, Dad!"

"I didn't think it would be helpful to tell her the truth. You know your stepmother. She wouldn't have stopped until she tracked you down. It would have been dangerous for all of us, you especially."

"Yeah, but it's fucked up! She thinks I died in that car accident?"

"She thinks what everyone thinks: that Cynthia had

a history of mental illness, had a nervous breakdown, kidnapped you, and then crashed the car with you inside it."

"That's awful!"

"It is," my dad says. "So you can understand why Raquel might be traumatized by something like this. She's had a hard enough time thinking you're dead."

"And now she'll learn I'm alive!" I shout-whisper. "It will make her happy, because it is the opposite of what's been making her sad! This might be my only chance to see her!"

My dad shoves the vial and syringe into my hand. "Go hide in your bedroom, and come out when I give a signal, all right?"

We hear the door from the garage to the house open, and Raquel's heels click-click-click into the kitchen. "Lyle?" she asks. "Are you in the bathroom?"

Her voice pulses with love even when she's not trying. It feels like home to me.

"Why can't I hide in here?" I whisper.

"Because," my dad whispers back, for some reason straightening his tie, "she might come up here before I've prepped her. Please, Dent. Go to your room and listen for a signal." He raises his voice and calls, "I'm coming down!"

"What exactly will this signal be?"

"You'll know it when you hear it," my dad says, striding confidently out of the room, his persona already recalibrated to Steady and Aloof.

I creep down the hallway to my bedroom. I don't know if I'm mentally prepared to go in there, especially if all of my stuff has been emptied out. But I'm relieved to see that it's exactly as I left it. Soccer trophies. Tiled bedspread. Blue Bronto.

"Hey, Blue," I say. "You happy dinosaur, you." I push away thoughts of my mom clutching her chest in a dirty subway car and walk to my closet. "My own clothes," I say. I exchange the loose-fitting Grateful Dead T-shirt and baggy pants lent to me by Brian for my favorite pair of jeans and a blue-and-red-striped T-shirt blessedly devoid of words. I'm back.

My dad and stepmother are talking, but of course all I hear is the muffled vibrations of human speech. I pop the vial of the superstrain virus and the syringe into my back pocket (don't worry, the syringe has a cover on it) and head out to the landing over the foyer, where I can actually hear what they're saying.

"How was book club?" my dad asks.

"Oh, fine," my stepmother says. "Everyone's still walking on eggshells with me, though."

"Sure," my dad says. "Of course."

"Theresa's the only one that speaks to me like a normal human being. 'Cause she gets it." I think she's referring to Theresa Miller, the mother of Ashley Miller, the girl in my class who died freshman year from a weird brain thing.

"Right," my father says. I keep expecting him to tack on a turkey gobble to the end of one of his sentences.

But he doesn't, and I don't think a signal's coming anytime soon. "Screw this," I say. I walk downstairs.

"Is someone here?" my stepmom says.

"Oh, um," my dad says. "There's, uh . . ."

"What? There's what? You're scaring me, Lyle."

"No, it's something good, but . . ."

"Hello?" my stepmom shouts. "Is someone here?"

"It's me, Mom," I say as I cross the foyer, just out of view of the kitchen.

I hear her gasp. I really don't want her to pass out when she sees me. Maybe that's just a movie thing anyway.

"Lyle . . . ," my stepmom says. "What— Do you . . . hear that, too?"

"It's Denton," my dad says.

I step into view.

My stepmom does not pass out.

She just slowly crumples to the floor, her eyes glued on me the whole time. "Who—who are you?" she stammers, her back to the cabinet that has all the casserole dishes in it.

"It's me, Mom. It's Denton. I'm alive." I want to reach out, but it seems like a bad moment for any sudden moves.

"Lyle, what is this?" my stepmom says, now slowly scooting along the cabinets away from me.

"It's, uh, a long story, Raquel," my father says, throwing a subtle look my way, like, *You should have waited for the signal.* "But it's Denton."

Her shock and confusion morph into anger. "Is this some kind of joke? That's not Denton. This boy has no hair."

"It's not a joke, Mom," I say. "I had to shave my head so no one would recognize me. I know it's hard to believe, but it's me."

"But you . . . ," she says, sitting near the fridge, her anger simmering down into something closer to hopefulness. "You died in that car accident. Didn't you die in that car accident?"

"I didn't, Mom. I didn't die." And then it's weird, but all of a sudden, tears are streaming down my face, and I'm a wobbly, unhinged mess. It's as if saying those words here, in the house I grew up in, to the parents I love so much, has released every emotion I've been holding on to these past weeks.

"Ohmigod. Denton," my stepmom says, sobbing, using the handle of the fridge to hoist herself back onto her feet before she grabs me into one of her patented Stepmama Bear hugs. "I felt you were still alive," she says. "I thought it was just wishful thinking. I thought I was going crazy, but I should have trusted my instincts. A mother knows."

"It's good to be home," I say, crying into her shoulder.

This is my mom.

Yes, Cheryl gave birth to me, and I'm so happy I got to know her, but she was never really my mother.

"Everything's going to be okay," my stepmom says, rubbing my back. "I promise."

"Oh," my dad says. "Dent, you should go."

"Huh?" I say, following my dad's gaze out the front window of the family room, where I'm pretty certain the hulking body of my old friend HorribleCop is walking up our driveway. A chill plummets down my spine.

"What?" my mother says, shifting within seconds from doting to ferocious. "Oh no, we're not playing this game again. Those cops can go screw themselves. They're not taking my son for the second time."

"No, it's more complicated than that, Mom," I say, my

fight-or-flight response already firmly fixed on the latter. "Look, I have to go, but don't worry, okay?"

"No," my stepmom says, her voice trembling. "Don't put me through this again."

"He doesn't have a choice, Raquel," my dad says.

Her head spins toward him, all of her fear bubbling up into anger. "Did you know about this, Lyle? Did you know our son was alive?"

She's completely in the right on this one, but I don't have time to watch this shit show play out. "Mom, Dad did know," I say, talking as fast as I possibly can, "and he really messed up by not telling you, but go easy on him. I'm sure he'll explain everything. At least I hope he will." I look to my dad, who nods. It's so painful to know it might be a long time before I see them again. "Thanks for everything, Dad. Really. I love you."

"Love you, too, Denton," my dad says. "Good luck."

The doorbell rings. I need to get out of here.

"And, Mom, just know that so much of who I am is because of you. I love you, and I feel so lucky you're my mom."

"Denton," she says, her arms reaching out for me.

"I'll see you soon," I say, racing through the laundry nook. "Or I'll try anyway." Just as the doorbell rings a second time, I'm out the back door, carefully dodging the barbecue grill.

I need to get out of sight, and that chain-link fence at the back of our yard is too exposed. I stare at the solid wooden fence that separates our yard from the Morenos'.

After checking that the vial and syringe are secure in my pocket, I try to scramble up the fence while making as little noise as possible. I hold on to the top of one of the pickets, and at least four splinters jam themselves into my palm. I slowly walk my feet up the fence until I reach the top and can vault my legs over. My right leg gets scraped on the tip of the picket, but I make it.

I'm greeted by a ferocious yapping. "Shhhh!" I say as Lucy, the Morenos' hyperactive American hairless terrier, jumps all over me. "Chill out, Lucy, please. Tsss!" I try my best to imitate the Dog Whisperer.

I hear the back door of my house open on the other side of the wooden fence. Somebody steps outside.

"That you, Dinton?" I hear the voice of HorribleCop ask.

I freeze. I try not to breathe.

"Hmm," he says.

Then I hear the back door close.

Time to leave.

But the ominous sound of car doors opening in front of the house means I can't go that way. Lucy is yipping, and my brain is spinning. I refuse to just stay in this yard, waiting for the DIA to find me.

An option occurs to me, but . . . well, screw it. Desperate times and all that.

I creep to the fence on the other side of the Morenos' yard and start the journey toward the closest place I can think of to hide.

THIRTY-FIVE

Millie pulls me inside as soon as she sees me on the deck, tapping at her back door. "Hey," she says.

"Hey," I say, out of breath from vaulting the fences of six yards to get to hers. I know it's risky to be here, seeing as tailing Millie was how the DIA found my mom's apartment, but I'm banking on the fact that Paolo's mom was the one behind that. And she's on my side now.

"I thought you might be around," she says. "I saw the Escalade parade they're throwing in your honor."

"Yeah, nice, right? I was so touched. They really captured the essence of what I'm all about."

"Absolutely. Ominous, intimidating, no fun at all . . ." Millie grins at me, and I can't help but grin back. Her dark hair's in a ponytail, and she's wearing pajamas that feature a pattern of square-chinned cops chasing bandits holding moneybags.

"Yeah," I say. "So, uh, as you can imagine from what's

happening outside, it's been kind of an insane past few days. And I might need your help. Or just, like, to stay here for a little bit. If that's all right."

"No, I'm sorry," she says, frowning. "You can't stay. Because I said I had a crush on you, and you were like, *No thanks, not interested.*"

"Oh. I mean, that's not—"

"I'm kidding," Millie says, her frown flipped back up to a small smile. "Follow me, please."

"Oh." I look around at the family room, tastefully furnished with lots of marble, and this house starts coming back to me. It's like rewatching a movie you forgot existed and realizing you know most of the lines. The first time I was here was many years ago, immediately after the neighborhood funeral of Fog. Millie had been so impressed with the poignant eulogy I delivered for that sweet frog she asked me to come over and say it again.

She led me up to her room, and I still remember the bubble of anticipation in my six-year-old heart just before we crossed the threshold, as this was going to be the first time I'd get to see what a *girl's* room looked like.

As it turned out, Millie's room wasn't the revelation I was expecting. "Your walls are blue," I said, equal parts puzzled and disappointed.

"I like blue," she said.

"Oh. Do you have any dolls or anything?" I asked, desperate for some confirmation that my girl's-room expectations were accurate.

"I have one doll," Millie said, putting her full body weight into pushing aside her closet door, like it was the entrance to a castle. "Here," she said, handing me a huge rubber figurine of a big-bellied man with a mustache and an apron.

"This is not a doll," I said.

"He's a butcher," Millie said. "He cuts up meat."

"Oh," I said.

"His name is Robert."

The whole thing threw me, and when I said my eulogy again, my sneakers digging into the thick white carpet, it didn't have quite the same pizzazz as the first time around.

Millie is once again leading me up to her room, and my heart is again bubbling up with, maybe not anticipation, but something. I wish it wasn't.

The walls of her room are still blue.

Millie closes the door.

"I'm doing that so we have privacy as we speak about these highly confidential matters," she says. "I'm not expecting us to make out or anything. Just so we're clear."

"Oh sure," I say, once again at sea in the middle of the white carpet. "That's smart."

Millie lights a candle on her dresser with one of those long plastic kitchen lighters. "Again, not trying to set a mood or anything," she says. "Candles make me less anxious."

"I didn't know you get anxious," I say. The candle fragrance batters my olfactory glands. "What exactly is that?"

"Wasabi," Millie says. "I got it online. I think I love it."

I do not. The room smells of burnt wasabi.

Millie sits down in a purple wooden rocking chair in the corner of the room. I sit down on the floor.

"You can sit on the bed if you want," Millie says. "It won't bite."

"That's okay," I say, staring up at her. "I'm good down here."

Millie rocks, and I listen to the ticking of the cartoon dog clock above her dresser.

"I'm surprised to see you," she says.

"Yeah, you seem it," I say.

"Are you being sarcastic?"

"I am."

"My face doesn't always register surprise," she says. "But inside I'm like, *Whaaaa?*"

"My insides have been like, *Whaaaa?* for the past month," I say.

"You saved that man," Millie says. "In Brooklyn."

"I did," I say. And it all pours out of me. How I saved Miguel, how they found the location of my mom's apartment by trailing Millie, how my mom and Dane escaped, how I was caught, how Karen Corrigan wanted me to save her, how I told Paolo's mom about that, how we escaped, how I found out my mom is dead and my dad created the virus, and how I have something that can save Paolo.

Millie slowly slides off the rocking chair and sits down on the carpet across from me. "That's a lot of things," she says.

"I know."

"I'm sorry about your mom. She was cool."

"Thanks," I say.

"And I'm sorry they found the apartment because of me."

"It's not your fault." I take the vial out of my pocket and hold it up, my attempt at a subject change. "Look.

Turns out my dad created a separate strain of the virus, even more powerful."

"That's scary."

"I know. If I inject it into Paolo, I think he'll live."

"Wow," Millie says. "But agents are swarming his house, too. We thought it was because they were waiting for you to show up there, but it must also be for Paolo's mom."

"Oh man," I say. "I don't know how we're gonna do this. There's already all those agents and cops out there, and I'm sure Karen Corrigan is in town so she can force me to save her. She knows I want to save Paolo, so she'll have people all over him."

"So we'll wait."

"What?"

"Her deathdate is tomorrow, right?" Millie asks.

"It is."

"So she'll be dead by the end of the day. Then I'll go to Paolo's and inject him with that. Easy."

"Wow. That's kind of dark, but, yeah, good plan. Except I want to be the one to inject him."

Millie stares at me. "Seems like that might be kind of dangerous, though, right? Since they're trying to get you and everything . . . ?"

"I don't care," I say, and I mean it. "I don't know for sure that this thing my dad gave me is even going to work, so this might be my last chance ever to see Paolo. I have to take it."

"Okay." She nods like she totally gets it, which I appreciate since it isn't fully rational. "You can stay here until tomorrow night if you want. My parents are always working or going to world-music concerts, so they probably won't even realize."

"Thanks, Millie," I say. I notice for the first time that her brown eyes are flecked with dots of gold. "How, uh, how is Paolo doing?"

"Oh," she says, uncrossing her legs and extending them out to the side. "Bad. Horrible, actually."

"Are you being funny?"

"I am not."

"Oh man," I whisper. I clasp my fingers together until the intra-digit webbing hurts.

"We've hung out, but I think it's hard for him to see me. Because he knows I like you more than him. Which I'm sure hurts, but then it also reminds him that he probably will never see you again. And that the last time he did, he was so upset at you."

"Oh man," I say again.

"He's been smoking a lot of pot."

"Maybe you can have him come over here tomorrow before his funeral. And I'll inject him with the virus then?"

Millie raises an eyebrow.

"Yeah, no, that's probably impossible. What with all the federal agents hovering around and everything."

We're silent for a few moments. I stare up at Millie's bookshelf. There are lots of books by Margaret Atwood.

"So . . . ," Millie says. "As far as sleeping goes, you can do a sleeping bag in here if you want, but there's also a couch in the basement. Which might be a better hiding spot."

I'm confused and upset with myself for how much I'd like to pick the sleeping bag option. "Yeah, the basement sounds good. I'll do that."

Once we're down there, Millie hands me all the sleep stuff. "Thanks," I say as the backs of my fingers brush against her palms.

"Anytime," she says. She nods and starts walking up the stairs.

"Hey, Millie," I say. "I'm really sorry you got pulled into all this."

"I'm not," she says without looking back.

The door closes, and I'm alone in Millie Pfefferkorn's basement, waiting for a horrible lady to die so I can save my best friend's life.

THIRTY-SIX

"I could come, too," I say. "I mean, I'm already disguised, with my shaved head and everything."

"That's a terrible idea," Millie says. She's wearing a black-and-yellow-striped dress and dangling skull earrings. She is very pretty.

"But it's my best friend's funeral," I say. "I feel like I should be there. What if this virus thing doesn't work and Paolo dies? I'm gonna carry that around for the rest of my life."

"Yes, but what if you go to his funeral and get taken away and never get to inject him with the virus thing at all? And then the DIA steals the vial and uses it for evil? And also kills you in your sleep like they did that Brooklyn man? That will be even less fun to carry around for the rest of your life."

"Well, I'll be dead, so."

"That's true. So maybe you should come to the funeral."

Millie and I decided she shouldn't tell Paolo that I'm here, because it would be too risky if someone like Karen Corrigan starts interrogating him; the less he knows, the better. (Look at me. Maybe I am my mother and father's son after all.) The unspoken part being, of course, that it also might make Paolo feel like complete shit to know I'm here in Millie's house.

His funeral was supposed to be at the Phillips Family Celebration Home, the same place where mine was, but now that everyone thinks Paolo's mom is a deranged lunatic who kidnapped me, Don Phillips didn't want to be associated with her or her family and refused to host it. Instead, Veronica was able to book the VFW hall on Main Street. It's smaller than the celebration home and a few notches lower on the classy spectrum. Paolo's goodbye to the world has been downgraded, and it's my fault.

And it sucks that I can't be there.

"Don't worry. I'll do some videoing," Millie says. "I'm a really good DP. You'll feel like you were there."

"All right," I say. "I'll stay down here and feel horrible about myself."

"Have fun with that." Millie grins, heads up the stairs, and leaves.

"I don't think you want to see this footage," Millie says, holding out her iPhone.

"You crazy? Of course I do."

She just got back. It's almost dark, and I've been going

out of my mind all day. You'd think by now I would have mastered being holed up in a room, but no.

"Well. Here goes nothing. . . ."

The video starts with a shot of Veronica in a dark gray dress, shouting into a microphone. My stomach jolts, as it tends to do whenever I see her.

"I started filming in the middle of her eulogy," Millie says, "right when she started yelling at the DIA agents standing in the back. It was pretty awesome."

I'm not happy that agents were there, but at least I feel justified in my decision not to go.

"It's my baby brother's funeral, all right?" Veronica is saying. "If you're going to stand here on your official business or whatever, at least have the decency to not be talking on your earpieces during the eulogies. And don't just stand there silently like jerks either. Clap along with everyone else! Are you even human beings? My brother is going to *die,* and you're . . ." Veronica stops speaking, I think, because she's overwhelmed by emotion.

"Look, my brother is going to come up here in a minute to speak for himself, and no matter who you are, if you are in this room, you better be celebrating him and his life. And laughing at every one of his jokes! You understand me?"

There's some clapping and cheering from the crowd.

"P, you know I love you so much." Veronica's crying now. It gets me tearing up, too, because it's such a rare sight. And because it's terrible to know all this happened without me there. And because what if my dad's virus doesn't work? "No one has a bigger heart than you, and no one's funnier than you, and I don't know how I'm going to go on without you. I really don't. But get up here. Please, *everybody,* let's give a big hand to my brother, Paolo Diaz!"

Paolo rises from his seat to nice applause. He's in a red suit, which is what he's been planning to wear to his funeral since freshman year. It's so good to see him.

As he arrives at the mic stand, he gives Veronica a sloppy hug, then trips over himself, and it becomes obvious that he's pretty drunk. Maybe high, too. He grabs the microphone before he speaks, a seasick man on the upper deck hanging on to the rail. "That was so sweet, V," he says, his mouth pressed up against the microphone head. "Everybody, let's give my sister a . . ." He doesn't finish his sentence. His eyes close, and he starts breathing deeply. It reverberates over the sound system.

Then his head snaps up, as if he's just been awakened by an alarm that only he can hear. "Hey, you guys!" he shouts. "Thanks for being here, people. I have to say, this is not a very encouraging turnout. Where the hell is everybody? Even my *mom* isn't here."

"You can't fully see, but it's not all that crowded," Millie says. "Between people hating his mom now and it being Senior Week, it was a perfect storm for low attendance."

"That's terrible."

Paolo continues his semi-aggressive self-eulogy, mumbling a lot of non sequiturs.

"This is hard to watch," I say.

"You think?" Millie says.

Paolo takes the mic off its stand and staggers around like a stand-up comedian, specifically one who seems unconfident and makes the audience feel uncomfortable.

"I thought this funeral thing would be sorta fun," he

says. "But so far, I hate it. I hate having a funeral! I. Do. Not. Like. It. Anybody wanna trade spots with me?"

He goes on for a little longer like this, then requests that somebody cue the music. As a song starts playing, Paolo dances across the stage like a free spirit at Woodstock. He begins to sing, accompanied by a track with backup singers but no lead. "Hey, hey, hey, hey," Paolo sing-speaks, vulnerable and ridiculous. "Won't you . . . come see about me? I'll be alone, dancing, you know it, baby."

"Oh no," I say. "He's karaoking that song from *The Breakfast Club*. Just like he said he would."

"Don't you forget about me," Paolo screeches, right before he freezes.

"I had to stop there," Millie says. "It didn't seem fair to keep filming."

I lean back on the couch in Millie's basement, trying to process what I just saw. "That was a mess."

"It was not good, no. He was starting to sober up by the time I said bye an hour ago. He felt terrible about everything. He's hoping he lives until graduation tomorrow so he can go there and make things right with a better speech."

"Oh right," I say. "Graduation is tomorrow."

"It is. And he will live until then. Because you're going to save him. Very soon."

"Yeah. Yeah, I will. And Cynthia wasn't there at all?"

"Paolo's mom? Nah. He was bummed."

"Shit." I wonder where she is.

"That Karen Corrigan woman was there, though. Standing in the back, saying that her people had to find you, that there wasn't much time left."

"That's terrifying."

"It was. But she'll be dead soon. If she isn't already." Millie takes out her dangly skull earrings as she's speaking.

"Yeah, guess you're right." I have to remind myself that if I save her, I can't save Paolo. Also that she's already lived a long life and is horrible.

A couple of hours later, it's 11:14 p.m., and Millie and I have talked out a plan. It doesn't seem foolproof, but it's the best we can do. And go-time is any minute, carefully calculated so I arrive at Paolo's right before midnight, the start of his deathdate.

I pace around the family room. "All right. We're gonna do this. We're gonna save Paolo."

"HEY!" Millie shouts into my face, startling the crap out of me.

"Ohmigod," I say. "Why did you do that?"

"Because you sound unsure of yourself, and I don't understand why. I watched you say things during your self-eulogy that people go their whole lives without saying, calling out all the people who genuinely suck. I watched you walk outside to stand on your front lawn in front of a very large gun."

"I did those things because I thought I would be dead soon," I argue.

"You don't know. You might still be dead soon. Me, too! And anyways, I'm not done with my list yet," Millie says. "I watched you commit to some off-the-wall mission because you thought it might help save your best friend's life. You're, like, the bravest person I know, Dent."

I still think that's a misguided assessment, but her words have served their purpose. I am ready. "Thanks, Millie," I say. "You've been so awesome during all of this. I really appre—"

Before I understand what's happening, Millie is kissing me.

It is very surprising.

And very wrong.

But maybe also the tiniest bit right.

Her lips are soft.

But as soon as that thought has popped into my head, it feels even more wrong.

I pull away.

"Whoa," I say, looking into her big brown eyes. "I don't—I mean, we can't. Do that. Especially not now. Paolo's about to die."

"Well," Millie says, staring down and chewing on her lower lip.

"It's not—" I don't have any words because I'm a little disconcerted at how much I enjoyed that. "I mean, you really know how to get around, Millie." Believe it or not, that was an attempt at defusing the situation with my classic brand of humor. Awful, I know.

"Don't say that," Millie says, her wet eyes meeting mine, radiating fury and heartbreak in a way I've never seen from her before.

"Yeah, I'm sorry, that was not—that didn't come out right. It's just that Paolo . . . He's my best friend, and he's really, really into you."

"Right," Millie says. "But I didn't choose Paolo. He chose me." She swipes tears off her cheek.

"Yeah," I say.

"I would choose you."

So don't know what to say here.

"And . . . you lived. Never in a trillion years would I have seen *that* coming." Millie simultaneously shrugs and raises her eyebrows. I'm holding strong, but I can't help noticing it's adorable. "And if that crazy, one-in-a-trillion, fateful thing has happened, how can I not try and kiss you? Sorry if I weirded you out."

"No, it was . . . I mean, you're right. We could both die at any moment. I think it's so cool that you did that. I just—"

"I'm going to ask you something," Millie says. "Is that all right?"

"I mean . . ." I'm thinking things are about to get more uncomfortable. "I guess so."

"If Paolo didn't have a thing for me, or whatever . . . would you ever pick me?" She looks down as she asks, her checkered Vans pointing inward.

"But he *does,* Millie—"

"But if he didn't." She looks back up at me. I know it's taking every ounce of courage she has.

"If Paolo didn't have a thing for you . . . ," I say. It's hard to answer this question, knowing that we are minutes away from Paolo's deathdate. It all feels like a betrayal. But I also hear Paolo's voice in my head telling me to *own that shit,* and I hear my voice in my head telling me to *be real,* and I know what to say. "Then it's possible I would like to kiss you again, Millie. Yes."

"Yeah, I thought so," Millie says. She gives me one of her patented subtle grins, and the back of my neck gets a little tingly. I smile back.

"Sidenote," I say. "Are you wearing, like, bacon-flavored lip gloss?"

"I am."

"That's amazing." We stand in the moment a while longer, not saying anything. I try to imagine what going on a date with Millie would be like. Probably pretty weird. But maybe pretty great, too. Life is funny.

"It's eleven-nineteen," Millie says finally, glancing down at her big yellow digital wristwatch.

"Okay," I say. "So, shall we . . . ?"

"Yeah," she says. "Let's." She holds up her hand for a high five.

"Oh, all right, we doing that? Sure." I high-five her. She sits down on the couch, her laptop on her lap.

She looks up at me. "Man your station, Dent."

"Right," I say. I go stand by the window. "Let's save Paolo."

Millie pulls up a website that allows you to make phone calls without revealing your location and types in some numbers, and we're off to the races.

"Marstin Police Department," a tinny voice says through her computer speaker.

"Yes, hello, sir," Millie says. "I saw a guy, looked to be about eighteen years old, with blond hair and black glasses, trespassing over the fence of Corgent Labs on Reid Hill Road. Thought you should know."

We thought a break-in to the lab would be a nice touch, like I'm searching for some chemical I need for the virus or something.

"Thanks for the tip. We do appreciate that. Can I get your name?"

"I don't really want to get involved. I just thought you should check it out."

Millie clicks off and shuts her laptop.

"Well, that was simple enough," I say. I hover by the window, peeking outside at the line of vehicles that's grown even larger than it was when I got here last night.

None of the vehicles move.

Three minutes pass. Still nothing.

"Shit, what if this doesn't work?"

"You are not a patient person," Millie says.

And right as she finishes her sentence, one of the black Escalades revs up and drives away, followed by one of the cop cars, which turns its siren on, followed by three other Escalades in quick succession.

"Oh wow," I say. "It worked."

Only a few cars remain on the street, and they're all farther down, parked in front of my house.

"You should go," Millie says.

"All right, um, yes. I'll see you, well, I'll see you soon, I hope."

"Bye, Denton."

"Bye, Millie."

I run out the back door, across the deck, and down the three stairs into the grass, where, just as Millie said, her purple, mangled bike lies on the ground. I creep it along the side of the house, feeling paranoid that I'll be spotted. I pat my pocket to make sure I've got the vial and syringe, hop on, and start biking away.

Hang tight, Pow. I'll be there soon.

THIRTY-SEVEN

I am immediately questioning this plan. Besides the fact that I am not a bike person, the bike is in fairly horrible shape from when I hit it with my car, so it's all slow and wobbly. For a moment, I'm less concerned with being caught by the DIA and more generally embarrassed to be seen like this.

But after eleven minutes of awkward cycling, I start to get a better feel.

The wind blows in my ears as I bike down Sterrick Road. I experience the strangest echoes of my past, remembering that this is the very street where I collided into this very bike, sending Millie careening onto the side of the road.

The sky lights up, and seconds later, a huge thunderclap explodes.

I had no idea it was supposed to storm tonight. I pedal faster.

On the street in front of Paolo's house, there are a

number of cars, but the ones that stand out are two black Escalades and a police car. I hop off Millie's bike and ditch it on a lawn five houses away.

I stealth-walk into that house's backyard and find what I'm looking for.

W-Town. The huge patch of woods behind Paolo's house, where he and I would hang out, extends all the way down the block, meaning I should theoretically be able to walk all the way to Paolo's backyard by way of these woods. Perfect.

I step between big-ass trees into the darkness of W-Town. Sometimes Paolo and I would take hikes through this swath of suburban wildlife to make ourselves feel manly and outdoorsy. You'd think that as a result I would have some familiarity with the paths I'm staring at now, but I really don't. Maybe that's because these hikes would last about fifteen minutes before one of us would get creeped out (usually me) and force us to go back.

It's dark in here, and the moon isn't very helpful, obscured as it is by thunderclouds. As if the universe has heard my thoughts, the world lights up again, followed by more insane rumbling, this time just a second later. It makes me jump, and when I land, my foot is immersed in water.

"Oh ball sack," I say. I just stepped into Shit's Creek, which is what Paolo and I call this two-foot-wide stream of murk that runs through the entirety of W-Town. I step back out onto dry land and kick my foot into the air twenty times in a row, then rub my sneaker on some rocks. It doesn't help.

I walk onward, my right foot making an audible squish with every step I take.

Finally, I arrive at the small patch of W-Town real estate that feels like home. There's the tree with the V-shaped intersection of branches that Paolo always enjoyed balancing his leg on. There's the tiny clearing of pine needles where Paolo and I once housed an entire package of Rainbow Chips Deluxe. And there, a little ways past me, is where Veronica took off her pants and got down on her knees to examine my torso.

I get sort of aroused thinking about it, which is both confusing and completely unhelpful at the moment. Not now, little Denton.

I creep slowly out of the woods, twigs crackling underneath me, until I reach the edge of the grass where Paolo's backyard begins. I perk up my ears, listening for any sounds from inside the house or from the cars in front of it, but I come up empty. I don't have time to linger in the woods, waiting and hoping that Paolo might walk out here. I get down on all fours and make my way through the grass. Even that feels a hair too conspicuous, so I shift into an army crawl, my elbows and knees propelling me forward. I make sure to stay off to the side, mostly out of view of the sliding glass doors that lead from Paolo's back patio into the kitchen.

I'm wondering who's in there right now for his Sitting. I'm guessing Veronica, but who else? Paolo's always bemoaned his lack of an extended family. Since his dad left so many years ago, before he was even born, there's no connection to any relatives on that side. And Paolo's mom has two brothers, but they both live in Puerto Rico with their wives and kids. Plus, as we now know, she's a top-secret operative, so cutting off all personal ties might have been part of her whole deal. I hope Paolo's at least having a nice time.

I smack at my calf, where a mosquito has stopped for a drink. Lying in the grass like this, I feel like there are bugs all over me. It's not my favorite.

I want to be prepared, so I rearrange my body in the grass and grab the vial and syringe out of my pocket.

A car drives up to the front of Paolo's house. Its engine pings and sputters even after the car's been turned off. It inspires me to work faster, as I'm reminded there are many people out there trying to get me and one could show up at any time.

I take the cover off the syringe with my teeth and spit it into the grass. Pretty badass. I flip the vial upside down and fumble with the syringe, finally sticking it in and pulling down to fill it up. I hope I'm doing this right.

A car door slams. I try to identify the person from their walk before they go inside. But then I hear the grass rustling along the side of the house and realize that whoever it is has, for some reason, decided to enter the house through the back. Very possibly because they know I'm here.

I hold the syringe at my side, cram the empty vial back into my pocket, and begin a ridiculous backward army crawl, hoping to blend in with some of the tree shadows at the edge of the yard. I stop once I recognize who the mystery person is and realize it's highly unlikely that said person will notice me.

It's everyone's favorite dreadlocked doofus, Willis Ellis. The classmate of mine voted by fate as Most Likely to Kill Me (Assuming My Dad Hasn't Created a

Deathdate-Nullifying Virus That Was Injected into Me by My Mother).

He's got one earbud in as he stares down at his phone. He strides toward the glass doors, which slide open to reveal Paolo. I resist the urge to call out to my best friend in the world.

"Yo, ChillisWillis," Paolo says quietly. "Thanks for coming on such short notice."

"Aw, dude, of course," Willis says, a little louder than normal human volume.

"Shhh," Paolo says, looking around. "Try not to draw too much attention to our illegal activities."

"Oh cool, sorry."

Something loud and buzzy flies by my head, but I keep still.

"You got the stuff?" Paolo asks.

"Yessir," Willis says, taking a baggie out of his back pocket and handing it over.

"How much?"

"On the house, my man," Willis says. "It's my Dying Client Special."

"That's bleak, bro. But sweet, thanks." Paolo smells the bag. "That's nice."

"Saved my best stuff for you."

"You're the best, Willis. I gotta get back inside, but, you know, have a spectacular life, my friend."

"Aw, shit, dude, this is so rough, you know?" Willis says. "First we lose Dent, now you. I'm really sad about it."

"Yeah," Paolo says, nodding a couple of times, seeming to get more bummed now that he's been reminded of me. "Thanks, bud. I am, too."

Willis exhales loudly, like he's really going through something, then shakes it off, pops the other earbud in, and saunters back around the side of the house.

Paolo stands alone and stares out into the night sky. He sniffs his bag of pot again and sighs.

This is my moment. I get to my feet, the syringe shaking in my hand, and scurry over to Paolo. I'd been thinking so hard about *when* I should inject him with the superstrain that I hadn't really considered *how* I should be injecting it. Or *where*.

"Pow," I say.

"Ha?" he says, startled and looking all around. He sees me, and his face moves from fear to astonishment to joy in the span of seconds. "D! Jumpin' jigowatts, you made it!"

"I'm sorry about this," I say. Paolo's about to give me a hug, but I raise the syringe and plunge it directly into his right thigh. That's where my splotch started, so I figure it's as good a place as any.

"Yeeeowwwww!" Paolo says, sounding exactly like an injured cartoon character. "Why did you do that?" he shout-whispers. I empty the syringe, pull it out, and drop it into the grass, which is kind of gross, but I've got bigger things to think about.

"Shhh," I say, looking around, expecting DIA agents to appear from anywhere at any moment. "Get down and follow me."

"Don't get me wrong—I'm superhappy to see you," Paolo says as we army-crawl side by side through his backyard, "but that really hurt. And I hope that wasn't hard drugs, because after much contemplation, I decided I'm going strictly Mary Jane for my death."

"It wasn't hard drugs," I say when we've finally arrived at a spot far enough out in the yard to seem less conspicuous, "and I'm proud of you for deciding that."

"Thanks, man."

"So, this is gonna sound nuts, but I just injected you with a superstrain of the virus."

"Wait, what?" Paolo asks. "*The* virus?"

"My dad gave it to me. Turns out he's the one that made the virus in the first place. And he said it doesn't matter if you're immune to the other strain, because this one is different. And stronger."

Paolo looks like he's stopped breathing. "Are you—are you messing with me right now?"

"I am a billion percent not messing with you."

"So you're saying I'm gonna . . . ?"

"The virus should be invading all of your cells, altering your DNA as we speak. Meaning, yes, you're gonna live."

I'm expecting Paolo to freak out or say something goofily triumphant, but instead he buries his face in the grass. I can't tell what's happening. "Pow," I say. "Are you okay?"

His body's shaking slightly, and I realize he's crying.

"I knew you'd save me, Dent," he says, lifting his head up and looking at me. "I'm gonna live. Because of you." He gives me a ground hug, wrapping his arm around my shoulders.

"I did exactly what you would have done for me," I say. "Not even, because you probably would have found a solution sooner."

"I don't know. You just injected me with a *superstrain*! That is so awesome!" I stare at him, wondering when the splotch is going to kick in—if it is, in fact, going to kick in. "Wait, so your *dad* made the virus?" he asks. "That is *effed up!*"

"Yeah, man, I know."

"Lyle, Lyle, gettin' all viral!"

"It's been a pretty effed-up week. And, look, I'm so sorry about how things went down the last time we saw each other. I feel terrible about that."

"Aw, Dent," Paolo says, propping his head up on one elbow like we're having pillow talk. "It's not your fault Millie's in love with you. Just sucks for me. But, honestly, I'm just so happy to see you. My mom came by two days ago, told me she helped you escape and that you were trying to find a way to save me."

"Yeah, your mom was incredible, Pow. She head-butted some dude."

"Oh cool! She didn't tell me that! She's so modest."

"It was really something."

"Cynthia, man, coming through in the clutch. I'm so proud." Paolo plucks at random blades of grass. "But then she had to leave, because she said the government was on her tail. She said she'd be back, but she obviously isn't yet. And I wasn't hearing anything from you either. So I was starting to lose hope."

The sky flashes, followed immediately by a huge boom.

Both of us startle—spaz out for a second.

"Whoa, baby," Paolo says.

I don't respond, because I'm too busy looking at the purple splotch with red dots that is rocketing up Paolo's neck.

"You okay?" Paolo asks. The splotch covers his face

and ears. It's moving way faster than mine ever did. "That thunder really shook you up, huh?"

"No," I say. "It's working."

"What is?" he asks. He follows my eyes down into the grass, where his arms and hands are purple with red dots, too.

"Oh Lordy," he says, slowly getting to his knees as he stares at his outstretched arms. "The red dots! I HAVE THE RED DOTS!"

I can't believe it worked.

Paolo raises his arms to the heavens. "SUPER-STRAIN!!!"

Not four seconds later, the sky opens up and rain starts coming down in sheets, so hard I can barely see Paolo. And yet I *am* able to see the back door of his house open. Agent Fields and two other agents step out, look around, and then stare right at us.

Paolo shouldn't have been so loud. I don't blame him; it was an exciting moment. But now we're going to have to run.

"They see us," I say, trying to shout over the downpour but not so loud that anyone else hears. "Let's go into W-Town."

"Okay, duder!" Paolo and I run for the woods. We hear the unmistakable sound of feet sprinting into the backyard behind us. "I forgot those agents were still lurking around!" he says.

"It's all good!" I shout as we pass from grass into trees. "We're actually right on schedule. The itinerary for today's events very clearly said, *TWELVE-OH-FIVE—DIA SHOWS UP TO ARREST US.*"

"You're pretty funny, you know that?" Paolo shouts. "Is that actually what time it is?"

"I don't know," I shout. "Maybe."

"Then it's officially my deathdate!"

"Hey, hey! Happy Deathday, buddy!"

We're blindly rushing between trees and dodging branches. My whole body is chilled, my shirt sticking to my body. The world illuminates again, this time accompanied by the hugest, most terrifying bang I've ever heard.

"Wow!" Paolo shouts. "That was incredibly loud, right?"

There's a sound like the combination of a Dumpster opening and a demon woman screaming. I'm about to say, *What is that?* when my peripheral vision catches a huge tree arcing downward toward us.

"POW! Heads up!"

"WHAT?"

I throw my arms around Paolo and tumble to the side, just barely getting both of us out of the way. We land on mud and rocks as the twenty-foot-long tree thumps down, spindly branches jutting out at scary angles.

"Holy shit, dude," Paolo says.

"Had to get you out of the way of the killy stuff," I say, out of breath. "They're gaining on us. Let's go."

"I'm afraid that won't be happening," a voice says, seemingly out of nowhere. Our heads snap to the right, and we see a horrible man step over the fallen tree trunk and walk toward us, his gun pointed in our direction.

THIRTY-EIGHT

"You must be real proud of yourself, huh?" Horrible-Cop says. His gun is pointed at my head. "Aren't you, DINTON? Outwitting all these bigwigs, thinking you're such a hotshot . . ."

I don't say anything.

"You let my sister die, you little shit!" The gun jolts as he says that, and I'm feeling like death could come at any moment. For me or Paolo. "Karen was a good person, and all she wanted was for you to give her your spit or whatever the hell it is you freaks do. Then I was gonna drive her off to Arizona, where she could start a new life. But that was too much to ask, huh?"

"I'm sorry for your loss," I say, trying to reason with a psycho. "But it's more complicated than that."

"You ain't sorry," HorribleCop says.

"What is he talking about, D?" Paolo asks.

"You shut up!" He shifts the gun a few inches toward

Paolo's head. "You're supposed to die today anyway," he says, "so this will work out fine. Two boys, dead according to plan. I don't care whether or not this is what the government wants for you, 'cause this is what *I* decide."

I feel Paolo shaking next to me.

"You don't want to do this," I say. "It won't bring her back."

"The hell I don't! Who wants to be first?" HorribleCop asks, shifting his gun between us. "Never mind. I'll pick." His gun lands on Paolo.

"NO!" I shout.

"Yes," HorribleCop says. "I choose yaaaarrrrrggghhh!"

I have no idea why he's gone full pirate until he falls to the ground.

Then I see Veronica behind him, holding her stun gun.

"V!" Paolo shouts.

"Come on, come on, we gotta go," she says. "There's more on the way."

Paolo and I are up on our feet and moving with Veronica away from HorribleCop, who's saying, "Gahhoooh," as he helplessly swings an arm at us. We sprint through the woods. I take a peek backward, and in the distance there are flashlights, lots of flashlights, slicing through the trees in pursuit.

"Go figure that when I finally use this thing, it's in my backyard," Veronica says. "Are you guys all right?"

"I mean, I think I might be traumatized, but it's nice to see you," Paolo says.

"I'm in a similar camp," I say.

The rain has slowed to a slight drizzle at this point. Veronica is leading us through the woods, dictating every turn. "Whoa, babe," Paolo says, trying to catch his breath. "It's almost like you know where you're going."

"I know you guys like to think this is your private secret spot or whatever, but I've been hanging out in these woods my whole life, too."

"Veronica," I say as we all skid down a small embankment, "I thought you were the one who gave up our location. I thought you were the spy."

"This might not be the best time to talk," she says. "There's a lot of people chasing us."

We run on. A sharp branch scrapes my thigh and cuts through my jeans.

"I know," I say. "But I wanted to say I'm so glad it wasn't you. Thanks for not giving me up to your mom."

"I can be a dick," Veronica says, "but I'm not a total dick. You're my friend, D. There's no way I was gonna let my mom and her cronies kill you."

Her use of the word *friend* is not lost on me.

"Hell yeah, V!" Paolo says, tripping over a root, then catching himself before he face-plants. "I'm proud of you, sister."

"Though I gotta ask," I say, knowing this truly isn't the best time but unable to help myself. "How come you never stayed long in the city? Like, why bother coming if . . . you know?"

"Good God, D," Veronica says. "Do we have to go over this again right now?"

"I kinda agree," Paolo says, narrowly ducking under a tree branch.

"I told you," she says. "I'm weird! I wanted to see you, but I didn't want to wake up and brush our teeth together and feel like we're in some kind of relationship or something. So I split, okay? But that wasn't because I was spying!"

So, once I survived, Veronica was still attracted to me but just couldn't really deal with the idea of us being together in any kind of committed way. I'll take that. "All right, cool. Sorry to be annoying."

"Apology not accepted," Veronica says.

The woods start thinning out, and we emerge onto a strip of pavement behind a huge, long building.

"Whoa," Paolo says. "W-Town connects to the back of Tensmore Shopping Center? What the hell?"

I am similarly shocked. Veronica is unfazed. "So, we can keep marveling at the geographical placement of this strip mall, or we can— Whoa." Her eyes get wider as she just now notices the color of Paolo's skin. "You got the rash. Does that mean . . . ?"

"Yep. Superstrain, babe," Paolo says. "You ain't getting rid of me that easy."

Veronica emits some kind of emotional squeal I've never heard from her before as she pulls Paolo into a tight hug.

"Love you, V," Paolo says.

"Love you more," Veronica says.

"Uh, we should probably keep running," I say, staring back into the woods, where the flashlights are getting closer.

"Shit," Veronica says, pulling out of the hug. "She's supposed to be here."

"Who?" I ask.

Veronica's looking all around the parking lot, a bundle of nerves. We hear footsteps approaching from the woods. "We have to run!" A second later, a minivan fish-tails around the corner of the shopping center and speeds toward us, stopping short at the last second.

"Get in!" my stepmom says from the driver's side window.

"Mom," I say. "How did you . . . ?"

The side door slides open, and Paolo's mom calls out, "Come on!"

Paolo, Veronica, and I get into the minivan and glide the door closed. My dad is in the front seat.

"Dad!" I shout. "It worked."

"That's great, Dent," he says, "but none of it matters if you get caught right now."

The minivan takes off, swerving around the shopping center, through the parking lot, and into the road.

"You had the minivan fixed," I say. "Looks great."

"Thanks, Dent," my stepmom says into the rearview. "It's good to see you, sweetheart."

"You too, Mom," I say. I'm tearing up, and I make no attempt to hide it. I look over to Paolo, who's staring at one purple hand in amazement while his mom clutches the other. "You all right over there?"

"I am so all right, dude," he says.

I lean my head back against my headrest. We got Paolo the virus. He's going to live. At least one more day anyway. I exhale. "So where are we going right now?" I ask.

My stepmom and father look at each other, then back to Paolo's mom.

"Um," my dad says. "We're not exactly sure yet, Denton."

"Oh," I say. "All right."

We keep driving.

THIRTY-NINE

Here's what you can expect to experience at your high school graduation:

You will arrive late. In a stretch limousine. This will not be some kind of ostentatious statement or joyride; rather, it will be the result of much discussion with your best friend, his sister/your sometimes lover, his mom, your stepmom, and your dad about the best way to make it to graduation without getting kidnapped by the government.

You will have spent a long night hashing everything out at the Econo Lodge (a location chosen both for its reasonable rates and the slim likelihood of running into anyone there). "It has to go public in a big way," your best friend's mom will have said, "or we're all screwed."

You will have seen your best friend, now purple and covered in red dots, start to say something in response to this and then stop, and you will have known he was about to make a joke involving the word *pubic* but then thought better of it.

Now you will stare out your tinted limo window, all of the aforementioned people spread out around you, as your restless legs butterfly in and out, in and out.

You will look at your best friend, sitting next to you, who is supposed to die today. Sure, he has the virus, but you will still be worried. "I'm not scared," he will say, as though he can hear your thoughts. "If I don't live through today, then it wasn't meant to be. And then I'll finally get to meet Marilyn Monroe, see if we're as compatible as I think we'll be. Either way, I feel good knowing I've got you here looking out for me." These words will not make you feel less nervous.

As the limo pulls into your high school's parking lot, you will experience a rush of memories: track meets, waiting for Taryn, cold hands around a hot chocolate, your classmates woofing as they rattle the bleachers with their feet. It will all seem so long ago.

You will file out of the limo. You will see eight news vans, logos of major channels on their sides. *They came,* you will think. *This might actually work.* You will head down to the football field, where the sound of a man's voice will reverberate through the speakers. He'll be giving a speech, peppered with tone-deaf old-man jokes ("When I was your age, I was thinking about two things: girls and sports"), and you and your best friend will simultaneously realize it's Harold of Harold's Bagels. This is worth repeating: the keynote speaker at your high school graduation will be Harold of Harold's Bagels.

You will stop at the side of the bleachers, out of view of the tightly packed masses, looking around for any ominous government presence. You will see your classmates sitting on the field in purple robes and caps. You will have forgotten that purple is one of your high school's colors. Of course it is. Your stepmom will be sticking to your side like a bodyguard, ferocious and focused, and you won't mind at all. "You sure you don't want to write down what you're going to say up there?" she will whisper, no doubt remembering your impromptu self-eulogy. You will tell her not to worry, that you've got this. But you will appreciate that she has your back.

Harold's speech will seem to be wrapping up, with a whopper of a bagel metaphor ("Your lives are going to be filled with variety—maybe some sesame seed, some poppy, perhaps some plain moments, too—but by the end hopefully you will have experienced a little of *everything*") and a closing offer of fifty percent off all bagels this week for MHS seniors. This will receive a huge response, because apparently your classmates love nothing more than a good deal on a bagel.

"Now!" your best friend's mom and your stepmom will say at the same time, the two of them serving as a human shield as you all rush down to the podium, right as Principal Barisch is announcing Lindsay Feldstein, the class valedictorian. Your stepmom and best friend's mom working together will strike you as remarkable, since, as recently as a few days ago, your stepmom believed that this other woman had kidnapped you and indirectly caused your death. *Life is unpredictable,* you will think to yourself, and this will remind you of what you want to say when you reach the microphone in approximately nineteen seconds. You and your best friend will cut ahead of Lindsay—who's completely confused by the sudden appearance of a purple

Paolo and a random dude with a shaved head—and stand at the podium, your mothers on either side of you.

Looking out at so many faces from the life you used to lead will give you a surge of energy, like the person you are now is fusing with the person you used to be, and you will think maybe everything is going to be all right.

This thought will be immediately followed by an overwhelming screeching from the PA system, as if the universe is saying, *Don't be so sure about that.* Everyone in the crowd will cover their ears until you adjust the microphone on the podium and the banshee squeal stops.

You will look to your best friend, who will be looking back at you with a *yeesh* face, perhaps also thinking that maybe this is all a Very Bad Idea.

Well, it's too late now. You will give your best friend the most confident nod you can muster: *Let's own this shit.*

A slow smile will spread on his face, like, *Oh, look how the student has become the teacher.*

You will raise your eyebrows, like, *Damn right I have, sucka.*

He will look at you, like, *Do you think we could get some of those half-price bagels right now? I'm hungry.*

You won't respond to that.

You will turn to the crowd, thinking, *All I have to do is be honest, and everyone will understand.*

While we're on the subject of honesty, I have to admit: I'll be very surprised if your high school graduation is anything like this.

I apologize for misleading you.

I put my hands on the podium and begin to speak.

FORTY

"Hey, everybody," I say. "I know this is a surprise, but, um, it's me, Denton Little." The crowd doesn't know how to respond—they look like they think this might be the start of some comedic skit intended to liven up the ceremony— but I hear a yelp from the rows of graduates behind me that I'm pretty sure is Taryn. "My deathdate was the same day as prom, but—"

"He didn't die!" Paolo shouts a little too loudly, so that the PA again emits that horrible screech until I shift the microphone. We're off to a strong start. "Sorry," Paolo says. "He didn't die. Is what I said."

The audience doesn't gasp exactly. They seem to be suspended in a state of confused murmuring.

"But today is Paolo's deathdate," I say. "You might notice he's purple with red dots, which, if you happened to see me at prom, is also how I looked. That's because of a virus that alters your DNA and nullifies your deathdate."

"Yeah, it nullifies it, people!" Paolo says, leaning into the mic excitedly.

I give him a look like, *Maybe let's not repeat what the other person just said?* and he nods a bunch, like, *Good point, good point.*

"So I lived," I say, and I notice out of the corner of my eye that at least three cameramen are set up near the bleachers, filming us. This is good. "And we're almost positive Paolo's going to live, too. But here's the thing: the government does not want you to know about this virus. There's a lot of money involved in the deathdate business, and us being alive compromises that, because it means the ATG kits aren't one hundred percent effective. I know that might sound crazy, but the reason my head is shaved, the reason I haven't been able to be here until now, is that I've been hiding out because the government has been trying to kidnap me.

"They say they just want to run some tests to see why I lived, but I think they really want me dead. . . ."

Maybe I need to redirect this speech so I sound less like a paranoid lunatic.

"Did you hear about that guy Miguel in Brooklyn who lived through his deathdate? But died the next day? Yeah, he lived because I gave him the virus. And I think he died because the DIA killed him."

Not sounding less paranoid.

"So if you hear in the next few days that it turns out it was some kind of mistake and we actually died, *do not believe it!*" Paolo says, coming to my rescue. "We've either been murdered or locked up, and it is not okay!"

I see a shift happening in the faces in the crowd, like

maybe they're starting to believe us. There are now at least ten cameras filming us, and I wonder if this is the kind of thing they'll show live or if they'll use the footage in a segment later tonight. Or if the DIA will try to crush the story altogether. It doesn't matter because my dad is also filming, with strict orders to post the video on YouTube and my Facebook Timeline and anywhere else he can as soon as Paolo and I finish speaking. I even showed him how to make a Vine edit. I had to explain how to do that, like, five times, but my fingers are crossed that the guy who created a way to avoid certain death will pull through on this one.

"I'm so happy to have lived through my deathdate," I say, "but I don't want to have to hide out or get a new identity or live in constant fear of being caught, unable to keep ties with everyone I love."

"Word," Paolo says. "What, I'm supposed to find a new 7-Eleven? With someone working the register who isn't Alexei? Not cool!"

"Alexei rules!" someone shouts out.

"Okay, jokes aside," I say, glancing at Paolo stony-eyed for a second, "we're hoping this moment, being in front of all of you, can be kind of a fresh start for us. You know, a chance to be born again."

"Not like born-again Christians, though," Paolo says.

"No," I say. "That's totally not what I meant." Lots of people in the bleachers are fanning themselves. "Not that we have any problem with born-again Christians."

"I love born-again Christians!" Paolo shouts.

"Absolutely," I say. I'm experiencing that familiar self-eulogy feeling of going off the rails. "I just meant, you know, that since we already had our deathdates—"

"Then this can be our new birthdate!" Paolo shouts.

"Yes! Right! And you, too, seniors. I mean, they don't call this graduation ceremony *commencement* for nothing, right? We all get to, you know, commence again. Well, start again."

"*Commence* is a weird word," Paolo says.

"It really is." I have no idea if the crowd is with us. I need to get us back on track. "It's actually kind of funny. When I gave the self-eulogy at my funeral, I sorta lost myself, said some ridiculous things, about life, about being real—"

"You said *penis*!" Paolo says.

"I even said *penis*," I agree. "But I don't regret it. Because the truth is, that was the most unpredictable I've been in my life. And it felt good. Life isn't supposed to be predictable. And maybe death isn't either."

"For example," Paolo says, "in the past three weeks, I fell in love! Whoa. Did *not* see that one coming! And then it turned out the girl I'm in love with is in love with this guy." This is not something we discussed putting in our speech. Nothing Paolo has said was discussed in our speech prep meeting. He throws his arm around me as some people in the crowd sympathetically *awww*. "Yeah, she's in love with my best friend. Can you believe it? It wasn't her fault or his fault, but it sucked, and I was really sad."

I see Millie out in the stands, and even from here, I can tell she's turning red.

"But then," Paolo continues, "I was like, *Wow, I've been in the world eighteen years, and I've never been in a love triangle, and now I get to be in one with two of my favorite people in the whole world. How awesome is that?*"

Only Paolo would come to this conclusion. I love him so much.

"And also," he continues, "I was feeling two things I'd never felt before in my whole life: true love and true heartbreak. And, sure, the second feeling sucked, but it was also *new.* And I thought, *How many other feelings are out there that I haven't experienced?* That made me really not want to die, because I want to experience them all: Sad! Happy! Jealous! Confused! Defeated! Triumphant! Disgusted! Superhorny!"

"Okay," I say, covering the microphone. "I think they get it." I hope footage of Paolo shouting *superhorny* makes the news.

"Wait, just one more," Paolo says. I reluctantly uncover the mic. "Happy!" he shouts.

"You said that one already."

"Oh, did I? Cool. Just wanted to make sure I got that in there."

There are at least twenty cameras filming us now.

"I'll add one more," I say. "Surprised. Because ever since I didn't die, I feel alive in a different way. I wake up every day not knowing if it might be my last. Not knowing what's going to happen. Not knowing who's going to piss me off or make me smile or break my heart. Not knowing what funny thing Paolo is going to say, or what annoying thing my parents are going to do, and whether that annoying thing is going to also end up being comforting, because my parents know me better than anyone else, and that's kind of amazing." Paolo's nodding, in all his purple-and-red glory, like I'm saying something really deep, which is encouraging. "Not knowing if I'm going to feel really alone or really insecure or really in pain, but knowing maybe that's okay, because the next day is a whole new opportunity to not know. To be surprised by life."

"It's kind of like at the end of *Thelma and Louise*," Paolo says, "when they're flying through the—"

I shake my head vigorously at him. He looks at me like, *No?* I shake my head. *No.*

The crowd is silent. It's time to bring this home.

"Look," I say. "The woman who gave birth to me thought it shouldn't be mandatory to know your deathdate. That's why this virus was created: to change the government's stance on deathdates. I don't really want to spend my life fighting that battle, but I think she had a point. It seems like you should get to choose. Because, I have to say, there's something surprisingly awesome about not knowing."

"Yeah," Paolo says, "here's your chance! This virus thing is totally contagious, if anybody wants some!"

I laugh. But the audience doesn't. It occurs to me that this is actually something we can offer. "Wait," I say. "I mean, seriously, if anybody does want to erase their deathdate, the virus transfers through saliva, so all you have to do is kiss Paolo. Or, you know, share a bottle of water with him."

Shocked murmurs ripple through the crowd.

"I would choose kissing," Paolo says.

"Maybe your deathdate is coming up," I say, gaining confidence with every word. "Getting this virus means you might live past that deathdate. Or, well, you might die even sooner. So you're taking a risk. But, in a way, your mind will be free from worry because every day could be your last."

"I'll do it," a voice says.

Paolo and I see freckly Danica Riegel, Paolo's most recent crush pre-Millie, standing up from the sea of purple graduates.

"Whoa, really?" Paolo says.

She walks down the aisle toward the podium, a look of determination on her face.

"Dani, no!" a voice shouts from the bleachers. It's a freckly woman, waving her arms frantically. Must be Danica's mom. "Please, think about this first! This is very dangerous!"

"Am I seriously gonna kiss her right now in front of everybody?" Paolo whispers off-mic.

"I have no idea," I say. "Maybe?"

Danica arrives at the podium and gives us hugs. "I'm so glad you're both alive," she says.

"You know it, girl," Paolo says.

"Thanks, Danica," I say. "So, you sure you want to do this?"

"I mean," she says into the mic. "I just . . . I think about it all the time. The day I'm going to die. And I don't want it taking up all that room in my head, affecting every decision I make, you know? So, yeah, I'm sure. If you are, Paolo."

He nods and shrugs. They move their mouths toward each other, then away, then toward each other again. It's awkward, and I'm thinking we've made a terrible mistake when suddenly Paolo and Danica are making out in front of everybody. It ramps up bizarrely fast from a small, chaste kiss into full-on tonguing, and I get the sense everyone's as shocked as me. But then some sitcom-style *oooooohs* turn into raucous shouts and applause. And Paolo and Danica are still making out.

Finally, they pull apart. They're both dazed, smiling at each other.

"Okay, then," I say into the microphone. "Well, that happened."

People cheer louder, and I see Lucinda Delgado coming down the aisle to go next. I can't even believe it, another one of Paolo's crushes. It occurs to me that maybe Paolo's had a crush on everybody.

"Anybody else that wants to be undated, feel free to get in line," I say. "Happy graduation. Have a great life and death, everybody!" I'm backing away from the mic, and I'm wishing we had brought candy to throw. I can't help but want to end on even more of an up note. "HALF-PRICE BAGELS!" I shout. I throw a hand in the air, and the crowd goes nuts, which I realize is also because Danica has turned purple with red dots.

Even though there's more ceremony left, one of the seniors gets overexcited and throws his cap into the air. A few others follow, and soon everyone's hurling up their graduation caps.

Principal Barisch pushes Paolo and me aside to get on the microphone. "It's too early for that," she says. "Please, don't throw your hats up yet! We still have to hear from our valedictorian, Lindsay Feldstein. Please." But it's no use. Even the high school marching band gets confused, breaking into a rousing number that I quickly realize is "Don't You Forget About Me" from *The Breakfast Club*.

I turn to Paolo, like, *Did you tell them to play that?* and he gives me one of his trademark eyebrow flicks, like, *Who else, baby?*

I stare out into the crowd, and my dad holds up his phone and gives me a thumbs-up. Something uncoils within me.

It's done.

Even if my dad messes up the upload, one of the thirty news cameras definitely got that on tape. And who wouldn't run the footage of that kiss? We're safe.

I give my dad a thumbs-up back, and I think about all the things I still want to ask him, all the conversations I want to have in the very near future.

My stepmom has been standing by my side this whole time, and now she pulls me in close, wrapping her arms around me. "I love you," she says. I try to say it back, but it doesn't make it past the lump in my throat.

"You did good, Denton," Paolo's mom says, tears in her eyes, too.

Meanwhile, Paolo is making out with Lucinda, and a line has formed. It includes three girls from our grade, two dudes (including Danny Delfino), and Ms. Donatella, the drama teacher.

I look back into the sea of purple robes, and without even meaning to, I catch the eye of my ex-girlfriend Taryn. I'm thinking maybe she's going to look pissed, but she doesn't. Her eyes twinkle, like, *I can't believe this.* I smile back, like, *Me neither.* She's holding hands with Rick Jackson, that football player who I'm sort of friends with, the guy who saved me at prom. It somehow makes sense.

Danica and Lucinda are both purple now, and they're

making out with other people and turning them purple, too. It's chaos.

In the bleachers, I see Veronica, in a gray T-shirt that has a hole in one sleeve, talking animatedly to Mrs. Lucevich, the high school art teacher. I'm too far away to hear what she's saying, but I know how it sounds: that unique combination of sarcasm and passion and intelligence that I've been captivated by since I was seven. I don't think she'll be my girlfriend anytime soon, which sucks. I do hope I know her until the day I die, though.

I feel a tap on my shoulder, and it's Millie, wearing the same adorable purple-and-yellow dress she wore to prom.

"Aloha," she says.

"Hey," I say.

"I think that was a success. Though what's happening right now is pretty much insane."

The sea of purple people in purple robes is growing wider. Danny Delfino and Andy Stetler are making out next to us. Danny is purple; Andy's splotch is forming before our eyes.

"I agree," I say. I like standing next to her. I can't see anything happening with us, because I don't think I could ever do that to Paolo, but considering he's behind us, furiously making out with yet another girl, who really knows?

"Fog would be proud," Millie says, giving me that tiny grin.

I'm about to grin back when a voice says, "Denton, hi," and I turn to see a woman holding a microphone in my face. "I'm Daisy Douglas, with ABC News. Your story is truly amazing. Now that you've lived, what are you going to do next?"

It's a good question.

At the moment, though, I'm way too overwhelmed to begin to answer it.

I mean, hopefully, I'll go to college.

Learn a lot of things. Maybe make out with some people. Fall in love.

Get to know my parents better.

Grab a beer with Felix.

Go to fancy adult dinner parties.

Paolo comes up for air and gives me the goofiest smile. For a brief second, I get a flash of how he might look in his fifties. Less hair, same infectious grin, a man with a distinguished career as a grocery cashier, zookeeper, and red-carpet interviewer, his bookshelves proudly displaying his many porn Oscars.

And then he's himself again. Behind him, I see several purple people frolicking across the football field.

I think about Cheryl. I wonder if seeing all this would make her happy. I wonder if she'd be proud of me.

I wonder if *my* heart will give out on me one day.

Or maybe I'll be thirty-two, visiting my parents back in my hometown, when, as I'm crossing the street, Willis Ellis will, finally, collide into me with his mom's car.

Or maybe, just maybe, I'll be in a retirement home with my wife, lying in bed, holding her brittle hand as my eyes slowly blink closed.

I have no idea.

And there's something liberating about that.

Terrifying, but liberating.

Maybe even a little beautiful, too.

The reporter is still holding a microphone expectantly in my face.

"I don't really know what I'll do next," I say. "I guess I'm hoping to surprise myself."

A breeze lifts my T-shirt off my chest for a second.

I could die tomorrow.

The sun warms my neck.

Or I could live for another eighty years.

My heart beats.

Or.

I could die right now.

Or now.

Or now.

Or now.

ACKNOWLEDGMENTS

Welcome to the end of the book! I can't tell you how much it means that you spent time on this journey. (Well, actually, I can: A LOT. It means a lot.) Thank you.

Immense thanks also to:

Nancy Siscoe, heroic editor, whose brilliant guidance shaped this book (and whose "Ha!"s continue to be so gratifying). Angela Carlino, cover designer, for killing it time and time again. All of the other fantastic people at Random House, including Mary McCue, Heather Kelly, Stephen Brown, Katherine Harrison, Jennifer Brown, Adrienne Waintraub, Laura Antonacci, Artie Bennett, Bobbie Ford, and the rest of the delightful folks in marketing, sales, and publicity.

Mollie Glick, kick-ass agent, for always having my back. Joy Fowlkes, for helping Mollie to do that. The superb folks at Foundry Literary + Media, especially Jess Regel and Richie Kern. The terrific Dana Spector at Paradigm.

Everyone who helped make the audiobooks, including director May Wuthrich, engineer Fametta Sawyer, producer Kelly Gildea, and the entire Listening Library team. All of the wonderful international publishers of *Denton,* including De Agostini, Piper Verlag, S&S UK, and Intrinseca.

Zack Wagman, for perpetual above-and-beyond awesomeness. Ray Muñoz, for being supportive as hell and for inspiring most people's favorite character.

The booksellers, librarians, bloggers, and teachers who have been so enthusiastic about *Denton.* You blow my mind. Special shout-out to all the amazing indies out there, including (but certainly not limited to) Books of Wonder, Community Bookstore, BookCourt, and the Voracious Reader.

All of the warm, lovely, generous authors I've met so far, especially the Fearless 15ers. Special thanks to Isabel Quintero, Tim Federle, Becky Albertalli, Kurt Dinan, Kathryn Holmes, David Levithan, Adam Silvera, Natalia Sylvester, and Greg Andree.

Stephen Feehan (for thoughts on how deathdates would affect the life insurance industry), Tea Lounge (RIP), the Brooklyn Public Library system, Kos Kaffe, Iconis and Family, Postmark Cafe, the Gang, Mates of State, and the person who left a *New York Times* article about viruses on the table at the coffeeshop just when I needed it most.

My extraordinary family: Mom and Dad, Dustin and Erin, Mariel and Brett, Jenny and Larry, and Hannah and David.

Minna Rubin, who retained her loving, inquisitive, larger-than-life presence almost till her deathdate. Love you, Grandma.

Sly Rubin, for being a hilarious, inspiring human being.

And, above all, Katie Schorr, my funny, wise, beautiful, tenacious partner, who makes my writing and my life exponentially better.